LATE TO SMILE

LATE TO SMILE

K. M. Peyton

DEFINITIONS

LATE TO SMILE
A DEFINITIONS BOOK 978 1 909 53107 9

First published in Great Britain by Methuen

This edition published 2014

1 3 5 7 9 10 8 6 4 2

The Random House Group Limited supports The Forest Stewardship
Council® (FSC®), the leading international forest-certification organisation.
Our books carrying the FSC label are printed on FSC®-certified paper.
FSC is the only forest-certification scheme supported by the leading
environmental organisations, including Greenpeace. Our
paper procurement policy can be found at
www.randomhouse.co.uk/environment

MIX
Paper | Supporting
responsible forestry
FSC
www.fsc.org   FSC® C018179

Set in Bembo 12/17pt by Falcon Oast Graphic Art Ltd.

Random House Children's Publishers UK,
61–63 Uxbridge Road, London W5 5SA

www.**randomhousechildrens**.co.uk
www.**totallyrandombooks**.co.uk
www.**randomhouse**.co.uk

Addresses for companies within The Random House Group Limited can be
found at: www.randomhouse.co.uk/offices.htm

THE RANDOM HOUSE GROUP Limited Reg. No. 954009

A CIP catalogue record for this book is available from the British Library.

Printed and bound in Great Britain by Clays Ltd, St Ives plc.

CHAPTER ONE

MIRANDA SAT WAITING for her mother to die. She glanced at her watch once or twice – not more than a couple of hours, they had said, but it was more than that already. They had said three months a year ago. Miranda had spent a lifetime waiting on her mother's whim.

The room was quiet, a March sunshine washing in through the high windows. A gardener was pruning roses in the hospice garden, very slowly and methodically. He had been at the same plant for ten minutes. Of course he was getting paid for it. No one paid Miranda for pruning the roses, a chore that had to be fitted in somehow, amongst the endless calls on her time . . . Her mother had demanded it. It was hard not to feel thankful, with her imminent departure, for the hope of better times ahead.

Even now, at ninety, vestiges of the old, fierce beauty remained, in spite of the cheeks sucked in with the fight for breath, and the lips slack across toothless gums. The great arches of bone above the hollow eye sockets once flaunted eyebrows of dark mahogany, bewitching men. Miranda thought that her husband, George, had married her for her marvellous mother. Her marvellous mother had flirted with him and he with her, the gallant, charming lover loving the whole household, making his way in by courting the lacklustre daughter, Miranda. Or that is how Miranda always thought of it. George had wanted a family. He had got what he wanted, as he always did. He had learned how to call the tune from her mother. Between them both, she had never stood a chance.

She had always thought she didn't love her mother, and certainly her mother hadn't loved her, had held her in scorn for her unadventurous ways. But when it came to the point of death, preconceptions gave way. To watch someone die was very moving. Miranda had held many animals in death, cradled the heads of old hunters and incontinent gundogs, but human death, although she was gone fifty, was an experience unknown to her until now. She had been away at boarding school when her father had been killed, and seen him briefly before the coffin lid had been screwed down, resplendent in full hunting fig, his whip laid over his breast. The crushed skull had shown rather, causing her to throw up in the lavatory shortly afterwards. 'How he would have wanted to go,' her mother said curtly. Better, Miranda acknowledged, than in a hospice bed of sheer old age, but at least the old girl had got her money's worth. She had wrung life dry.

The manner of dying was, of course, open to many interpretations. Splendid to be active to a great age, but now the same unusual energy made dying very hard. Natural fighters did not give in, even at the end.

'Come on, old girl. Don't make it so hard. Let it go, let it go.'

Miranda held her mother's gnarled hand tightly in her own. It was cold and unresponsive. The wedding ring, a thick band, was loose, caged by the swollen knuckle. It would never come off without cutting. Alice wanted to be cremated, she had said so, and Miranda had wanted to keep the ring, but when she thought of cutting, she wondered now what they would cut, and decided not to ask for it. The ashes were to be scattered by the wood, where the old boy's had gone before her. Pheasants pecked there, and were later shot and eaten, which had always amused them in the past; the recycling of one's parents through family and friends.

But now Miranda was in no mood for jokes. Was this what one called 'peacefully, in bed'? The breathing was fierce and laboured, wracking the emaciated body. It was anything but peaceful. Alice had always been positive about everything she did, and dying was no different.

Miranda smoothed the sweat-soaked hair which, even now, was trying to spring in its habitual fashion from her skull. Once tightly curled and a deep auburn in colour, it still made a triumphant halo round her bony forehead. It was exactly the same as Felix's, Miranda's second son – about all he had, fortunately, inherited from his grandmother. Felix, like Miranda before him, had been a disappointment to the old woman, so quiet and steely. The steeliness she called obstinacy. Alice liked outspoken, positive, fast-moving people, like George.

Well, there would be a lot more peace around with Alice removed. George was going to lose his ally.

'How are we doing, dear?' One of the nurses put her head round the door. 'Are you all right?'

'Yes, thank you.'

'Do you want anything? A cup of tea?'

'No, thank you.'

'You prefer it on your own?'

'Yes, please.'

'I'm only next door if you want anything.'

'Thank you.'

Miranda had always preferred it on her own. Sometimes she wondered why she had ever married. But of course, she had been in love, and had hoped to leave her mother.

Now, at last, her mother was leaving her. And

Miranda was shaken with guilt by her feelings, and a deep, almost hysterical compassion for the old lady, her mother, done for at last. The rasping breathing was beginning to subside. Peace was on its way. Miranda, a soft touch, now leaned over the bed and stroked her mother's burning forehead. The huge, dark blue eyes were open, but saw nothing. She talked to her, soothingly, encouragingly, a lifetime with animals having made smooth talk a habit – it wasn't what you said, but the tone of voice, after all, and what she said now was mostly rubbish. And the old girl was past taking it in, halfway to her maker, the breath perceptibly slowing, the rattle stilled. Miranda glanced at her watch again. Five minutes?

It was longer, true to pattern. Miranda had stopped talking, almost stopped breathing herself in order to catch the last faint whisper of the old woman's exhalations. Each breath had longer and longer between it; each breath Miranda thought the last, until another, fainter, followed, and a longer gap until, at last, no more.

Miranda did not move. She gazed at the marble face, stark, the eyes now like glass eyes, the skin already blueish with the pallor of death. The nose stood up like a headland out to sea, steep and bullish, but with life gone its threat was now empty. The nostrils had once swelled with aggression like those of her beloved horses.

Miranda had trembled, retreated into a protective shell and found it hard to emerge. But the shell, strengthened by her own brand of stubbornness, had stood her in good stead. Her feelings now were softened by pity, that she, so long the underdog, was strong and in her prime and her protagonist departed. She sat for a long time, taking it in, the pity provoking silent tears to roll steadily down her cheeks and drop warmly on her folded hands. Perhaps this feeling was love – but Miranda had become sceptical of love. Perhaps her tears were for herself, for relief at the peace which was palpable in the antiseptic room, that wrapped her like a blanket, sitting there.

It was half an hour before the nurse looked in.

'Oh, my dear.'

She came over and stood looking down at the formidable white husk of Miranda's mother.

'Shall we shut her eyes?'

'I tried once.'

The nurse put out her hand and pressed the lids firmly down. She stroked the hair tidy, and pulled up the sheet.

'She's got a very strong face. She must have been a fine-looking woman.'

'Yes, she was.'

'I'll tell the doctor. When you're ready.'

'I've finished now. I'll leave her.'

'There's no hurry.'

'It's all right.'

Miranda got up. She felt terribly tired, and her mind was blank. She went to the Matron's office and was told what to do about registering the death, about finding a funeral director; was given a cup of tea. Her car was outside.

'I'm quite all right. Thank you for everything you've done – you've been marvellous.'

'It's what we're for. We do our best.'

Smiles, handshakes.

Miranda went out of the swing door, and met Philippa coming in.

'Oh, Mum! Good! They said you were here. Is she – how is she?' Philippa, after the embrace, drew back and guessed what had happened from her mother's face. 'Oh, Mum, she's – is it all over? Oh, Mum!'

Tears of sympathy welled up in Philippa's stone-grey eyes.

'Dad dropped me in the car. He said you were here. But he didn't say – didn't say anything about – she was *dying*.'

'He doesn't want to accept it. I told him, but he kept saying she'd hang on, she'd get better. After all, he hasn't been in to see her since they took her in, so how could he know how she had deteriorated? You know your father – head in the sand, anything he doesn't want to know.'

'No. He never could stand illness, could he? Yet he'll miss her more than anyone. She was his buddy.'

They walked across the car park towards Miranda's car. It occurred to Miranda – 'You don't want to see her, do you? Now, before she – while she—'

Philippa considered, in her steady, unimpulsive way. 'Not really.'

She looked shaken.

'I wasn't expecting—' She shook her head. 'It's hard to take in, such a – a strong person. Not a little sweet granny – you could expect it then.'

'A ruthless woman, but she was ninety, after all. High time – oh, thank God! I can't believe it, to be honest.'

Miranda sank back in her driving seat, shattered by the realisation. At last! The glory of it, if she were truly honest, was shivering under her shocked surface. But she would not show it, even to Philippa, who would understand better than all the others. Philippa, her eldest, was the most like herself of her four children: the quietest, the most boring, the plainest, the least adventurous, the most reliable.

'It'll be really peculiar without her. The house – I can hardly imagine it. Will you change it? Move, even?'

'You must be joking! I couldn't leave Lilyshine.'

'But it's huge. When Jack and Felix and Sal go, you and Dad'll rattle around—'

'That'll be the day, when they go! Your father will never let them.'

'Felix would like to – he's talked about it to me.'

'Felix, perhaps. He never did get on with George. But he hasn't the energy.'

Philippa the eldest, the only one she understood, the one she could least do without, had departed to London and married a man in a grey suit called Paul. Even now, after five years, Miranda could only think of Paul as a man in a grey suit. He had kept scrupulously clear of Lilyshine, after the first visit. Miranda didn't exactly blame him for that, but she blamed him bitterly for not making her Philippa happy. For Philippa patently wasn't happy. But Miranda would never enquire, protecting fiercely the shreds of her own privacy and respecting it in others.

Philippa said soothingly, 'It'll be much easier for you now. Without Gran. I can't believe it!'

She sat silent after that, looking out of the window at the countryside shrouded in a grey mist of drizzle. Lilyshine was in a village once remote but now, since motorways and Intercity, on the verge of commuterland. The nicer houses, when they came on the market, were bought by London people. The countryside was not marked by any characteristics that told you exactly where it was: it was a mix of rolling arable and pasture land, with enough woods to qualify for 'pretty', enough hollows and ridges and resident skylarks to delight the visitors, near enough to the sea to bring the white gulls in droves behind the plough. The winter barley was well advanced, the trees beginning to green, the snowdrops still nodding in optimistic banks on the loamy verges. But Miranda didn't see it any more. She only noticed the landscape when she went away which, given George and the calves and the children and, latterly, her mother, had been rarely. She could get high on the bright lights of Shaftesbury Avenue on the occasions she had been up to the theatre with Philippa and Paul, heady with excitement at the whiff of mountain or moor. She had never been abroad in her life. 'I'll have time later,' she was used to saying. Perhaps later was coming.

Her car was an ancient Ford, full of gravel and dog hairs and old Pay and Display tickets. Jack kept it going, along with the farm machinery, and when her current car was beyond his doctoring powers, she was passed on another heap discarded by one of the malefolk, barely an improvement. It crossed her mind then, for the first time, that her mother might have left her some money.

The same thought occurred to Philippa

simultaneously, for she said, 'Did Gran have much money?'

'Not from the way she behaved.' She had never paid a penny towards her household expenses. 'But she never spent any, so perhaps she has. Her pension must have mounted up, for a start.'

'I hope she's left it to you, Mum. Not Dad. Did she make a will?'

'Yes. But I don't know what's in it.'

'I'd like that pair of art nouveau vases. That's all.'

'Heavens! They're horrible.'

'I love them.'

'There's some nice old jewellery. I never wear it. You and Sal could share that.'

'Why don't you wear it?'

'I'm not the sort, am I?'

'What a stupid thing to say. As if you've got leprosy or something. You'd look wonderful in those ruby ear-rings she used to wear at Christmas.'

'I'd feel ridiculous.'

'That's your trouble, Mum. You do yourself down. You'd look marvellous.'

'Do you think so? With my hair?'

'Yes, I do.'

Miranda's hair had missed out, her mother's auburn glory passed on in a faded version of dull carrot, frizzy instead of curly, and now beginning to grey. She herself called it coconut matting. A bolder girl would have grown it long and wide like a bush, but she had always scraped it down and cut it short.

'It's awful to be talking about what we're after. I hate people who fight over the leavings.'

'Yes, it's really disgusting.'

They both laughed, then realised the unseemliness of it, so soon, and froze. Miranda switched on the car lights for the long, narrow road under trees that curved down into the hollow where Lilyshine Hall stood against its wooded surroundings, and reverted back to her numb, tired daze. Of course she had been expecting the death daily and had got into the state of mind to accept it, but it would be a shock for everyone else. Although she had told them Alice was dying, they had all pooh-poohed the idea, not even bothering to visit. 'She's as strong as a horse, of course she'll pull through!' How stupid they all were, Miranda thought sadly. Sometimes she felt very alone amongst her family.

On an impulse, coming to the first of the village cottages, she pulled in and said to Philippa, 'I'll just tell Meg. She ought to know. I won't go in, just give her the news.'

Meg had been to see Alice. Meg was a brick, to use one of Alice's own expressions.

Meg was in her kitchen, taking a cake out of the oven. She was the same age as Miranda, but looked older, stout and strong like a man. Miranda depended on Meg, if she depended on anybody. Sometimes one needed someone, although – for God's sake – that's what a husband was for. But George's shoulder had never been for crying on. Meg hadn't got a husband, at least not present. He had been a captain of a banana boat when last seen, which was many moons past. Meg just laughed.

'Oh, my dear, she's gone?' Meg straightened up, her face full of concern.

'Yes. I'm with Philippa, I won't stop. I just wanted you to know.'

'It's splendid news, let's be honest. For you, and for her too, since she started to go downhill. But there'll be a huge hole . . . my word, huge!'

'I'll tell you about it later.'

'Go and have a stiff drink. Use hers.'

Miranda smiled. 'That's one cupboard that was never empty.'

'She knew how to enjoy life, I'll give her that. Mostly at other people's expense. We'll all miss her.'

'Cheerio then. See you soon.'

'I'll help with anything you want. You know that.'

'Yes, I know.'

Miranda went out and drove the hundred yards to thegates of Lilyshine. The rest of the village, what there was of it – a church, a pub, a sort of shop and some houses – was farther on. Lilyshine stood aloof, the squire's house, a Victorian fantasy of gable and Gothic which required, and did not get, an enormous expenditure in upkeep. Miranda was used to a habitual sinking of the heart as she came home, seeing the ineffectiveness of her valiant stabs at improvement; the paintwork was always peeling, the drive forever sprouting weeds, the garden over-reaching itself; all shouted neglect, in spite of her efforts. Now in the grey rain, with death at hand, it lowered out of the dusk with its usual malevolent scorn for what the estate agents might term 'desirability', the windows blank and dark, the rain dripping from the ivy which was in essence a tenement block for the sparrows, spewing shit and feathers and last year's nests like an old dog its hairs, adding to the forlorn air of the decaying drive below.

Even Philippa shivered, coming home.

'I banked up the stove,' Miranda said. 'It'll be warm in the study. Let's go and have a drink.'

Meg's idea was a good one. Miranda found she was shivering.

'You go and sit down, Mum. Honest, I'll do it. You look terrible.'

They went in round the back and put the lights on. Miranda went straight to the study and knelt in front of the stove, pulling out the bottom to make it flame up. She was crying again, but thought it was more relief than sorrow; her hands were shaking. She felt as empty and unwelcoming as the house itself. Oh God, it's over, she kept saying to herself, it's over. The last three months of Alice's decline had been horrific. I can live again, it's over.

George had kept asking Miranda what was wrong with her. Was she ill? Alice was ill but there was nothing wrong with *her*, was there? What would he say tonight?

'She's dead. She died this afternoon.'

'Are you having me on?'

'No. About a thing like that? She's dead.'

'But –' His face worked passionately – disbelief, sheer anger. 'Nobody said—'

'I told you she was dying three months ago. I told you she was near the end on Saturday, that you should go and see her. You went to the point-to-point, if you remember, said you'd call in on the way home. If you had, you'd have noticed that she was on the point of death.'

George sat down heavily in his armchair. There were two armchairs on either side of the fire, one

George's and one Alice's. Miranda sat down in Alice's and realised she could now make a habit of it.

'I told you all again yesterday, and Philippa came up from London, the only one of you to take any notice. She came home with me and fed the dogs.'

'Where is she?'

'She had to go back.'

'You didn't *say*—'

'I did, George. I said it many times. I'm sorry it's such a shock to you, but you chose not to listen. I could have done with some help, believe me, the last three months.'

'The silly old bitch, to slide away like that, without – oh, Jesus, I shall miss her, the silly old bitch.'

Miranda watched him dispassionately. She felt quite sure that if it had been her own death, he would not have been so moved. Philippa said she did herself down but when it came to relationships Miranda believed she was fairly acute. She could see that George was genuinely upset, as she had known he would be, more upset than herself.

'She should have told me,' he said. 'Made arrangements. Everything we've got here is hers. Suppose she's left it to the cats' home?'

'Oh, don't be so silly.'

'Her house, her farm, the woods . . .'

'The debts.'

'The mortgage, yes. My God. Did she leave any money?'

'I've no idea.'

'Did she leave a will?'

'I don't know,' Miranda lied.

There was a copy of the will in the dressing-table drawer, Miranda had seen it several times, in a strong brown envelope, but she had no idea what it said. She did not doubt that it was fair, possibly some money to the children, and the house and farm to herself and George. Why should it be otherwise? Her mother had been biased but not unfair, and in full control of her faculties right up to the last few days. If George knew there was a will he'd be making her find it at once. George was impulsive and without finer feelings. He had lived in Alice's house and farmed her farm since the day he had married Miranda. George was more her mother's son than son-in-law. If anyone was the outsider, it had been herself, not enchanted with the sporting life.

'I can't believe it,' George said several times, and took a large Scotch. He then asked if dinner was ready.

'Dinner ready?' Miranda was bewildered. 'I've been watching my mother die all afternoon.'

'Jack and Felix will be expecting something, all the same.'

Miranda bit down an inclination to scream.

'Get something out of the freezer. And give me a Scotch too. I'm not cooking tonight.'

'Bloody hell. Keep your hair on.'

An arm round her shoulders, a rough hug of understanding, a quiet, 'I'll rustle something up, darling' . . . Miranda had a nice line in dreams, which prompted her to smile cynically at times. But she was past smiling tonight. She clutched her Scotch and sat on the hearth-rug, staring into the flames. Suppose her mother had left her fifty thousand pounds? She couldn't go, even if her mother had left it her, because Sally was still at school and the boys needed her. And sometimes, just sometimes, George was lovely. One didn't leave a marriage early on because of the children, and later one had resigned oneself. It was too late to start afresh. She was fifty-two, and had never worked for money, only for George. More fool she.

To her relief George downed his Scotch and went out to the kitchen. A big man, he had a powerful presence and personality which filled any room he was in, but most of his day was spent outdoors in his natural element: the wind and the sun and the rain. Thus Miranda had survived. Yet she loved him in her way, and had loved him passionately when she was young. Young gods like George Fairweather at the age of twenty-two did not fall off trees. She had been as enamoured as her mother.

Miranda had spent the whole thirty-two years of her marriage wondering if George and her mother had slept together in those early days. Or even in later days, such was the rapport. Her mother's physical beauty was something that had overshadowed Miranda's life. Increasing age had, if anything, underlined rather than diminished it. Miranda knew now that she should have escaped early on, as Philippa had escaped, but just as she had been on the brink of plucking up her courage to ask to enter a London art school, George had arrived on the scene. And George's arrival on whatever scene tended to dictate the action. She, so slender, guileless, romantic and naïve, had fallen like the ripe apple from the tree, giving up all ideas of a career to bask in his blue-eyed gaze. Heavenly George! She had descended from the heights in a series of painful bumps which had numbed her eventually, enduring adultery, penury and occasional cruelty over the years, but having always her children and her room and her own friends to comfort. George loved his home and the children. He was never going to leave her, she knew that. Perhaps that was the crowning blow to her marital situation.

Miranda hugged herself in front of the fire, adrift on alcohol, shivering and yet warm, half in tears, half hysterically glad. The gruelling routine of tending her mother over at last, she could start living again, going out, sleeping uninterrupted at night, seeing Meg in other than ten-minute snatches, reading a book right through in an evening. She could work on this terrible house, redecorate, rearrange, let in the fresh air. She was just beginning to glimpse these compensations beyond the pain. She had at times during the last year or two prayed for her mother to die: gone into her room and watched the sleeping form for the stillness of death, always to no avail. She had been ashamed, guilty, and was now equally guilt-ridden for the little sparks of joy that kept needling her cold grief. She put such confusion down to the whisky, and topped up her glass again.

'What's up?' Jack had never seen his father look so thrown.

'Your grandmother's died.'

'*What?*'

'You heard me. She's dead.'

'What? Gran? – you mean—' Jack, like his father, foundered. 'Nobody said – I didn't know it was that bad—'

'Your mother says she told us. I don't remember either.'

'You mean, she's died? When? Just?'

'This afternoon.'

'Bloody hell!'

(Miranda might have been amused, had she heard, at the son's imitation of his father on hearing the news. Jack was a chip off the old George.)

'Bloody hell, where does this leave us?'

'Without our dinner, for a start.'

George had opened the freezer and was crashing about amongst the contents.

'Where's Mum? How's she taking it?'

'She's drowning her sorrows by the fire. Coolly, I'd say. She says she told us it was due and we didn't listen.'

'I don't remember her saying.'

'We assumed the old girl would come home when she was better. Apparently it was never on the cards. She went there to die. Now she tells us. I didn't take it in before either. How long does this ocean pie stuff take?'

'What happens now? This place is hers. Who's she left it to?'

'Us, of course. Half an hour at two hundred, it says.'

'Take the wrapper off, for God's sake.'

'Serves two! They must be mad. I'll put six in, two each. Felix was nearly finished, wasn't he?'

'Yeah. She might have left it to me and Felix. Cut you out, Dad.'

'Why would she do that?'

'Bit of fun. She liked to surprise people.'

'She did. Well, I wouldn't mind packing up. Farming's not your own business any more – the bloody government's got you on the hop all the time. Them or those European bastards. Lucky for her it wasn't like that in her day. She had the best of it. Could do what you damned well pleased in those days. She was a goer, old Alice – poor old Alice! Fancy her giving up. There wasn't anything wrong with her that I ever noticed.'

'Oh, Dad, she ponged. There must have been.'

'I never noticed.'

'The dogs pong and you had old Benbow on your bed till Mum moved out into the spare room. You never notice anything.'

'I lost my smell when I broke my nose at Aintree. You were only four then. Alice caught the horse, I remember. Told me I rode like an idiot.'

'Well, you do, Dad. You're useless compared to Felix.'

'No, well, we all have our own talents. Pity Felix is so bone idle. You aren't all that keen to put it in either, not where the horses are concerned.'

'I don't mind qualifying them.'

'No! The fun bit! It's the work I'm talking about, mucking out, exercising.'

'You know I like the other sort of horse power best, Dad. Give me a break.'

'Yes, okay. Make some tea. I've made the dinner.'

'How long will it be?'

'Half an hour it says on the box.'

George sat down at the table to await his tea. His lurcher, Rough, and Sally's mongrel, Carstairs, sat looking at him, fed but always hopeful. George never fed the dogs. Miranda did all that. He was offhand with them, but they both adored him. The farm dogs lived outside and Miranda fed them too. Jack shot rabbits for them and Miranda skinned them, although the men told her not to bother.

The men waited for the pies to cook, and Miranda remained in the study and took another whisky. The fire, now burning bright, and the alcohol were having a marvellous effect: she was warmed and relaxed and full of bright, sentimental ideas for the future, what she would do to the house, what she would do with all the hours and hours of freedom now at her command. She had a brain once, she remembered. Little scraps of intellectual thought gleaned occasionally from a newspaper or the tail end of a television programme had always raised her hopes of doing something about her brain some time, nourishing it, exercising it. All the great novels to be read . . . she had read *Middlemarch* and *Anna Karenina* when she had once, many years ago, had to stay in bed for six weeks and realised then that there was more to life than running Lilyshine, but since her incapacity she had never managed any more than a few Dick Francis's and a grubby needlepoint cushion depicting a pheasant. Intellectualism always seemed just out of reach, beckoning from a plateau just above her head where she could only reach up and grope fruitlessly.

'Hey, Mother, are you all right?' Felix put his head round the door. 'Dad says Gran died this afternoon.'

'Yes, she did. And I'm a little drunk.'

He came in and perched on the edge of George's armchair, looking down at her anxiously.

'You must have had a bad time. Philippa came?'

'Yes, she did.'

'Was she there when . . . ?'

'No. She arrived just afterwards. She came home with me.'

'Why didn't she stay?'

'The usual. Paul needed her. "I must fly", you know. But she did come.'

'I'd have come, if you'd said.'

'She wouldn't have known you.'

'For you, I mean. I'd have come for you. You've had a tough time.'

'Yes, yes, I have. That's why I'm drinking, it makes it feel better.'

'She trampled you underfoot. And Dad always took her side, which made it worse. She was a terrible old woman, Mum, let's face it. I'm glad she's gone. So domineering. It's wrong, for old people to be like that.'

'You can't change your nature.'

'You should learn, after all those years, to take a back seat when the time comes.'

Felix scowled. Miranda thought it wouldn't be wise to say that, of them all, Felix was the most like his grandmother. They didn't get on, those two, Philippa always said, because they were so alike. Miranda hadn't thought so, because Felix was quiet and Alice was not, but Philippa said, 'They both get their own way, you notice. Whatever happens, those two both do exactly what they want.' Miranda rather thought that applied to everyone in the family except herself but, on reflection, saw that George and Jack were, compared with Felix, quite easygoing and careless in their steamrollerish way. If Felix decided against something, nothing could make him change his mind, even – in his boyhood – threats, beatings and dire punishment from his father. None of the others had got beaten, only Felix, because he was so unmoving, uncooperative, silent. So *bloody-minded*, said George.

But like his grandmother he was beautiful: slender and graceful, with dark red closely-curling hair and the same dark eyes beneath strong, arched eyebrows. He had her autocratic nose, and wide, close lips. He sat staring into the fire. One could never tell what he was thinking from his face; unlike George, whose emotions flared in his eyes and the colour of his cheeks and the movements of his body for all the world to see. A closed book George was not. Felix had the power to enrage him, which none of the other children had.

'I don't think some people accept that they're old,' Miranda said, 'even when they really are. It's more a way of thinking. It's a very fine thing, to carry on regardless, not to give in.'

'You're sticking up for her.'

'She was a very fine woman in many ways. If she'd been anyone else's mother, I'd have admired her terrifically.'

'Yes, that sums it up. It was *living* with her . . .' Felix had kept out of her way, on the whole. This study where she had held domain was not a room that had seen much of Felix. Lilyshine was so big that one could lose a person without difficulty over long periods of time, save that in the winter the need for warmth flushed most of them into the kitchen or the study, the only heated rooms. Miranda had always been intending to make one of the downstairs rooms into a private den of her own, but had never got beyond installing her own bureau and a rather nice sofa that Meg had thrown out. Time to sit there had never occurred. An inadequate system of storage heaters kept the mould out of bathroom, passages, landings and bedrooms but no more . . . comfort was not a priority in Lilyshine.

'Have you all eaten?'

'Yes, Dad produced some funny muck out of the freezer.'

'What are they doing?'

'Jack brought a video home. *Some Like It Hot.* They're watching that.' He got up. 'I'll go and feed the horses. Do you want anything?'

'No.'

He went out. Miranda lay back in Alice's chair (she would throw it out; it smelled) and thought of George, who had loved Alice, watching *Some Like It Hot.* In all the years she had known him he had never behaved with what one might call propriety, predictably, in a civilised fashion. Was the video covering up the pain for him of his lifetime love affair with his mother-in-law, or was he so thick-skinned that he was able to enjoy it? In all her years of knowing him and living with him Miranda still found the man impossible to understand.

CHAPTER TWO

DURING THE STRANGE limbo week before the funeral Miranda thought several times about the will in the bureau drawer, but made no move to read it until she had completed her practical chores. George, of course, went to work outside as usual, his only contribution being to remind her that no one would come to the funeral if it was on Tuesday because Napoleon's horse was running in the two-thirty at Huntingdon. 'Wednesday, make it Wednesday, then we can all have a good chat afterwards.'

Miranda knew that the church would be full. The farmers liked a good funeral, plenty of flowers and gossiping and drink. They would expect 'a good show, a grand turnout'. They would wear their point-to-point suits and clean their cars. Only the rosettes would be missing.

She walked up to the church, which they none of them attended, a barnlike mediaeval building with a very good timbered roof and a stumpy tower which stood in its nicely dishevelled graveyard at the top of the village. Beyond it the lane divided to encircle a large green which made up the core of the village. The old Georgian rectory dominated the green, but this was no longer occupied by the vicar. It had been bought by a man from London who was reputed to make pornographic films. The vicar lived in a dismal square red-brick house newly built for him, and he was young and blunt to go with it, unused to country living, having been dispatched from the suburbs of Birmingham. He had twelve-month-old twins and his wife was expecting again, which Miranda thought both ungodly and unkind. She did not respect him for it, in spite of his enthusiasm for 'God's gifts' in the church magazine.

She had been married in this church, and so had Philippa and so, she thought, had Alice. It had punctuated the highlights of her uneventful life. She had even, at emotional times, prayed in it, but not for several years. God had come to have less and less meaning, although she still loved the atmosphere of church, the stillness and peace, and the music. She knew she should call at the vicarage but the thought of the smell of nappies and the squalor one had to pass through before getting to the study put her off, so she went and sat in the church hoping the vicar might come in. She would decide what sort of funeral she wanted – a good old-fashioned service, and then a cremation, and drinks and food afterwards at Lilyshine. George would not lift a finger. She must get it right. And hymns with good tunes and appropriate words . . . very difficult, when so many made such play with meekness, humility and frailty, none of which attributes could be said to apply to Alice.

When she walked slowly up the aisle towards the dusty altar she could not help seeing George standing there as he had stood on the day of her wedding. He might have been God himself that day, with the sun shining on him from the high rose window (as it was shining, weakly, now) polishing his already golden hair and sunburned face, shining in his Mediterranean eyes. So tall, so athletic, so beautiful, laughing as she approached, she could not believe it was herself he was waiting for: she remembered thinking that she was living in a fairytale, so romantically and hopelessly was she in love, so gloriously were the bells ringing in her ears and the organ resounding through the church. No girl ever went to the altar in such a cloud of rose-tinted euphoria as Miranda Crawshaw.

Alice, whose remains were to lie mutely on the same spot in five days' time, had been standing in the front pew an arm's length from George, dressed in a fuchsia pink silk coat and a navy straw hat wreathed in pink and white flowers. Her superb legs were for once revealed (she normally wore trousers or jodhpurs) and her high heels almost put her on a level with George. George had glanced across at her and winked, and Alice had given him a look which Miranda could see clearly even now, a conspiratorial, laughing, thumbs-up sort of look, most unlike the emotional, tremulous expression of the normal bride's mother.

Miranda, come to think of funerals, saw her wedding again clearly, sadly. George had been unfaithful many times, had been sorry, but sharply, had treated her like a doormat, but was a happy man at heart and not given to sulking and gloom, and there had been good times and fun. But she had always been the outsider, little Miranda: the conniving looks between Alice and George during that moment at the wedding had set the pattern for their family life. She, fastened by three children and then – horrors! – the unexpected fourth, had been the mainstay of Lilyshine while Alice and George had fun. They called it work – horse-dealing, racing, hunting – but self-indulgence had prevailed. They had friends in and parties and Miranda had cooked and laughed and thought privately that she must look older than her own glorious mother, still hunting in her seventies. But the children were a fulltime job and she had never complained, hating horses save at peace in their looseboxes and not envious, unambitious, a biddable woman. The only child (unwanted, she saw much later), she had been brought up to be obedient and to stand neglect. She had sat in her pram for hours out in the field, while her mother schooled horses in circles around her; she had been sent to boarding school at eight, like a boy, and spent her holidays refusing to ride the ponies Alice kept buying for her. She too had been stubborn, wisely (perhaps Felix got it from her, not Alice). She liked talking to the ponies but not riding them. Later she had sat on the Pony Club committee and was recognised by the children whose mothers forced them to ride as a good friend in adversity. She had never forced hers but perversely they had taken to it and all rode like troopers.

She sat there dreaming and heard the door open. She pulled herself together, presuming it was the vicar, but it was Meg, come to do the flowers. Meg, unlike Miranda, went to church and the WI, did B & B, cooked dinners for dinner parties, took liveries, raised calves and had an egg-round, but always had time to talk. She lived alone, although her son Martin came down from London quite often. He was a violinist and couldn't lift heavy weights or put up shelves – 'useless' according to George – but Miranda liked him: he was sweet and funny and kind, unlike her physical brutes. It was through him that Philippa had met Paul the pianist, but Paul was none of the nice things Martin was. Why hadn't Philippa married Martin, for God's sake? Miranda's mind was wandering, she realised. She stood up and Meg came crashing down the aisle. She never lowered her voice, even in church.

'Why, Miranda! Splendid. What day's the funeral? I'll make sure the flowers are in their prime.'

'Wednesday.'

'Fine. Have you spoken to Tom?' Tom was the vicar.

'No. I can't face the crêche out there. I was just thinking about it.'

'I'll tell him what you want, if you like. I've got to call in. Save you the trouble.'

'Oh, Meg!' What a relief! 'Would you—?'

'No problem. Leave it to me. How do you feel, Miranda? It's a sort of limbo time, until the funeral, isn't it? Nothing seems quite real.'

Meg was utterly reliable, efficient, sensible and goodnatured, the universal aunt. She was large and stocky, with big outdoor hands. She had wiry grey hair, thick like a bush and cut like one, and a brown, lined face with a slightly spaniel expression, concerned and loving. But her ways were brisk and far from sentimental. Miranda found in her a wall to shelter from cold blasts, a shoulder to cry on. Meg gave her wonderful biscuits hot from the oven, as if to a fractious child, and Miranda was always grateful for Meg's existence, Meg's oaklike roots in common-sense, just down the lane. Meg would even choose the hymns.

'Yes, of course. Good tunes. Everyone likes to sing. She'll get a good send-off. Funerals of really old people are usually fun, because there's really no mourning owed, just gratitude.'

'Gratitude they've gone?'

'I didn't mean that. But in your case, could be.' She laughed.

'I was sitting here remembering my wedding, actually. Do you remember what she looked like, in that pink coat?'

'Radiant, like the bride! The competition's over now, Miranda. You should be celebrating.'

'I feel numb. Asleep, sort of. It'll sink in later.'

'That's normal. I'll see Tom for you, and drop in on the way home. Put the coffee on.'

Miranda went home, grateful. She saw Meg open the vicar's kitchen door and shout, 'Cooee!' Tom generally wore a track suit and trainers and his wife was a slut, a cheerful godly slut, but a slut nonetheless. Meg took all this in her stride, but Miranda couldn't. Her instincts were too prim. She walked slowly down the lane back towards Lilyshine. Lilyshine was in the dip of the village where the trees grew down the stream valley and was a secretive place compared with the houses round the bright green higher up. The village hadn't changed much in her lifetime, save for the council houses above the green and the more recent 'executive' Georgian shams grouped up a chase and mercifully hidden by the woods, sold to incomers at exorbitant prices. The farmer whose land they were on was friendly with the planning officer. George had put in for a housing estate behind Lilyshine and been turned down. He had only laughed. Meg had an acre beside the lane but hadn't applied, saying she didn't fancy neighbours on both sides, one was enough. Getting rich was a lottery, the way planning opportunities arose. The thought of getting rich made Miranda think of Alice's will, still untouched in its brown envelope. When Meg came, she might open it. She needed courage to open it, although she expected no shocks. There was nobody else save the members of Alice's immediate family at Lilyshine to leave the money to, however fancifully her old brain might have danced in its dotage (it was true: she did like surprises). She had outlived all her own generation and offended her husband's family so that the younger generation had lost touch. That was no loss, for Miranda's father's family had been thick and boring, like the man himself. Alice had married her husband for his seat on a horse, not a great basis for success in a marriage, but it had been an amiable enough pairing, Alice – like George – finding her delights elsewhere and returning faithfully to the nest without her husband noticing anything amiss. Miranda had never really known her father, save as a figure high up in a red coat.

The air was mild and smelled of spring. The banks of snowdrops on either side of the lane never failed to lift her spirits, although she knew George and the boys ploughed through them on their hunters, and their white faces were unkindly splashed by the homecoming Jaguars making for the Georgian estate. What little things made her happy . . . no wonder George scorned her concern with small things and turned to brave point-to-point girls for his smiles and tumblings.

Lilyshine was a strange house architecturally. Once a smart Victorian dwelling, it was much too exuberant for its verdant setting and now, a hundred years later, something of a white elephant. It was too exotic to accept its role as farmhouse, uneasy with the barns and stables that had grown in spreading disarray behind it. The original farmhouse that went with the land, known as Violets, lay out of sight up a long drive over the hill at the back. It was occupied by the ancient cowman Arthur, who was craving for a council house, quite understandably in Miranda's opinion. She rarely went up to Violets. Lilyshine was much more conveniently placed, in all respects. George was always going to 'do up' Violets, but never had. George, of course, was always going to do many things. And never did.

Miranda stood in the drive and quite suddenly the amazing, glorious, mind-blowing realisation of her new freedom washed over her. Looking at Lilyshine, empty and silent, divested of that eternal presence, she felt a miraculous glow of affection for the familiar rooms, at last, after all these years, hers to do with as she wished. The garden, no longer an enemy to be controlled in ten-minute frenzies two or three times a week, beckoned in the March sunshine: the robin carolled, the first daffodils were fighting their way into the light from brambly embraces; the seat – the seat! – was still there by the lilacs . . . no one had actually sat on it since the children were babies. Oh, she would sit on it! Sit with her coffee and the morning paper, with her feet up, relaxed, not watching the clock. Life with Alice had been one long breathless scamper, fitting it all in . . . her breakfast in bed, washing her, dressing her, getting her downstairs, making her cups of tea, her lunch, her library books, her *Horse and Hound*, her jigsaw puzzles . . . all slotted in between meals for the men, the washing and ironing, the dogs, the chickens, shopping and cleaning, tea for Alice, supper for Alice, Alice to bed, her hot water bottle, her pills, her glasses, her conversations . . . 'Stop and listen to me for five minutes!' 'Oh, God, Mother, I can smell the pie burning!' – one long dash from dawn till dusk. The chores were stupifying, endlessly repetitive, without any sort of reward. Ugh, the false teeth, the slimey bits she scrubbed off them . . . 'If you put your mother in a show for grandmother in best condition you'd win,' Meg used to say. 'You have such high standards.' But Alice had demanded high standards. 'No back-sliding,' she used to say. Back-sliding . . . I shall back-slide, Miranda vowed now, back-slide on the garden seat in the spring sunshine, and Sally can bring me coffee and biscuits.

Sally was the only one who did not know that her grandmother was dead. She was on a school skiing trip in France.

'Didn't you send a message?' Meg asked when she came.

'It seemed pointless, when I thought about it. They didn't get on, those two. She would be relieved, I think, and that would make her feel guilty. So why bother, when she's having fun?'

Meg shrugged, smiled. She looked round the kitchen and said, 'It is nice without her, isn't it? We can just sit, and – and—'

She sat.

'No clock-watching. No bobbing up and down.'

They both laughed. And as she laughed Miranda was aware of a throat-clenching wave of grief rising up to stifle the enjoyment, as if her mother in a jealous heaven were reproaching her. She had to turn away from Meg, back to the coffee-pot. She could feel tears pricking her eyes. It was ridiculous.

'Just get the boys married off, and you stand a chance of actually living, Miranda. Think of it.'

'Jack and Felix? They'll never go.'

'No, they're too damned comfortable here. What's Jack now – twenty-seven?'

'Yes, just. And Felix is twenty-five. They don't seem to have girlfriends, or if they do I've no time to notice. They don't bring any home.'

'No – with Alice dominating the scene, would you? Things might be different now.'

Miranda made the coffee and brought it to the table. The mongrel Carstairs sat expectantly and Meg gave him half a biscuit. Rough was out with George. The men came back for lunch at one, so clock-watching was not entirely ruled out, but at least their dinners were easy, not like Alice's tempting, fussy little trays: steamed fish and parsley sauce, breast of chicken, rice pudding, egg custard . . . all the things she liked the men dismissed as rubbish. Shopping time would be halved without the need for Alice's titbits. Sitting talking to Meg was pure luxury. In the past they would have had to sit with Alice. She had always insisted on having any visitors in with her.

'I haven't told George . . .' Miranda fetched the will and put the envelope down in front of Meg. 'I haven't got round to opening it yet. I'd rather do it with you here than George.'

Meg was impressed. 'Are you sure?'

'Yes. I'm a bit nervous. That's why I keep putting it off.'

She turned the envelope and picked at its strong sealing.

'She could be such a cow, if she felt like it.'

The will was brief and to the point. Shorn of its legal claptrap, Miranda read out the salient points: the house Lilyshine and the farm were left to George; the farmhouse, Violets, its yards and orchard were left to her, as were all the effects; Alice's money was to be equally divided amongst her four grandchildren.

'What a very strange will,' Meg declared. 'Why not between you, for God's sake, Lilyshine and Violets and the farm?'

'I suppose because we don't agree about everything.'

'But, in value, she's left far more to George than to you.'

'She always liked George better than me.'

'It's outrageous!'

'Is it? It won't make any difference surely? George is the farmer, not me, and if Lilyshine is his it's still mine too. He won't kick me out.'

'Miranda, it's iniquitous. You are forgiving to a fault.'

'I've never had anything but brickbats from my mother, ever since I can remember. I wasn't expecting it to be any different. This will doesn't alter anything at all, surely?'

Meg almost snorted. She folded her lips firmly to stop herself nagging. She sat silently until her rage against foul Alice and her steamrollered daughter had subsided, then she asked blandly how much money would be going to the grandchildren.

'I've no idea.'

'She never paid you anything, did she? Her pension must have mounted up.'

'She bought George horses.'

'It might be a fortune.'

'It might be. I'll have to go and see the bank manager. It's nice for them. Nice for Philippa. She has a tough time with Paul. He won't let her work, says he needs her around.'

'He was always a bully. She should stand up to him.'

'You give in to them, you get a quiet life. You can't win.'

'It's a matter of opinion. I won.'

'And your husband buggered off.'

Meg laughed.

'Those "effects" she left you . . . diamonds? Gold? Impressionist paintings?'

'There's some nice antique furniture. Jewellery, yes. Gold chains and things. Nothing I'd want to sell, though.'

'You could get it valued. You never know.'

'Never know what?'

'Oh, Miranda, money is nice to have! Don't be so unworldly! It can buy you independence. Comfort. Fun!'

Miranda shook her head. She would not argue. There was nothing in particular she wanted that money could buy. She wanted George not to rub her up the wrong way, and the children to move out; she wanted peace of mind. She wanted her own private self to remain unviolated, a desire that stood more chance of fulfilment now that Alice was out of the way.

She smiled at Meg's disapproval. 'It's all right, Meg! I'm glad I've opened it at last. I'll tell George when he comes in. He might be cross he gets no money.'

'Only about a million pounds, the value of the house and farm.'

'Well, he's always had that, hasn't he?'

'It's quite a gift, to have it made official.'

'It doesn't really change anything.'

'It might, Miranda. And to anyone but you, it does.'

'Anyone but me?'

'You expect so little of life.'

'Then I'm never disappointed.'

When Meg had gone, Miranda thought, 'I did once.' She had expected her love affair with George to last for ever. It had lasted a couple of years. Having adjusted over the last thirty, she had come to terms.

He came in for his lunch and she handed him the will.

'What's this?'

He instinctively distrusted official-looking letters. He was not all that bright, after all. Quickwitted, yes, impulsive, sharp; but a thinking man, working out the consequences, the alternatives, the compromises – that was not his style. As he read the will Miranda saw quite clearly his reactions reflected in his expression: initial doubt changing to excitement, to surprise, almost shock, and, after a re-reading, to a look of hesitant guilt.

'Blimey.'

He was still a very handsome man and, with his sky-blue eyes brightening at the prospect of coming into this grand inheritance, he still had the look of an eager, cocksure boy. He hadn't, in essence, ever grown up. A sense of responsibility was low on his list of priorities. At fifty-four he was fit and active, spurred by his mercurial temperament. He had fine teeth and his thick blonde hair was only just beginning to show a bloom of grey; he still caught the female eye and his high spirits were always infectious in company. It was nearly always at home where he showed his reverse side: moodiness and the sulks when things were not going his way, a flaring temper, a tendency to self-pity. Miranda was used to absorbing his extremes of mood – a doormat truly, as Meg was fond of pointing out. He had always dominated the family, giving way only to Alice, but for years she had not sought to influence him. She had aided and abetted.

'What is it?,' Jack asked.

George threw the paper over. 'Your granny's will. She's left the cash to you lot.'

'What cash?'

'Yes,' said George to Miranda, 'What cash?'

'How should I know? What's left from buying you presents. You should have more idea than I have.'

'Horses, not presents. We dealt.'

'If you were successful, quite a lot then.'

George did not look optimistic. 'Not much went back in the bank. We invested it, you can say.'

'Nobody who puts money into horses can be said to "invest". Come, come, George!'

He grinned. 'No. Well. You never know.'

'Hey, how much? Doesn't anybody know?' Jack and Felix were both eagerly curious, poring over the will. 'Somebody must know!'

'The bank, I suppose.'

'Hey, Mum, can we ring them up and ask?'

'They won't tell you just like that. I'll go and see Mr Herriott.'

'This afternoon?'

'Perhaps. I suppose I could. I'll have to tell him she's dead, for a start. Yes, I could go this afternoon.'

She put out the lunch – a fairly solid oxtail soup – and George started carving up hunks of bread. They sat round the table, the will pulled between them as they started eating.

'Jolly funny will. You going to live at Violets, Mother? We can leave home with the cash and you and Dad can live in a house each.'

'Don't be stupid. It doesn't change anything as far as I can see.'

'Dad could sell up and live on the Costa del Sol.'

'Just his scene!'

George never took holidays, save a couple of days at the Cheltenham Festival or a trip to the Grand National.

'Christ, I'd like to know how much money,' Jack said.

'Don't be so greedy. And don't be too optimistic either. The bookmaker took a fair amount, from what I heard of her telephone conversations.'

'She always said she broke even.'

'Have you ever heard anyone who doesn't say that?'

'No, not really.'

'Find out though, Mother, You will go this afternoon?'

'Yes, I've said I will.'

'Come and tell us?'

'Yes!'

The three men between them were very physical, unrestful. The kitchen always seemed to have a gale blowing through it when they came in. They ate with great gusto, elbows out, spoons crashing. They got up and down for ketchup and mustard and all the things Miranda hadn't thought of putting out, to put the kettle on, to fetch the newspaper to read the racing entries, to make a phone call, up and down like yoyos. The chairlegs scraped on the tiled floor. They laughed loudly, they swore. Miranda presided usually in silence, wondering why she had had no influence in their upbringing. They rode over her. They depended on her, all the same.

Suddenly angry she said, 'At the funeral, for God's

sake show some respect, some manners! You'll be the hosts here. You must get your suits cleaned, pull yourselves together. Sometimes you are just like the farm dogs, the way you behave.'

They looked at her, amazed.

'Of course, Mother. Keep your hair on.'

'That school you went to – cost a fortune! – I can't see it taught you anything at all!'

A good public school, paid for by Alice, that had squandered her money as blindly as the bookmakers from all the evidence . . . the girls had had to put up with the local comprehensive. Alice didn't believe in educating girls. But they had passed far more exams than their brothers.

'We can be nice when we try,' Felix said, aggrieved.

'We won't let you down, Mother, promise.' Jack got up and ladled more soup into his bowl.

'I think a lot of people will come back for a drink,' Miranda said, to warn George. 'You'll see to all that, won't you?'

'Pouring drinks? Yes, I can do that.'

He was a good host after all.

'I'll go to the wine merchant as well this afternoon.'

'I hope she left some money to pay for it all.'

'The funeral will come out of the estate, it always does.'

'Our money, you mean?' Jack asked.

'Of course. Her money, before you get what's left, if any.'

'I could have done with some cash,' George said.

'Bad luck, Dad!' The boys laughed.

When they had all crashed out again, slamming the door, Miranda sat for a bit, sadly cogitating on their lack of . . . of what? They were kind enough underneath. Civility perhaps. She thought suddenly of Meg's Martin, a quiet, slender young man of immense intelligence and charm, whose presence was as soothing and uplifting as that of her boys was exhausting. Yet Meg criticised Martin. 'He never helps,' she said. Meg needed physical help on her smallholding with her heavy work. Jack or Felix could have done her tasks in minutes. Martin didn't know how to start. Yet Miranda loved Martin's company. What a diverse lot they all were. The genes never ceased to amaze.

The talk of money having rubbed off, Miranda stacked the dishwasher and went up to Alice's room to see how much of value was hidden in her dressing-table drawers. The room made her feel weepy again, the empty bed, the threadbare old nineteen-thirties satin quilt, the ancient torn camelhair dressing-gown, once Miranda's father's. She had tidied it up as if, like the men, she had believed in her heart that the old girl was going to come back from the home which specialised in dying. All was now peace. The sun came obliquely into the room, washing over the faded carpet, the frail curtains. Everything was old in this room, fit only for the tip. Alice had hung on to the lot, even when it was in ribbons.

The jewellery bequeathed to Miranda was likewise splendidly old and no doubt valuable: chunky rings of rubies and garnet and even diamonds, set in thick gold, gold bracelets and necklaces, a rhinestone necklace, dangling ear-rings that would not have looked out of place amongst the crown jewels, gold stockpins and cufflinks and the old man's pocket watch. Of course she would not sell any of it. Nor even wear it, in spite of Philippa's observation. But she handled it with pleasure, tried on the rings and a pair of the ear-rings, smiled at her reflection in the huge Edwardian mirror. How pale she was! The rubies swung from her ears like thick drops of blood. Her face was sallow and lined, without the magnificent cheekbones that had given Alice her distinction. Miranda's nose was small, straight and firm, nothing like the architectural proboscis of her maternal family. She had mercifully escaped it. She was small altogether, not only the nose; thin and shaped like a boy, small-hipped, agile. Yet she was strong too. She could run up hills and garden all day, given the chance. Her eyes were dark like her mother's, but soft and shy. There was no storm and glitter in her regard, no fire in her cheeks. If she had any natural expression at all it was one of hope, even optimism, in spite of everything. She was always ready to be happy. Perhaps she would be now.

She put the jewels away (one day she would get them valued) and changed into a clean jersey to go to the bank. She nearly always wore old jeans or old cords and baggy sweaters, and chose something respectable to impress Mr Herriott, a chestnut poloneck bought quite recently from Marks and Spencer, fawn cords and her ancient, once very expensive, wool tweed jacket. Her mother had always worn very good clothes for a very long time, a habit Miranda had tried to copy. The trick was to make sure you liked the garment very much before you spent the money, and to spend enough to ensure the quality that made clothes still look classy even when nearly threadbare. It was quite difficult to get right. Her mother had been much better at it than she was, disporting herself in positively Edwardian evening dresses and nineteen-thirties tweeds some thirty or forty years on. Miranda did not intend to carry the trend to such extremes. Her wool jacket was barely ten years old and the lining was coming apart already. It needed to be buttoned up. She buttoned it up and slung a cream scarf round her neck, and departed for the bank.

Mr Herriott knew about her mother's death and welcomed her with the slightly unctuous sympathy of the professional man doing his duty. He was not, after all, a dear friend, more a schoolmaster figure with his lips usually pursed over another of George's impetuous buys. He sent a minion off to examine Alice's portfolio.

'We can perhaps get a rough idea – very rough. She has some shares in Unilever, I think, which your father left. Do you want us to handle the probate? We should be very happy –'

'I might do it myself. It's not difficult, is it?'

'Not at all. Tedious rather. You will want all the certificates and the deeds of the property. We have them all here.'

'I don't want them yet. I'll come back when the funeral's over. It's just that the boys – you know . . . we read the will. They want to know if it's anything to get excited about.'

After a wait of half an hour, Miranda discovered that it was, in fact, enough to get moderately excited about, far more than she had expected. It was something in the nature of fifty thousand pounds between the four of them.

'That is the current value of the shares. The expenses will have to come out of it, and any bequests she might have made.'

'No bequests.'

'Very well. I shall await your instructions – presuming the shares are to be sold? We can do that for you when you're ready. Of course, they can be divided and put into the young people's names, if they would prefer that?'

'I very much doubt it. I'll let you know.'

Mr Herriott made some sympathetic noises and Miranda departed. Good old Alice! So nice for Philippa. The others would probably squander it. Sally's would have to be put away for her to have in a year or two.

As she drove home it dawned on Miranda that she had got indubitably the worst of the bargain, a rotting, barely inhabitable old farmhouse with a sitting tenant. She could neither sell it nor live in it.

Perhaps she would wear the jewellery after all.

CHAPTER THREE

ON THE DAY of the funeral there were cars parked all round the village green and a good few on it. Miranda knew when they arrived at the church that it was standing room only; she prayed, as she followed the coffin up the aisle, that they would not all come back to Lilyshine. It was a good day for it, the ground still too wet for spraying, a non-hunting day and, Napoleon's horse having won, a cheerful atmosphere. Alice would have approved.

The plain fact of Alice being reduced to silence in a quite small wooden box after her lifetime of domination overcame Miranda, and she wept quietly all through the service. George too blew his nose several times. The four grandchildren stood in a row perfectly turned out for the occasion, the boys in the good dark grey suits that served for NFU dinners, Young Farmers' dances and friends' weddings, Philippa in sombre purple which became her and Sally in black, albeit leather with studs. Sally had been plunged into shock and mourning only two days before, on her exuberant return from skiing. The funeral was rather soon for her; it had been a mistake not to send a message to the ski slopes. Sally, having said for several years that she loathed Alice, was suddenly exhibiting a most unseemly – so it seemed to Miranda – grief. Having cried noisily all night, she had now donned black boots, black tights, a black mini-skirt, a black jersey, a black leather jacket and a black leather flying helmet over her cropped bright yellow hair. Her tanned face and sky-blue eyes (George's) shone gloriously out of so much gloom: the effect was impressive. The farmers' eyes missed none of it as she shuffled into church.

Tom the vicar needed a haircut. His friendly, confidential style of praying and sermonising annoyed Miranda; he was more like a chat-show compère than a cleric. Miranda liked her vicars old, wise and unimpeachable, but that sort were now all, like Alice, into the next world. Meg had, thank God, chosen stalwart hymns, nothing in the pop style which Tom showed signs of favouring, and the good attendance and earthy lack of inhibition resulted in a splendid, rip-roaring send-off. Not many elderly ladies could inspire such affectionate respect in a male world.

The crematorium was twenty miles away and Miranda had decided not to go with the body; it was only disposal, after all. The farewells had been made in church. Tom had thought this unorthodox, but agreed that it was practicable. But when the coffin was reloaded into the hearse and covered with a mere fraction of the generous and flamboyant mass of flowers that had appeared with the congregation, Miranda felt a near-panic of remorse and a quite ridiculous surge of emotion. As the po-faced pallbearers closed the doors of the hearse she turned her face into George's best suit and wept afresh.

'Oh, come on, old girl.' George patted her.

Meg breezed in.

'Let's go and open a few bottles. That's what she'll be thinking now, Miranda – the demon drink. Enough of church.'

'The whole bloody lot are coming, Mother,' Felix said anxiously.

'We got it sale or return,' Meg said, practical as always. 'There's enough for the whole county.'

Most of the cars remained on the village green. The congregation stood in knots in the churchyard, the men chatting, the women nosing over the cards on the flowers, no one in a hurry to depart until they had worked out who might be expected to stay. In the county pecking order, some were certainties. Others, not so bold, hovered hopefully until the drift down the road towards Lilyshine became well-established, then tagged on apologetically. 'We'll just have a quick word. We won't stay.'

Meg coped, appropriating helpers, organising Jack and Felix, guiding Philippa, goading Sally. Miranda had nothing to do. George talked, drank and laughed; Miranda shrank behind the long chintz curtains in the dining room and watched numbly. It was true that her mother had known all these people personally, but she, not given to joining in, eschewing the horse scene, realised that she was scarcely recognised in their social register. Even while they voiced the obligatory sympathies, their eyes were out across the room looking for someone they wanted to talk to. All her life Miranda had been Alice's daughter, or George's wife. It had never been quite so obvious as it was now. She murmured the right things when approached, nodded, smiled, but had no duties to discharge as a hostess, as they all knew each other better than they knew her. If anyone was a stranger here it was herself. Even Sally could chat to the farmers better than she could, and the reserved Philippa, now known as a Londoner, had lost none of her old familiarity with the Pony Club set, the young marrieds, whom she was patently pleased to meet again. She laughed and gossiped with an ardour Miranda had never seen her display in Paul's company. Her family were all at their best, but she was nowhere, anchored behind the threadbare curtains.

'My mother asked me to bring you a drink.'

It was Martin, Meg's violinist. He smiled at her, holding out the whisky. He was the only person in the whole room Miranda was pleased to see.

'Are you all right?' he asked.

'Yes. Just a bit overwhelmed.' It struck her – 'How nice of you to come. Paul hasn't turned up, but you've made the effort.'

'No effort. Mother told me, and I'm free today, so I drove up. I think Paul's got an engagement.'

'He's always got an engagement.'

'He's pretty successful. It could be true.'

'Well, I wouldn't know. We never see him.' She smiled. 'I'd far rather have had you for a son-in-law. Think how your old mothers would have loved it! You young folk are so inconsiderate.'

'Gracious, I'm no catch! Philippa's on to a good thing. Paul's brilliant.'

'Is he? He's not exactly a bundle of fun.'

'No. Hard to live with. But he's really good at the job.'

'Oh well.' Paul was not a subject that Miranda cared a lot for. 'Whatever would he have thought of this lot?'

Martin laughed. 'Living in London, you forget . . .

it's always a shock, coming back, if you see them en masse. But then what would this lot think of a reception in the green room, after a performance of a Bartok sonata? They're just as way out, in the other direction.'

'At the moment, I don't feel I belong anywhere.'

'You do, don't worry. After losing someone like Alice you're bound to be disorientated. It'll come right in time.'

He spoke with sympathy and wisdom. He was, after all, the same age as Philippa, nearly thirty, hardly a child. Miranda liked Martin better than she liked Jack and Felix. He was gentle and liked things of the soul: music and the books she was always intending to read, Thomas Hardy and Anthony Trollope . . . He could talk about them, and he didn't overpower, he didn't show off, he drew the other person out instead of bombarding them with his knowledge. He was much too good to remain unmarried. Meg had wondered aloud occasionally if he was gay, but Miranda had never thought so, although it was impossible to know. He had a flat in Notting Hill Gate not far from Paul and Philippa, and taught at one of the London music colleges, and broadcast quite often, and played in recitals. He was very civilised, by Miranda's reckoning. She sometimes wondered if he was the *bona fide* son of Meg's banana boat husband, being so unlike, but of course she would not enquire.

He stood beside her, watching. Old May Bloom was pontificating nearby – always known as May Bloom although she was officially the Dowager Duchess of somewhere remote in Ireland – a bandy-legged, ancient friend of Alice's with outrageous dyed orange hair and a laugh like a hyena. She bred and trained gundogs and usually wore plusfours, although her funeral apparel was less eccentric: a tweed trouser suit in ginger and bottle green checks and a brown corduroy cap. George had given her a huge whisky. Her intake was renowned, but it made no apparent difference. Her car driving, which was appalling, was said to improve after six doubles, although she had now lost her freedom to demonstrate. Her gardener had been provided with a chauffeur's uniform and was no doubt sitting up on the green reading *Sporting Life*, waiting for her to reappear. Even to look at her made Miranda flinch, but George swore she had a heart of gold. She was always worrying at George to 'pull his socks up' and organise a decent shoot on his land, but George was too slapdash to nurture gamebirds.

George, well-liked amongst this fraternity, was not admired for his farming, only for his optimism and enthusiasm in the point-to-point field. The general opinion, as Miranda well knew, was surprise that he managed to get by on his farming without going bankrupt. Only the bank manager, talking to Meg, knew how much he owed. Grudging honours in the farming world were accorded to the man George called Napoleon, on account of his constant expanding of his boundaries. Meg was surprised to see that Napoleon had taken a day off to make his farewells to Alice, for he was talking to May Bloom, a rotund man shaped like an egg, small of head and feet and rounded in the girth. He was a merchant banker, officially Arthur St John Martindale, and his farm was mostly run by a very able manager. What hedgerows it had were sheared almost to the ground, the woods had been pulled out and the fields were all ploughed to the last inch. 'No bloody cover for man nor beast,' George complained. But it paid to be polite to the man. Politically he was on their side and his large donations to various causes did not come amiss. He did not hunt, shoot or fish but redeemed himself by buying steeplechasers which were professionally trained. One assumed from the evidence that he was a selfmade man. George, whose father was a barber in Romford and whose love for horses had been nurtured by his grandfather who had a totting cart and a Welsh cob, had entered the county set through his marriage. The true but now decaying scions of the old country estates, born and bred, were represented at Alice's funeral by Sir Henry Montgomery

Fielding-Jones, commonly known as Old Windy. Sir Henry, now approaching eighty, had a flatulence problem and his noisy presence had long been accepted in society. Only the children still giggled. He was crumbling fast yet his latest (fifth) wife was a girl still in her twenties and quite gorgeous. She was a Roedean girl and swore like a trooper. She rode, shot, fished and went racing and was a great favourite of George's. Sir Henry, from his five wives, had sired thirteen daughters and no sons. 'It must be a biological fault,' Alice had always maintained. 'Poor man.' 'In this age of Equal Opportunities does it matter?' asked Meg, to be different. 'With you, no,' George replied rather rudely.

Sir Henry, reporting at intervals like the finishing gun on the terrace of the Royal Yacht Squadron during Cowes week, was talking to Napoleon's gamekeeper (a great pal of Alice's) and his wife Sandy was talking to George. Miranda wasn't at all sure that George had not slept with Sandy. They had a very intimate way of looking at each other. They were both born flirts. Sandy was a willowy blonde with enormous green eyes. She rode like an angel, and had fitted in the obligatory two-girl children out of the hunting season. She and George made a beautiful pair, even Miranda admitted it. It still hurt Miranda to see George flirting, even after all these years and in spite of knowing when she had married him that he was a ladies' man. She had blindly ignored her mother's warning: 'They don't change, remember that. Marriage doesn't make any difference with that sort.' Miranda wasn't enthralled when George made love to her these days. 'I don't want to get AIDS thank you.' 'Who do you think I go with, for heaven's sake?' was the answer, not a denial of adultery, only a defence of its quality.

And as she watched them, Miranda wondered how any girl as lovely as Sandy could marry an old man like Henry and bear him children. He had no charm, like many elderly men: he was fat and shambling and invariably had food stains on his lapels; his hands shook, his eyes watered; he had slack wobbly lips and high purplish colour in his cheeks and in his big swollen nose. He had jowls like a bloodhound. He was more than fifty years older than his wife.

But he could trace his family back to the Crusades and his house to the thirteenth century. Quite shortly he would die and leave her the beautiful manor house with a stableyard full of hunters, a park, a farm and several million pounds. She would be about thirty with the best of her life before her.

Meg admired her. 'She'll have earned it. Take your hat off to her.'

'Never.'

Miranda appreciated the cunning but despised Sandy. Miranda was a true romantic. She had married for love.

'And look where it got you!'

'I wouldn't have changed anything, all the same.'

'You're stubborn, just like your mother.'

Late in the afternoon people started to leave. They had had too much to drink and wanted to get home before dark; also they had animals to feed. George and the boys changed and went out to see to the animals and Miranda started to clear up, helped by Meg and Philippa. Martin collected the glasses and the empty bottles and Sally went up to her room to play records.

'What did children do before there were records?' Miranda asked. 'We didn't have records. Only "Tubby the Tuba".'

'We read books?' Meg suggested. 'I didn't – I was always outside – but girls like you probably did.'

'Yes, probably. But my mother always maintained that reading was a waste of time. I had to hide. I remember that.'

'Horsey people, on the whole, don't read. Only *Horse and Hound*.'

The reverberations of Sally's rap music thudded in the ceiling beams. The funeral was over and her tears were no longer required. Miranda did not understand Sally. But she had always got on with Philippa.

Philippa went out to the stableyard after everything was shipshape. It was just getting dusk, and the old familiarity of 'going out to feed the horses', the smell of the hedgerows just coming into leaf, the evening crooning of the pigeons in the oak trees across the lane, gave her a surge of childish nostalgia. She came home so rarely now. But nothing changed here, from the bickering of her brothers in their unsatisfactory routine – the farm, as run by George, was incapable of providing three decent salaries – to the undemanding, all-sustaining nature of her mother whose devotion to duty never wavered. In the face of George's infidelities this was a constant surprise.

'So, what's new round here?'

Jack was in the feed room filling the buckets, measuring corn from the bin. He had changed back into cords and jersey.

'Nothing's new, mate. That'll be the day! Unless you count Maureen.'

'Maureen?'

'The filly we bred from old Fleabite – you remember? Dad's going to run her when the ground firms up a bit, so she counts as new, I suppose.'

'God, you can't call a racehorse Maureen!'

'Dad can.'

'Does Felix still do the riding?'

'Yes.'

'You're rich now. You can buy one of your own.'

'Christ, that's the last thing I'll do with it! Bloody horses!' Jack laughed. 'Buy myself out, more like.'

'It's not the army.'

'Feels like it sometimes.'

'Dad still the sergeant major?'

'You know what he's like. Felix and I, we tried to make it so that we did our own thing. Me the cattle, Felix the sheep, both of us the crops – leave Dad his horses and keep out of our hair. But he won't let it work, always interfering. You can't do that. You've got to do this. He doesn't give us a chance.'

Philippa grinned. 'That doesn't surprise me! Granny never mellowed, did she? And I can't see him taking to the bowls club and over-fifties coach trips.'

'We reckon we could make this place work, Felix and me, if he'd let us.'

'What, and if you marry and want a house each, and raise kids?'

'Hang about. We weren't looking that far ahead.'

'You're twenty-seven, Jack!'

He didn't look it, all the same, a large blonde man

the image of his father, but without George's sparkle and aggression. Jack was, by nature, painstaking; he liked dismantling engines, restoring old motor bikes, mending clocks. He was a man for detail, for poring over conundrums; he was careful and thorough. George wanted quick results and a tilt at this, a tilt at that. It wasn't a farmer's nature, too short-term. But Jack had the right credentials, given a chance.

'Will Granny dying make any difference, do you think? She egged him on, didn't she? Spending money on the horses.'

'A new tractor would be more to the point. The trouble is, Dad's not been left any actual money, has he? The farm and the house, but he virtually had that already. Here, you can take these two buckets – the end boxes, Maureen and Harry.'

All the same, Philippa thought, Lilyshine wouldn't be Lilyshine without the horses. Her father lived on the hope of all racing people: that one day he'd stumble across a real winner, a star. The family were more realistic. For every Desert Orchid there were a million also-rans. Her father's head was in the clouds.

But dull if no one believed in dreams. Philippa had believed in dreams when she got married, but it hadn't worked out. Her mother had warned her; she hadn't listened. Did any child ever listen?

The looseboxes had been built in the old threshing barn, two rows of five on either side, knocked up by the boys with timber from the demolition yard. The barn had a roof like a cathedral held up with cruck beams five hundred years old. The barn was listed, but no one could keep such a barn in order any more without a fortune. Its once thatched roof was now tile, and what wasn't tile was corrugated iron, a growing area. The site of Lilyshine was ancient; a farmyard and house had always been there. As a child Philippa had been very aware of a sense of times past, and the same feeling came back to her now, walking down the aisle of the great barn, hearing the sough of the evening breeze high over the arched summit of the massive timbers. It reduced her ego to a proper pinpoint of human aspiration. How ridiculous their ambitions, their squabbles, even their deaths, taken in the perspective of five hundred years! Alice had been able to trace her family back to the twelfth century, but it mattered not a jot in essence. Only the feel of it in the barn was still there, an awareness of the men before them.

'So you're Maureen?'

She tipped the contents of the bucket into the manger fixed inside the door. Maureen plunged her handsome face into the feed, one eye taking in the stranger, but greed overcoming nerves. She was hidden under some disgusting jute rugs, ripped all over, barely kept together by the surcingle that encircled her deep and impressive girth. Philippa remembered her as a sweet foal, shy amongst the buttercups in the top meadow.

Harry was George's old hunter and point-to-pointer, now past his prime and looking it. He put back his sage ears and waited crossly while his feed was delivered. His name was Harrington Pike, after a long-dead local huntsman. Philippa had ridden him many times.

'You old fool.' But he was looking fit, considering his hard life.

She patted the hard muscle of his bright chestnut neck. He was a devil to ride, pull the arms out of you. He suited George perfectly.

There were two other horses she didn't recognise opposite. Jack brought their feeds up.

'Dad's bargains – you know. He got them cheap, dicey legs. They need to go out to grass for a couple of years.'

The story of three-quarters of the world's steeplechasers.

They took the buckets back to the feed room and swilled them out.

'You going home tonight?' Jack asked. 'I thought

that fellow of yours won't let you out of his sight?'

'Who said that?'

'Just an impression I got.'

'I'm staying tonight.' Her voice was cool.

Jack gave her a sideways look, not sure whether to pursue it. They were close together in age and had got on well as children. Felix had caused the trouble, the spoilt baby pestering them, coming between. Felix had always demanded more than they had.

'What's wrong with your Paul, that he never comes with you. Or what's wrong with us – is that a better way to put it?'

'No. He just won't leave his work, that's all. Hours of practice – it's like having a milk quota. No days off.'

'It's a good excuse. I'm not convinced.'

Philippa closed up when talk came round to Paul. Jack was not the only one of the family to notice it. Her clear eyes became non-committal; small frown lines gathered on her forehead. Jack felt an instinctive antipathy towards Paul for not pleasing his sister more. Even as a child she had not easily shared her joys and fears. And there was no mistaking now that there was something about her marriage that she did not wish to discuss. She had the same tolerant disregard for self that stamped Miranda, an old-fashioned acceptance of the yoke. Standing there with her frown, her straight brown hair hanging in wings on each side of her round, earnest face, she looked just as Jack remembered her as a child, listening to some Pony Club instructor. He felt a surge of affection for her, his old playmate, but he wasn't used to exhibiting emotion.

'You can't wait on him all your life, all the same.'

She shrugged. 'It's a difficult job, you can't imagine—'

'It's his job. Why don't you get one of your own? Have a bit of fun?'

'Hark who's talking!'

They went back to the house, feeling the old companionship. They, and Miranda, were the quiet half of the family. The other three were the ones who spoke their minds.

The visitors had all gone and supper was the leftovers, shovelled on to two or three plates on the kitchen table. There was soup and bread to fill it out.

'That went off very well,' George said, pulling up his chair. 'Alice would've enjoyed it. They did her proud, turning up like that. Hope they'll do the same for me when the time comes.'

'Yeah, we'll round 'em up, Dad,' Felix said.

George had been a long time seeing off Sandy Fielding-Jones and her natural bent for flirtation had aroused him. She had promised to ride Harry in the

Ladies Race in two weeks' time. The thought of her long, strong thighs in tight-fitting white breeches excited him. He was in a good mood, the drink still lifting him. After supper he would sit in front of the television set and go to sleep.

Miranda felt very tired. It was true that everything had gone very well, but that was no thanks to George. But she felt deeply relieved to have all the traumas behind her and sat at the table with a serene smile on her lips at the thought of rearranging her life. She was warmed by Philippa's presence, so rare these days. She sat opposite Sally, wondering why her two girls – and her two boys too for that matter – were so different from each other, considering they were mixed with the same ingredients. Philippa's presence was invariably calming, exuding reliability and strength, but Sally was like a bright butterfly, her wings endlessly beating against the window-pane in a bid for fresh fields and wider skies. She could not even sit still in her chair, reaching for the farthest-away food, fidgeting with her hair, nodding in time to the music plugged into her pretty ears. She was, unlike Philippa, all long legs and neck and childish grace, with a natural instinct for the opposite sex like Sandy Fielding-Jones. Miranda worried about her a lot. She seemed to have nothing in common with her at all, and hated to hear her own voice exhorting the child to work harder, dress properly, comb her hair, help wash up. Sally liked a good time, and had grown out of ponies and into boys with startling speed. She went out a lot, on the backs of rackety motor bikes and in rust-rotted cars, all driven with great panache by farmers' sons, and Miranda sat waiting for her to come back with sweaty visions of disaster polluting her evening. Philippa had never pursued a social life with such gusto, nor exuded the sex appeal which attracted the Young Farmers in such droves. It was the Alice genes reappearing, dancing recklessly in the girl's personality after avoiding Miranda and Philippa with almost insulting totality. She was, naturally, the apple of George's eye. He never chided her.

When they had eaten, Miranda said to Philippa, 'We can sit in the study. The fire's still in. You don't want to watch television, do you?'

'No.'

Perhaps she hoped Philippa would talk to her about her marriage. Or did she really want to hear? If everyone was happy, Miranda was happy. And if Philippa's marriage was a mistake, it would make her unhappy to know, and there would be nothing she could do about it. But she gave Philippa her chance, and Philippa sat in Alice's armchair and talked about what life would be like without Alice and what did Miranda plan to do with the house?

'It's never really been yours. It's all your mother's furniture, her taste. It's like a museum.'

'I'll redecorate it all, just keep the best bits, the antiques. It'll keep me happy until next Christmas. I like decorating.' She stopped, waited. Philippa was staring into the fire, frowning. 'And what will you do with your money? Have you any plans?'

'I'll put it away. In case . . .' She hesitated. 'In case.' She smiled.

Miranda waited. Philippa said nothing.

George put his head round the door.

'I've been thinking,' he said. 'This house, she left it to me.'

Miranda waited, curious.

'I'll sell it! It should fetch a bomb, all these yuppies up from London.'

'And what shall we live in?'

'Your house. Violets.'

'Violets! It's derelict!'

'Nothing we can't put right with a bit of effort. The money will put the farm on its feet, buy that new tractor the boys keep on about. Pay a bit off at the bank. It's a great idea, Miranda, for God's sake! I don't know why I didn't think of it before!'

'You didn't think of it before because it wasn't your house to sell.'

'I mean, before now. When you first told me what was in the will.'

'Are you serious?'

'Of course I'm serious.'

'I'm going to bed,' Miranda said.

CHAPTER FOUR

'THE GROUND'S DAMNED hard, Dad. I've walked it as far as the wood. I'm not going to hammer her – it'd be stupid.'

'She's got legs like iron bars, this one. But do what you like. Just let her see the fences. There's sixteen runners in your race.'

Miranda stood with Meg in the paddock, watching the men get Maureen saddled for the Maiden. George was thrilled to have a new horse running and was all excitement, fussing and fiddling, while Jack stood patiently at the mare's head and Felix fixed the strap of his helmet. It was a beautiful spring day and the point-to-point course was thronged with enthusiasts, the parked cars covering a whole hillside. Miranda had only come because it was a day to be out, and Meg had brought a sumptuous picnic which the two of them had consumed in the members' car park along with a bottle of wine, guaranteed to improve the afternoon. Watching horses race was all right when the sun shone and, although she never wavered from her conviction that it was a ridiculous sport, Miranda was nevertheless terribly proud of Felix when he came out to ride in his jockey's silks and spotless breeches. The family colours had been chosen by Alice – red cap, bright yellow and white quarters and hoops of red down the arms. And even if the colours did not exactly enhance his own auburn and gold colouring, Felix was something of a hero figure on the course, slender and handsome and known as a strong and intelligent rider. He was much in demand as a jockey but did not choose to ride for many others. He was basically lazy and only did as little as he could get away with. He rode because George expected him to. Jack wasn't as good as Felix and George was now too old, although he had ridden Harry in the Members race until the last year or so.

Maureen, not used to such an atmosphere, was proving very fractious, and George gave Felix a leg-up with the mare on the run, charging round the crowded paddock. Once aboard, Felix was able to steady her and she took her place in the queue of circling horses.

'That's a very nice filly,' Meg said appreciatively.

Miranda's eyes were on Felix. When they came past, near the entrance, he bent down and grinned at her.

'You're supposed to enjoy it, Mum. Cheer up!'

His golden-brown eyes had Alice's malicious gleam.

She smiled back, loving him. But it wasn't great fun, watching one's nearest and dearest competing in such a hair-raising game – the reason she skipped several of the meetings throughout the year. Now, without Alice, she no longer had an excuse. George and Jack came back as the horses cantered away to the post. George said cheerily, 'Put your money on, Meg? Doesn't she look all over a winner?'

'The bookies seem to think so, I'm afraid.'

'Do they, by God? I'll have a tenner all the same. What about you, Jack?'

'What, on what you pay me?' Jack's voice was derisory.

'Suit yourself. You'll regret it.'

George set off towards the bookies.

'He really expects her to win, doesn't he?' Meg said. 'Her very first race . . . he really is the world's greatest optimist.'

Meg wore an old leather coat of thirties vintage and a faded silk scarf spilled out at the neck. Her thick bush of grey hair stood out in the warm breeze. She adored the racing scene. Her deepest disappointment in life was having a violinist as a son.

'Felix is beautiful on a horse, Miranda. I envy you this so much!' She couldn't help saying it again, although she knew that Miranda was well aware of her feelings.

Miranda laughed.

'I'd rather go to a concert than a point-to-point any day of the week! Have you ever been to any of Martin's recitals?'

'I did once or twice, early on. I found it hard to sit still – no tunes, all that scraping! I think you've been more often than I have.'

'I went before Alice got so demanding. Once or twice.'

She had first seen Paul playing with Martin. Philippa had been with her and had been deeply impressed by the dynamic pianist. Poor Philippa.

They went to stand by the third fence, a good vantage point for the whole undulating course. Skylarks' voices shrilled above the buzz of the crowd. Meg checked her race card.

'What a cavalry charge! Sixteen is too many for this course. The fences aren't wide enough. Hey look, your mare is down as More Rain. By Morston out of Winter Weather. He's clever at names, your old man.'

'More Rain . . . Maureen . . . Yes, I see. That's the sort of thing he uses his brain for, I'm afraid. Not for issues of mind-boggling importance, like not going bankrupt.'

'Are you going bankrupt? He's been saying that for years.'

'Not if we sell Lilyshine. That is now the definitive argument.'

'Is he selling Lilyshine? I thought it was a joke.'

'No. Lilyshine is on the market.'

'Miranda, no!'

'Yes.'

'My God!'

'Look, they're coming!'

As the ground started to vibrate to the impact of sixty-four approaching hooves, Miranda's mind was wonderfully concentrated into its old familiar ache of agonising fear, excitement and pride. Sixteen novice horses, mainly out of control, bore down on the big brush fence beside them. Six feet in front of it a heavy orange-painted bar insisted they take off in time to miss that as well. The thrill was electric. At such close quarters one smelled sweat and hot blood, saw eyes dilated, men and beasts alike, felt terror, elation, and glory all in one. Miranda got a glimpse of Felix, gimlet-eyed, in the front rank, booting Maureen to take off well back. She catapulted through the air, jumping huge, and Felix let the reins slip, accommodating to her youthful enthusiasm, expertly balanced, a real professional compared with many of the other riders, as green as their horses. Two horses fell; one jockey got trampled on, kicked aside like a football and came to a groaning halt at Miranda's feet, spewing blood and teeth. Miranda melted away as the concentrated attention of the Red Cross homed in.

'Ugh!' Always the thought that it might be Felix.

'He's doing fine, your lad!' Meg breezed. 'Two lengths clear!'

She pulled Miranda across the trampled grass to get a viewpoint across the far fields. George bounded up, excited as a boy, as if it was the first time he had ever run a novice, instead of about the fortieth.

'She's got a jump in her! Did you see? It would have cleared Valentine's, that leap!'

He was all smiles, the golden boy Miranda had once loved so passionately. Not a great farmer, he loved the fringe benefits: the flavour of the farming world, wearing his tweed and Barbour, jawing at the market and, best of all, leading in his winner behind the hunt servants. Considering his upbringing and family life in Romford he had come a long way, but his brothers were richer in the beer trade. George chose to despise them. He despised their warm, double-glazed executive homes, their door chimes and their designer bathrooms. He only went to visit when his ancient mother sent word she needed to see him, fortunately not often, although he was said to be her favourite. Miranda hadn't been for years, because of leaving Alice. She had realised lately that looking after Alice had saved her conveniently from a good many things she didn't want to do. Even, the last year, point-to-points.

On the second circuit the horses were well strung out. There had been four fallers and five had pulled up or were in the act of doing so. When Felix jumped the jump close to them the next time he was smiling. He was lying third, and Maureen was still pulling hard. George started to jump up and down and Miranda felt the familiar sick, sweet excitement taking hold of her, so that her hands were trembling in her pockets. It was at the end of a race, when the horses were tired and the riders saw their chance of winning, that they rode without caution, when mothers found it hard to watch. Miranda had never wanted excitement in her life.

Maureen was gaining on the two leaders fast. At the second to last fence the leading horse fell and the other started to tire rapidly. The finish was uphill and Felix rode Maureen out and caught his rival on the run in to beat it by two lengths. The crowd roared; George capered and even Miranda let out some uninhibited cries of delight. Meg gripped her arm fervently.

'How that boy of yours rides! What a beautiful race he gave her!'

Miranda was flooded with joy that the race was over. Her heart could relax. They elbowed their way to the winners' enclosure and were waiting to meet Felix as he rode in between the two hunt horses and smiling huntsman and whip. All their friends crowded round to congratulate them. This was the moment George lived for, being everyone's hero: old May Bloom clapping him on the back, Sandy smiling into his eyes, Napoleon nodding amiably – the betting ticket to be honoured, the champagne to be accepted, the day his own. Jack had to take the mare and do the hard work, cooling her off, settling her down; George would be in the Farmers' tent, rejoicing.

'Well done, Felix!'

Felix smiled at his mother.

'She went well, didn't she? Dad might have a good one here.'

How many times had they believed that? Miranda laughed.

'It was great! You were splendid!'

Felix pulled off his saddle and went to weigh in. Later he would join them, washed and changed, the euphoria faded. Miranda knew he only rode because George demanded it. He like her had never wanted excitement in his life. 'Sometimes I'd like to do my own thing, Mum,' he had said to her more than once. But they all danced to George's tune.

Miranda and Meg followed George to the

champagne bar and Meg drew Miranda aside when the congratulations had faded and said, 'What's this about George selling Lilyshine? Are you going to leave? Is he selling the farm?'

'No, just the house. We go and live in Violets, can you believe? He makes a lot of money and we all carry on as before.'

'Violets is a bit of a ruin, I thought?'

'He's having it done up. He's quite decided about it so what's the use of arguing? The boys don't care one way or another – they say they'll get a new tractor out of it, that's all they're bothered about. Sally's been up there and has got all excited about making her own place in a hayloft over the old cow-byre. I'm the only one who's considered the fly in the ointment, making a fuss. So I've stopped making a fuss.'

'You don't want to sell Lilyshine though, surely?'

'Of course I don't!'

'He is a shit, your old man.'

'I suppose it'll get the bank manager off his back for a bit. And it'll give me plenty to think about. Showing prospective buyers round Lilyshine is going to be the real pain – God, listening to their remarks!'

'I imagine it'll be snapped up.'

'It's so shabby!'

'Old. Romantic. Different. "A house of character",

they'll say in the brochure. What about the stableyard, the barn?'

'We can't do without that. They only get the house and garden, no land, no outbuildings.'

'He's a great one for surprises, George. Don't sell it to any rats, for God's sake. Remember I shall be one of their nearest neighbours.'

It had taken Miranda several days to accept that George was serious; not until the valuer called did she accede to the inevitable and walk across the fields to see what Violets was like. The visit had done nothing to relieve her forebodings.

Violets was a very old house, massively built, with walls about a metre thick, small frowning windows and a load of rat-ridden thatch which passed for a roof. It had never, ever, been 'refurbished'. The front door was Elizabethan oak. The windows, true, were no longer mullioned, but the glass was distorted and quaint. One end of the house was still set out as a stable, although it was used for storing junk. One entered it from the kitchen, which was flagged with stone, mostly cracked, and still featured a fireplace big enough to park a car in. It had one cold water tap, a gas cooker fuelled by bottled gas and an extremely ancient electric wiring system.

'There is no way I am moving in until it is re-wired,

re-plumbed, re-floored and re-roofed,' Miranda said. 'That is the very least I will put up with.'

To her surprise George put the improvements in hand immediately. Arthur said he would go and live with his daughter who had a council house in the village. There was no impediment to moving, yet Miranda found it hard to believe: after all these years, she was going to move house.

Violets was set back from the road about four hundred yards. It couldn't be seen from the road by the steepness of the ground up from the valley. The drive left the road beside Lilyshine and followed the stream up the hill. Where the ground flattened out, the stream curved away to make a loop round Violets, containing the 'orchard' mentioned in the will. Beyond the stream were the woods which May Bloom wanted George to make into a shoot. Behind the house was a yard of old stock barns where the boys did the lambing and housed the calves. It was all very old-fashioned and picturesque, like something out of a child's picture book – 'A bloody run-down dump' according to the boys. It was probably more their complaints than hers that had provoked the builders' vans, the re-roofers and the electricity men in their droves.

All on tick, no doubt, until Lilyshine was sold. George was full of enthusiasm. The house agents were in, the colour photos taken, the advertisement space booked in the right magazines and newspapers. The agents wanted to include the barns and stables and some land, but George wasn't standing for that.

'Sell it to some smart Londoners. They only want parking space for the BMW and the Porsche. We don't want an equestrian centre, for God's sake.'

Over the years Miranda had learned to be adaptable. Violets could be quite attractive if the rats were removed, the damp checked, the smell of rot overcome.

'It's my house. I'll have it my way.'

'Suit yourself!'

She was now in a vacuum, unable to feel involved in Lilyshine, Violets not yet ready for her.

Two days after the point-to-point, the first couple came to view Lilyshine. They were German and discussed it in their own language while Miranda stood by. She was outraged and put the price up by ten thousand pounds.

'There is a misunderstanding? We were told—'

'No. That is the price. The agents have it wrong.'

She didn't tell George.

After seeing several couples who couldn't offer anything until they sold their own houses, she stayed in to meet a couple from Kensington who had already sold a Georgian house in a smart square. They arrived on time in a Mercedes which drew up on the drive alongside Miranda's rusty Escort. She watched out of the window as the couple surveyed the house from the car. They did not get out for some time, looking at the house from their seats. Miranda expected the car to back round and drive away but, after several minutes, the couple got out and approached the front door. Miranda felt nervous as she went to answer the bell.

Jason was very smooth, charmingly apologetic, endearingly understanding about the miseries of having to show strangers over one's house. Miranda melted before his charm. Ianthe was polite, restrained, her eyes flicking everywhere with laser efficiency. They were in their late twenties, perfectly turned out in Kensington style: expensive shirt and silk tie for Jason beneath a smooth grey suit, Ianthe in Jaeger and Gucci, silk-scarfed, scented, with plenty of gold jewellery. Miranda felt appallingly scruffy, although she was in one of her rather smarter pairs of cords, and clean.

'I'm afraid it all needs redecorating badly.'

'Yes, but one would enjoy doing one's own redecorating,' Jasper said, smiling.

Seeing the house through these sharp, expensive eyes, Miranda was ashamed by its shabbiness. She trailed the couple miserably, opening cupboard doors, revealing piles of grey towels and badly ironed sheets, uncleaned shoes, broken umbrellas and similar debris. The men never threw anything away. Their clothes cupboards looked like Oxfam shops in bad areas of town. Miranda saw Ianthe's eyes missing nothing. They were large, dark blue and rather fine, just beginning to show early wrinkles. Her beauty was spoiled by a thinness of the lips, a suggestion of shrewishness in her expression. She had highlighted, artfully tousled hair, not outrageously tousled like Sally's, but very expensively tousled. There were no hairdressers within miles of Lilyshine that could do such a job. She would have to commute back to town. She was not friendly like Jason, but cool and sophisticated, the sort of woman Miranda couldn't cope with at all. As a next-door neighbour for Meg, she was not the sort to shut up the chickens when Meg was delayed.

They made no derogatory remarks, whatever their opinions, and Miranda offered them coffee, ashamed (once more) that it was only instant.

'The place is very run-down, I'm afraid. If you come from town . . .'

'Remarkably accessible though. Only an hour and a quarter in the car. And one could drive to the station – the train service is very good.' Jasper's smile beamed on like electric light. After George, he looked incredibly well-groomed, his skin clear and smooth, his haircut impeccable. He was tall, broad but not fat; he carried himself well and gave the impression of total assurance and reliability. His charm was easy, but appeared real. His hands were smooth and well kept, with long, elegant, artistic fingers. Miranda supposed he was something in the Saatchi and Saatchi line, or possibly a stockbroker. Certainly not a used-car dealer.

'You would have to go up to London every day?' she suggested.

'Certainly, to the West End.'

'Quite a lot of people commute from here now. But basically it's still very much a farming community. We shall still be using the yard behind the house for livestock. The agents told you that?'

'Horses, they said. Not pigs . . . We enquired.'

'No, not pigs. But there is a manure heap.' She wanted these basics made plain. People came to the country and wanted muck-spreading stopped. However much he wanted to sell Lilyshine, George didn't want people like that around.

'I should think we could bear that,' Jason smiled.

Ianthe was not a chatterer. She sipped her coffee in silence.

'My wife is an interior designer. We are not into animals, I'm afraid.'

'Oh, my word, you'll have plenty of scope here!'

Ianthe smiled a cold smile. 'The rooms have good proportions, yes.'

It was the only compliment they paid poor Lilyshine. Miranda did not expect to hear from them again, and was happy, for they did not strike her as fair to Meg, nor a likely comfort to herself, should she need a helpful neighbour. But a few days later the house agent rang up and said they had made a very good offer.

'What's more, they've got the money.' He was very eager. 'Considering how much needs doing to the property, it's very encouraging. There will have to be a survey, of course. They want that put in hand, if that's agreeable to you.'

'Yes, of course.'

But Miranda was not excited by the thought of the Pertwees buying Lilyshine.

'They're not our sort at all. So smart. So smooth.'

'So rich! Rubbish, Miranda.' George was highly delighted, seeing his money.

'I never asked if they have children. They never asked about schools or anything.'

'No nubile daughters?' Felix was disappointed.

'No handsome sons for Sally? I should have asked,' Miranda said.

'I don't want any bloody public schoolboys, thank you,' Sally said angrily.

'Don't swear, Sally.'

'Bloody's not swearing, for God's sake!'

Sometimes Miranda felt she actively disliked her youngest daughter. Meg said it was a phase. 'Leave her.'

Sally looked atrocious, to Miranda's eyes, militantly sexy. 'She'll get herself raped,' Miranda said to George.

George said, 'She might like it.' So much for supportive fathers.

'Do you really mean that?'

'She'd scratch their eyes out, anyone who tried it on,' he said proudly. 'Why are you so stupid about some things? Why do you get so worked up? Girls are like that these days.'

'Philippa wasn't.'

'Oh, Philippa . . .' George's voice was dismissive.

'Meaning?'

'Whatever you like, dearest.'

'Meaning, by implication, that Philippa is unattractive to men because she doesn't wear her skirt up to her crotch and her blouses see-through as bedroom windows.'

'Did I say that?'

Miranda, when she argued, got herself in a muddle. She was aware of her inability to argue logically and blamed her years of domestic stodgery for her brain damage. But to lean on, George was the original broken reed.

'Does this mean we can all have a wage rise, Dad?' Felix asked hopefully.

'I've got to spend a lot on Violets, remember.'

Miranda saw a glance pass between Jack and Felix that she remembered, long afterwards, she ought to have heeded.

'We've got to be more than bloody labourers before we're forty, Dad. Just a thought,' Jack said.

'You don't know you're born, the pair of you!'

'Oh, great.' The glance flickered between them again. Jack went out, slamming the door.

'Who's that girl Jack's seeing?' George asked Felix. 'Skinny blonde, talking to him at the point-to-point? Nobody I know. I saw him with her the other night outside the Queens.'

'Don't ask me, Dad.' Felix dropped his eyes, clamming up.

Miranda was surprised, but said nothing.

'We could build him a bungalow, if he wants to get married.'

'Christ, Dad, he only met her last week.'

'I'm not mean, you know.'

'No, Dad, you're a bloody marvel.'

The family conversation round the supper table was

not uplifting. Miranda wondered if a bit of Pertwee polish might rub off on her tribe if contact were made. But George, prepared to take the Pertwee cash, was very sceptical of the yuppies interested in Lilyshine. He used the word with great scorn.

'I thought yuppies were just what you wanted? You said so, when you first talked about selling the place.'

'Yeah, but for neighbours . . .' He shrugged. 'I'd forgotten we've got to live with 'em.'

'The price you've put on Lilyshine, only merchant bankers can apply.'

'I was right though, wasn't I? Caught a fish in no time.'

'Let's wait and see the money first.'

But the sale proceeded smoothly. The Pertwees were extremely professional and gave no trouble, save that the very smoothness of the operation had Miranda moving house long before it suited her. Violets was still in disarray, its thatch removed and mere tarpaulin currently in place, the kitchen flagstones taken up and nothing yet laid to take their place, new electric wiring protruding from holes in the walls like tubes from a patient in intensive care. The Pertwees politely gave them an extra month's grace after the moving date originally suggested. Meanwhile they culled builders, plasterers and carpenters from the far shires to 'improve' Lilyshine.

Nobody local was involved. All their renovators were specialists in their trade, and their vans were white and shiny and had their names and telephone numbers written on the doors in gilt paint. The inelegant vehicles of the motley bunch of repairers working on Violets passed these vans parked outside Lilyshine every morning. Ribald remarks abounded. Lilyshine's guts began to gather on the front lawn in heaps. Whatever George was getting done at Violets was mere patching compared with the transformation going on at Lilyshine.

'Thank God it's summer,' Miranda remarked to Meg, sitting in her new kitchen admiring its new tiled floor. All doors and windows were open to air the replastered walls where the rising damp had been temporarily routed. Most of Miranda's furniture was stored in the lambing sheds. Her Aga, scorned by Ianthe, was installed in the enormous fireplace and the family could be fed again, which constituted normality. Fridge and freezer purred.

'What on earth is your Ianthe doing down there?' Meg asked. 'Have you been in?'

'No. She's not there very often, and I'd feel I was nosing if I went when she wasn't there.'

'Nobody else would be so restrained! Only you, Miranda.'

'I was very strictly brought up. Why do you think Sally's so awful? What have I done wrong there?'

'It's the biological thing at the moment, rebellion, leaving the nest, asserting her personality.'

'It's not a very nice personality. I feel ashamed of her.'

'It'll pass.'

'None of the others were actually horrid.'

'You're lucky then. One out of four. Count your blessings.'

'Ignore her, you mean?'

'If you can.'

'She'll get pregnant and I'm not going to look after it.'

'She won't! Don't be daft.'

In Violets' yard, which lay on the uphill side of the house, Sally had taken possession of what had originally been a hayloft. A boy of dubious appearance had arrived on a motor bike and fixed a lock on the door. 'And he's going to fix a wood-burning stove for the winter. So it will be my own place. My own bedsitter.'

'We own the property as it happens,' Miranda pointed out coolly. 'Your father will want a duplicate key.'

'What for, for God's sake? So you can come spying?'

'The last thing I want to do is spy on your sordid

affairs. It's our right, that's all. We still keep you. You eat our food and your father buys your clothes. You have to dance to our tune a little longer, until you are able to support yourself.'

Fortunately George supported Miranda in her stand, and a duplicate key was provided to hang on a hook inside Violets' kitchen door. 'She might set fire to the damn place, the way she smokes,' he remarked. Miranda hoped the smoking was of nothing illegal. She knew nothing about drugs, save that the one called grass sapped the ambition. Sally needed ambition to remove her to university; she was the clever one of the family and should be applying for university the following year. Looking like she did, no deceit university would offer her a place but that was a problem for the future. Meg was very reassuring, but what experience she had to go on was not convincing.

'You never had a daughter after all. Only Martin who's a sweetie. He wasn't any trouble when he was sixteen, was he?'

Meg laughed. 'He played the piano and the violin all the time. I thought it was very unhealthy and downright queer for a young lad, and lambasted him all the time. Made him clean out the chickens and dig the potatoes. He hated me and I was worried sick over him.'

Miranda remembered that her own mother had told

her she was unnatural, not wanting to ride the prize-winning ponies she was offered. She had been locked in her room on occasions, when Alice had despaired of her stubborn silences. She had read her books happily, much as Sally must now be smoking her dubious cigarettes in the fastness of her hayloft. Ah well. There were other things to worry about . . .

'That Lilyshine money is burning a hole in George's pocket. He wants a decent horse, he says, to replace Harry. He's going to the Doncaster sales.'

'Oh Gawd.'

'He's got four, too lazy to do them himself. The boys hate the horses. They say they're farmers, not glorified stableboys, and Geoge is too mean to employ a couple of girls.'

'Well, he does treat his family as personal servants. But you're not going to change George at this time of life, are you?'

There was no way of refuting the truth of that.

Miranda had introduced the Pertwees to Meg and a cautious appraisal had taken place. There was no great enthusiasm on either side. Jason's charm covered up Ianthe's tight-lipped silence.

'She's very clammed up,' Meg reported. 'Does she unbend on further acquaintance? We can but wait and see.'

Miranda called at Lilyshine when the Pertwees made one of their now more frequent appearances, to offer friendship and support. None was likely to be forthcoming from the vicar, for Meg reported that he considered such people parasites of society, using a rural community to further their glorified lifestyle. Miranda thought Tom's own lifestyle would benefit by a bit of glorifying, and that Ianthe Pertwee could well do without Tom's blessing; she was there to offer useful local information, free-range eggs and lambs for the freezer, the Lilyshine kitchen now apparently in action once more.

'Would you like to see what we've done?'

Jasper asked her in kindly.

'I hope you won't feel offended. The changes are fairly extensive, but we were looking for a property to renovate, rather than one just to move into. I expect you understood that?'

The staircase was about the only thing Miranda recognised, all her snug dark rooms having been swept away to make an enormous sitting room and a twenty-seater dining room. Light poured in. The long windows were now treble-glazed, the quaint interior shutters renewed, stripped to the old pale wood and looking indubitably part of a glorified lifestyle.

'Of course we shall still be having curtains. Ianthe's

got to have her head in this department — she's got a magic eye for colour! But you can see we are just about ready to start carpeting, and choosing the furniture. Most of our London stuff is too small in scale.'

The walls, pale and gleaming, were papered in discreet, silky colours. The plasterwork on the ceiling cornices, which had had a habit of falling into the soup whenever Miranda had had dinner-parties, was now renovated and picked out in gilt. The doors had been stripped down. The old brown skirtings were white and the marble mantelpieces which Miranda had hated looked fabulous, cleaned and polished and white as snow. The hearths were newly tiled, the fire grates replaced with new ones which would have paid the vicar's salary for a year. Miranda nodded her head at everything Jason said, and was taken to the kitchen for a coffee, made in a machine that needed an alcove to itself. Remembering how she had offered them instant in this same room, she felt disorientated, visiting on another planet. Her old kitchen, nub of her married life, was a palatial, white, purring space-deck, all dials and knobs and electric points. She could relate to nothing. Ianthe was obviously a hi-tech cook and the bottle-washing was done unseen, in the depths of the machinery.

'It's amazing,' she said lamely.

Jason beamed.

'When it's all finished, towards Christmas time, we are planning to give a party. We thought it would be really nice to have one for all the people we hope will become our friends in the neighbourhood. You could tell us who to invite, couldn't you? – so that we can meet everyone and give some hospitality in advance, a way of getting to know people.'

'That's a very nice idea. Everyone will be agog to see what you've done here. They'll love to come.'

As soon as she had said this, Miranda realised that she had as good as stated that everyone would be far more interested in seeing what the newcomers had done to Lilyshine rather than in meeting the couple themselves. This was the truth, of course. She tried, inadequately, to cover up.

'What we should do is give a party at Violets to introduce you to our friends.'

'But we've made this place especially in order to have parties. Look at the huge dining room! It would be a great pleasure to us to see everyone here.'

Tom the vicar would construe this generous idea as showing-off, no doubt. Perhaps it was. Miranda vowed to put him on the top of the invitation list, even if George was bound to remove him.

'It might be a bit one-sided – we are farmers and

know all the farming and sporting people. We don't mix a lot with –' Miranda faltered, aware that she was about to put her foot in it again. We don't mix a lot with the incomers like you, the pornographic films man, the trumped-up car dealer. We are great snobs, after all. We only mix with our kind, the earthy lot with mud on their boots.

'We would love to be introduced to them.'

So be it. Miranda reported to George.

'Great! We'll give 'em the lot – old May Bloom, Windy Jones, Jim the gypsy—'

He went to the trouble to pencil out a guest list. Jim the gypsy was an illiterate man made good who had a house with an indoor swimming pool, hard tennis courts and electronic gates. He and his wife Cissie teetered uncertainly on the edge of every gathering, happy and hopeful. He had been passed over by the golf club but the Pony Club loved him and used his pool to train the tetrathlon team. Cissie baked amazing cakes for the hunt puppy show. Miranda was dubious as to how well she would go down with Ianthe but when she raised her doubts George laughed and said, 'They want to meet all the lovable old country characters, surely? That's the brief, isn't it? What's wrong with Jim and Cissie?'

George, as usual, had put her in the wrong. She was

far more friendly with Jim and Cissie than he was. He still called them the bloody gypsies, which she never did. She was dubious as to whether Jason and Ianthe knew what sort of a party they were begetting – now that George's enthusiasm was roused she felt nervous.

'It's got to be a pleasure for them, not an ordeal.'

George laughed.

He changed the subject.

'Napoleon's going up to Doncaster – I told you, have a look round the sales. He's asked me to go with him, give him a bit of advice, so I'll be off tomorrow.'

'I thought we were rather busy just now?'

'The boys can cope.'

'They're ploughing. You've got the horses in – who's going to do them? And Masters is coming for a load of hay – he can't do it himself – it'll kill him.'

'Jack can help him. Or put him off for a couple of days.'

'He's had to borrow a lorry, for God's sake. It was all arranged.'

'Tell Jack.'

Miranda told Jack. She expected him to swear and sound off, but he took it in silence. She saw Felix look at him anxiously.

Jack said, 'Is Masters paying cash?'

'He does usually.'

'Okay.' Jack smiled.

Miranda rather thought her worms were turning. She was surprised it hadn't happened earlier, but the prospect gave her no joy. She was the scapegoat in all family arguments, the arbiter for peace with an impossible brief. Birds leaving the nest in the Fairweather family were considered by George to be ungrateful, unnatural, bloody-minded and stupid. It had been bad enough when Philippa had taken her quiet, stubborn stand, but the prospect of Jack departing had far more serious consequences.

George departed for Doncaster. Jack loaded Masters' hay and took the roll of cash in payment. In the evening after supper he went out. Felix, having done the horses, went on ploughing until ten o'clock. Miranda, decorating one of the bedrooms, could see the tractor headlights beaming steadily across the brow of the hill and smell the turned soil through the open windows. She tried to decide whether she was happy or not, running the emulsion roller steadily across the uneven plasterwork, and came to the conclusion that her happiness or otherwise was in the hands of other people. If the family was trundling along without disaster or dismay she was happy. She corrected herself: she was undisturbed. It was a state of mind too numb to count as happiness. Yet she was not unhappy. She was not living in a cardboard box on the Elephant and Castle roundabout or languishing in Holloway jail. She was by nature adaptable and contented, yet she could not help wondering if life was passing her by. She was never going to see the Himalayas or the Grand Canyon at the rate she was going on; she had never even got round to opening a Thomas Hardy novel yet – too much decorating to do. She had no great estimation of her own worth; she despised her lack of ambition to climb out of her rut. Yet she had married for love, known great passion, great despair, and given birth to four beautiful children. She had never, as far as she knew, done a dishonest thing or hurt anyone by her actions. She wasn't a failure. But these days she was doubtful about the future. Probably because it was the first time in her life she had had some moments of leisure in which to consider herself.

She wasn't a person people noticed much. She had cultivated hiding away in her childhood, and had got stuck like it.

She finished the wall and put the roller in a bucket of water. The small bedroom (Jack's) was crooked and the floorboards were wide and sloped slightly down to the inner wall. She liked it, the cosiness of the sloping ceiling, the little eyelike window looking out over the fields. She put her head out. Felix's ploughing was disturbing the night, which was otherwise perfect, still and smelling of autumn: wet leaves and old bonfires overlaid with diesel fuel and dung, a true farming mix. The sky was glittering with stars, very sharp. It was nice without George sometimes, she thought. She tried to think what it would be like to live alone and believed she would like it, but it was impossible to know. When she turned to go downstairs she saw the little room enhanced by its fresh pale apricot paint, and the stir of self-congratulation she felt she supposed was happiness, after all. It didn't take much, for her.

Felix came in and flung himself down in George's armchair. They had a small room opening out of the kitchen under an archway, and the comfortable chairs were there and the magazines and the TV set, arranged round a stove which was always in. The dogs slept in front of the fire. Carstairs hadn't moved out with Sally, preferring this hearth. Not a lot had changed after all. The Lilyshine atmosphere had transferred unscathed – unimproved, Miranda realised sadly.

'Is there a beer?'

Miranda fetched one. She expected Felix to have a bath and go to bed, but he seemed in no hurry to go. Stretched out in front of the fire, he looked to her very young, without a future. Like her, the boys lacked ambition.

'Has Jack got a girlfriend?'

He looked at her, rather surprised.

'As a matter of fact, yes.'

'Do I know her?'

'No.'

'What's she like?'

'She's a townie girl. Sharp. Blonde. High heels. Pushy.'

Miranda considered these adjectives doubtfully.

'Is it serious?'

'Well, the way Dad's riling Jack these days, it probably is.'

'Perhaps George ought to be told how Jack feels.'

'God, Mother, Jack's made it plain, I would have thought. Dad just doesn't want to know, does he? The original ostrich, our dad, sticking his head in the sand.'

'And what about you?'

'Oh, I'm all right.' He grinned.

But the girls liked Felix. One day soon he would want more than George was offering.

'As long as he doesn't buy any more bloody horses.'

Miranda smiled at this. 'A leopard can't change its spots.'

'At least there's no one to egg him on any more.'

'Poor George! He must miss Alice, mustn't he?'

And Miranda, having considered earlier the

constitution of happiness, felt her whole being flood with joy at the reminder of her release from Alice. Happiness indeed . . . how inconstant the human condition, that it accepted so quickly its most desired aspirations! She had always believed she would be happy when released from her mother's eternal presence and there she was, painting the bedroom wall, having forgotten already.

'Mother, you are wet,' Felix said disgustedly.

At this moment the loud revving of a motor bike from the yard broke the peace of the night and the ramblings of Miranda's mind. Sally was home. It was eleven-fifteen and she was still a schoolgirl. Miranda removed herself sharply from her armchair and went outside. Across the yard, by the steps that led up to her hayloft, Sally was dismounting from the pillion and about to invite her boyfriend into her nest.

'Sally!'

Miranda, having decided that her daughter was a hussy, bellowed across the yard. Sally paused on the steps.

'Come here!'

Sally came, scowling.

'I was only asking him in for a coffee.'

'The coffee's on here. Ask him in here. I shall be pleased to meet him,' Miranda lied.

She flounced away to put the kettle on and get out the mugs. If George had been home she wouldn't have done it. George said, 'God, Miranda, if she wants sex she'll have it whatever you do to try and stop her. It's biology, for God's sake, like a filly in season. You can't beat nature.'

'But we're not animals, George. We are intelligent enough to reason, not to thresh about under a hedge with the first male that comes sniffing. We try to cultivate something called self-control, self-respect – brains even.' Philippa had never behaved like Sally did. Philippa had studied diligently and eschewed boys until her fatal passion for Paul at the age of twenty-three. George implied that Philippa was unnatural. He had never felt for Philippa the way he felt for Sally.

Sally coming in from the night bright-cheeked was even to Miranda's jaundiced eye a sex-symbol. She had Alice's enormous flashing eyes and imperious eyebrows and her ridiculous blonded hair stuck up in a halo round the bony beautiful face. She was thin and moved with the endearing grace of the growing young, athletic and uninhibited.

'You coming the heavy mother or something?' she mumbled in the slack diction cultivated by her circle.

'Yes.'

Miranda cracked a smile in the direction of the

embarrassed lad who followed Sally into the kitchen. He was enormous, blinking, speechless, the original oaf, Miranda felt uncharitably. Clad in black leather from head to foot, with greasy black hair falling in a hank over his spotty forehead, Miranda found it hard to credit that George could encourage this relationship. Yet even as she, in Sally's words, acted the heavy mother, she knew in her heart that her attitude would fix Sally in her desire, whereas George's encouragement was far more likely to result in the relationship disintegrating. The young only wanted to show their independence, after all, and a mate that met with parental disapproval was far more satisfying than the encouraged nice boy.

Sally flounced on to a chair and waited for her coffee. Her bad manners appalled Miranda. She turned to the oaf.

'Do sit down – er—' She waited for enlightenment.

His face turned crimson.

He mumbled, grunted something. It sounded like Dan.

'Do sit down, Dan.'

'Sam,' Sally said.

To show her disapproval of the proceedings she then picked up Horse and Hound lying on the table and started to read. To reveal the rage that this provoked, Miranda knew would be point to Sally. She smiled sweetly at Dan – Sam.

'Sugar?'

He grunted, the blush mounting afresh.

Miranda took this for assent and put the sugar-bowl in front of him. She sat down opposite him with a cup of coffee which she knew would keep her awake, and strove to think of something to say. Absolutely nothing came to mind. Sally read intently. Sam ladled sugar into his mug and a fair sprinkling over the table which he then attempted to scoop up with his enormous hands.

'It doesn't matter,' Miranda said.

Sam grunted again, incoherent with embarrassment. Miranda looked at Sally. How could she do this to him? The only consolation was the one Miranda had wished for: he meant nothing to her at all, apart from convenient transport to town. Miranda then felt love and compassion for Sam.

'What's your motor bike? It sounds pretty powerful.'

He told her about his motor bike, first in grunts: 'Five 'undred grunt, fuel grunt grunt . . .'

'What does it do to the gallon?'

As if she cared, but Sam told her earnestly, his flushes, dying down, and Sally scowled into *Horse and Hound*. Miranda listened to tales of mountain-trailing . . . the Ridgeway . . . halfway up Snowdon by moonlight . . . 'Great . . . grunt . . . an' down them rocks, Christ! An' a Lan'rover chased . . . grunt . . . arse over tit . . .'

Sally yawned.

'I'm going to bed.'

'Yes, it's late.' Miranda got up. She beamed at Sam. 'Very nice to meet you. Call in any time. Jack's keen on motor bikes – Sally's brother.'

'Yeah. Great. Thanks.'

He roared off into the night.

'God, Ma, what d'you want to carry on like that for, inviting him?'

'Someone had to talk, Sally. It's called manners.'

Sally got up, stretched, grinned.

'You sound just like Granny.'

She lolloped out into the night, leaving Miranda seething.

CHAPTER FIVE

GEORGE CAME BACK from Doncaster with a new horse. Miranda was not surprised. The boys didn't say anything, watching it emerge from the lorry with narrowed, disapproving eyes. All the same, the habits of a lifetime could not be discarded.

'Bloody hell!' breathed Felix, the eyes widening.

'Christ Almighty, that's a horse!' Jack said.

George squeezed Miranda round the shoulders with one of his bearhugs.

'What d'you think, eh? Alice would've fallen for this one, wouldn't she? What do you say?'

Miranda, well-grounded from youth, saw a very expensive young horse of outstanding quality, a grey, strongly made with absolutely everything in the right place. It came down the ramp and looked all round with the bold intelligent eyes that every horseman looks for, not frightened, not silly, but like a king surveying his country. I'm here, he proclaimed, the long alert ears switching to take in his new home. What do you want of me?

'How old is he? Is he broken?'

'No. He's five, but no one's done anything with him.'

'What did that set you back?'

'A fortune?' Jack challenged.

'No. I was lucky. End of the afternoon, you know . . .'

Meg came to see the horse. It was called The Druid.

'What a ghastly name. All those bloody weirdos round Stonehenge. Aren't they druids?'

'I thought druids were Welsh. At the Eisteddfod.'

'That's no Welshman. What's George going to do with him?'

'Take him hunting and qualify him for point-to-pointing.'

'What did it cost?'

Nobody knew.

'It'll be in *Horse and Hound*,' Meg said.

'It comes today. Let's have a look.'

But Miranda couldn't find it, having searched through all the discarded papers.

'That's funny. It always comes on Thursdays.'

'Mine'll be at home. I'll look for you.'

Miranda, suspicious, said, 'I'll come with you. He's been rather evasive. I'd like to know.'

They walked back to Meg's cottage, past Lilyshine where the decorators were now working on the exterior, sand-blasting the stone Gothic extravagances and repointing the brickwork from which the sparrows' ivy tenements had been stripped. Lilyshine was beginning to look rather expensive and desirable in a way Miranda had never believed possible.

Meg's *Horse and Hound* lay on the kitchen table unopened. Miranda picked it up and flipped through it to find the lists of horses sold at Doncaster. There were five pages of them. She ran her eye down the first item, the horse's name.

'The Druid, grey gelding – here we are—'

Her voice trailed away.

Meg looked up sharply. Miranda's face looked haggard suddenly.

'Forty thousand pounds.'

'*What?*'

'He cost forty thousand pounds.'

'I don't believe it!'

Meg pulled the paper out of Miranda's hands and frowned at the small print.

'Jenny Pitman the underbidder,' she read out. 'Oh, my God, he's taken leave of his senses! For point-to-pointing! Forty thousand pounds . . . a gelding!'

Miranda sat down at the kitchen table and put her head in her hands.

'Keeping the boys on a pittance – and yet spending . . . oh God, the *irresponsibility*—'

'It's Alice, from the grave. She was prompting him.'

'Her money, I suppose.'

'Yours by rights!'

'Whatever will the boys say?'

'The gossip! How George's ears will burn! When Billy Beenbeg paid a mere twenty thousand for Daystar – do you remember? – everyone thought he was off his head. But this—'

'How they'll love it!'

Jack and Felix heard the news when they went to get a spare part for the tractor at a forge ten miles away. Felix came home for supper and said Jack had gone to meet his girlfriend and they could expect him when they saw him.

'And what does that mean?' George demanded.

'I think it means two fingers up to you, Dad. And I can't say I blame him.'

'All that money you've blown on that horse, Dad,' Sally said. 'Everyone thinks you're off your trolley.'

'Who's everyone, for God's sake?'

'Meg and I, for a start,' Miranda said.

'Kitty and Rosie Fielding-Jones,' Sally said. 'Sam. The vicar. My maths teacher . . .'

'The blokes at the forge said they're going to charge us double in future,' Felix said.

'And it was only in *Horse and Hound* today! Wait till the news has gone round. At the meet on Saturday – you'll have to buy drinks all round, Dad,' Sally said with glee.

George looked put out. Miranda knew he had not thought it through, this impulse buy. This was the story of George's life.

'Jealousy, that's all. Haven't got the guts to take an opportunity when it arises, most of 'em. A horse like that – how often do you see a horse like that?'

'If it performs like it looks, Dad, great,' said Felix heavily. 'But that's not how it goes, on the whole.'

'Could break a leg in the field.'

'Have you insured it?' Miranda asked.

'Cost an arm and a leg to insure that,' George said.

'And who's going to look after it, Dad? Who's going to break it in for a start?'

'You can do that, surely? Just up your street. A pleasure, a horse like that.'

'Alison Purvis charges seventy-five quid a week for breaking. Try her. Or pay me the same, then I might do it.'

'For Christ's sake, I buy you a ride like that, and you

try to hold me over a barrel – I'll break the bloody horse myself!'

'Yes, Dad. Great.'

They all knew, George included, that he hadn't the patience to break in a horse. The steady, slow, calm half-hour of work every day, handling, familiarising, walking about, talking, gradually extending the time, humouring, asking obedience, insisting, repeating, commanding . . . a horse like The Druid demanded top-class treatment. With The Druid, George now had five horses in his stables. The two with bad legs were not being worked, but they came in out of the field at night. There were five boxes to clean, five horses to feed, two to be kept hunting fit and hunted and one to break in.

George was silent, fuming, looking for a way out.

He turned to Miranda. 'You've got nothing to do now the old girl's gone – you could get him started, lungeing and handling? We could do it between us. As soon as he's riding, then I'll do it all.'

'Thank you, no.'

'I'll do it,' Sally said eagerly. 'For seventy-five pounds a week. Seventy, even.'

'What, instead of gallivanting with boys in your spare time?' Miranda asked tartly. 'You can spend any spare time you can find on your schoolwork. It wouldn't come amiss.' To George she said, 'Pay the boys, or hire a groom. What do you expect? Or do it yourself, like a job. Let the boys get on with the farm, and you stick with the horses. That's what they want – they've wanted it for years, to run it their way.'

But George was incapable of doing this. They all knew it. This argument was a perennial, and now – Miranda guessed – was fast coming to a head. Jack did not come home that night, nor the night after, and when he did it was to pack his things, kiss Miranda and take the best car.

'I did all the work on it. I've left Dad the money it cost, here on the mantelpiece. I've taken the logbook out of his desk.'

'Oh, Jack.' Miranda felt like wringing her hands, her feeble remonstrance being all she was capable of.

'I've moved in with Carol. We're going to set up a business. I'll send you the address when Dad's cooled down a bit. I don't want him round there knocking us up – you know how it'll be. Sorry, Mum, to land you in the soup but you must see, I can't go on scratching away for peanuts all my life, getting nowhere.'

'I think you're right, but –' But . . . who is this Carol? What sort of a business? What sort of home? What about Felix? Who will do your work here? Who will mend my car? Who is going to tell George? The only question she knew the answer to was the last one.

'Oh, Jack!'

'Honest, Mother. I should've done it long ago. He's impossible, you must see.'

'Yes, I do see, Jack, I'm not arguing.'

'I'll ring you in a week or two.'

'Yes, dear.'

'You're great, Mum. I don't know how you've stuck with the old bastard all these years.'

'No.'

He departed. Miranda sat in the kitchen, gazing into space. Felix would go too, she thought, and what would happen to George then? And herself, come to that, the sole buttress for George Fairweather in his idiosyncratic middle age? She missed Alice more than she would ever have known possible.

Jack was welcomed into the home of Roy and Mary Green, father of Carol, with a bone-cracking handshake and a blast of beery breath.

'I'm glad, mate, I'm telling you!'

Jack rather thought this amounted to an engagement of marriage to Carol, although the room he was allotted was not Carol's but the spare room with the suitcases stored under the bed and unsuitable lampshades stacked on top of the wardrobe. It was in the front, where no one else slept owing to the noise of traffic on the busy main road. A lamp-post shone in and spasmodic sounds of night-life made Jack an uneasy insomniac.

The Druid was the last straw. Jack knew he was a coward, not standing up to his father, sliding out when George wasn't there, but it had been hard enough to do without slugging it out face to face. He was a quiet lad, when all was said and done, and wanted a quiet life, but not necessarily one directed by his father. Old Alice's money had given him the necessary backing and Carol the opportunity.

He lay in bed listening to the late-night cars hissing through the November rain. The house was one in a terrace of boring red-brick homes built just after the First World War to accommodate the town's artisans in light industry. They had privet hedges in front and privies turned into garden toolsheds in the strips of back-garden behind. Televisions and radios could be heard through the walls, along with hammering, quarrelling and babies crying. Fifty yards up the road a set of traffic lights provoked a constant revving of engines and changing down of gears, and fifty yards down the road a parade of shops and a fast-food place attracted another nucleus of activity and noise. Jack, who had never thought his life privileged, realised that the space he had taken for granted was in fact rather special. Five of them to three hundred acres was pretty generous. And with his opting out it was a privilege he knew he was unlikely to get back again, even when George died, George being an unforgiving man when crossed. Yet in spite of this Jack felt carefree in a way he had never experienced before, as if ridding himself of his father on his back had shed a heavy burden. A sense of lightness and freedom, almost dizzying in its insistence, kept him on a strange high, lying sleepless on the lumpy bed with the orange streetlight in his eyes.

He could never remember feeling, even in childhood, unaware of his father's reactions to his every move. And he had never come up to scratch, not at school, not in sport nor in riding. Felix had, but he hadn't. He hadn't Felix's courage, Felix's debonair grace, Felix's good looks. He had disappointed George in every way and the look on George's face, the impatient, angry frustration badly disguised, was etched deep in Jack's childhood memories. His mother's arm, protective, understanding, laid across his shoulders, had burned like fire. George loved and was proud of Felix and Sally, his two youngest, because they were beautiful and bold and physically brave, but the qualities of his two eldest he had passed over because they were boring. A dogged perserverence in the face of adversity, a characteristic he shared with Philippa, was low on glamour; willingness to work hard and demand little was taken for granted. The only way to live with George was to go along with him, as Miranda had, submerge the personality and say yes, yes, yes. Jack should have left long ago but, until he had talked his troubles over with Carol, he hadn't fully understood what they were. Carol, hard and bright like a polished stone, had pointed out the hopelessness of his prospects: until his father died, he had nothing. And his father was a young fifty-four, totally incapable of changing his ways. It was the Alice and Miranda situation, Carol pointed out. 'And look where that got your mother!' As Carol had never met any of his family, Jack asked her how she knew, and came to realise that the gossip of the neighbourhood was far-reaching. Carol's father Roy was a salesman for cattle feed, and there was little he didn't know about the farming hierarchy. Roy said he could get Jack a job in the feed business if he was willing to bide his time a while, but Jack fancied working in the motor trade and knew a few people to approach in the town.

Carol was full of ideas. She was shrewd and aggressive when it came to making money. Hairdressing was her trade but, having set up a salon, she wanted to move on. Next door to the shop she ran was a run-down wool and haberdashery which she wanted to take over. The leasehold was on offer, along with the flat over the shop.

'We can live over it and build it up, and I can still run the salon. That old couple . . . all that rubbish in there, baby wool and sock wool – it's out of the ark. I'd throw it all out and get quality stuff – fashion stuff, and tapestry gear, and embroidery stuff – there's nowhere else in town that goes in for anything like that. You could put the shelves in and we could make it look really good – class, you know. The situation's right . . . I think it could be a little goldmine.'

Jack knew that old Alice's money was going to set up this business. But he accepted that Carol was bright and knew a thing or two. The hairdressing business was a success, and she had built that up from nothing. She was an ambitious girl, hard and ruthless. Jack knew that he was no go-getter and realised that he stood a chance of getting somewhere if he could survive a partnership with Carol. The prospect both scared and intrigued him. He admired Carol and was slightly nervous of her, but she was a fine girlfriend with a happy appetite for sex which he found amazing. He wasn't sure that he could live up to her, and knew he had scant chance of getting his money back if the partnership fell apart. Yet how had the money been made in the first place? – only by old Alice's gambling. And this was just another gamble.

Alice would be applauding him, he felt, going into this thing with his eyes wide open. Scornful of a *woolshop* no doubt, but glad for a risk taken, a jump in the dark – it had been her life, to find excitement through taking a chance.

Whether he was in love with Carol or not, Jack could not tell. She would not be easy to live with, but she was good for a laugh, not narrow and mean. She was as far removed from the selfless Miranda as a woman could be. Miranda had married for love and where had that got her? George had married for the main chance and set himself up for life. Jack rather thought that's what he might be doing himself, if not in such a grand style.

One thing he did know: he was glad he had broken with his father. It was like coming out into sunshine after a winter's dark.

'If you put the addresses against these names, I'll give this list to Iona or whatever her name is.'

'Ianthe.'

'Bloody silly name. Probably christened Iris. Or Mavis.'

Miranda studied George's choice of guests for the Christmas party. Seeing her face, George said, 'No changing it now!'

'There's people here that don't mix. Nobody asks Napoleon and the Parmenters – not after that monumental row after he cut the oak trees down. And Sandy and the Bambridges – old Windy knows Sandy had it off with Jerry Bambridge. Nobody asks them together any more.'

'For God's sake, nobody expects Irene to know these things, do they?'

'Ianthe.'

'It'll give 'em all a chance to forget old scores. Good for 'em. It's a fine bunch I've put together for her. We don't want to all fall asleep, do we? Get a few sparks flying – that's the makings of a good party.'

'It'll be your fault if there's any embarrassment.'

'That hard-faced hen will love it.'

'Jasper seems pleasant enough.'

'Never here, is he? Only bought the place as a spec, I reckon. It'll be on the market again in no time – bloody estate agents.'

George was increasingly bad-tempered since he had had to do Jack's work. He had never noticed before exactly how much Jack had done for his pittance, and could see the farm falling apart more rapidly than usual. The thought of employing someone else was anathema to him; he would have to pay twice what he paid Jack.

Miranda would have suggested a girl to do the

horses, but did not want to put temptation in his way. One Saturday morning when Sam roared into the drive on his motor bike on his way to collect Sally, George and Felix were just going out exercising. George bawled at him and he throttled down apologetically, continuing on his way up to Violets after the horses had disappeared along the road. He came into the kitchen where Sally was still eating her breakfast, and mentioned the meeting to Miranda. Since the first meeting over coffee, he had thawed towards Miranda and spoke more freely.

The words he used – 'a smashing grey' – alerted Miranda.

'Do you know anything about horses?'

'My dad's got a Welsh cob.'

Sam was currently on the dole. It occurred to Miranda that if he got a job working for George doing the horses she might kill several birds with one stone. Sally would see far too much of him and look farther afield; George might stop being so bad-tempered and Felix could get back on the tractor where he belonged.

The deal was done, although with much grumbling from George.

'You can show him how I like things done. If he's no bloody good he's not staying—'

Miranda showed Sam. He knew all about handling horses and how to groom and muck out; he had a quiet way with them and was pleased with his new job. Undone from his motorcycling leathers, he was a large gangling boy with huge hands and feet, a wide amiable face given to pustules and a forelock of black hair that hung down over the bridge of his nose. He worked slowly but thoroughly. Felix had done the same jobs at the gallop, taking half the time but leaving a nervous air behind him. Miranda sensed that the horses were better under Sam's care. He came in the morning and in the evening, and his employment made a drastic improvement to the atmosphere at Violets. Miranda was pleased with her idea.

The party at Lilyshine was to take place a few days before Christmas. None of the invitations had been refused. Ianthe asked Miranda if she would help her with the table-placings, but George insisted on doing the job and went down to Lilyshine all smiles and charm. Miranda suspected it was to put himself next to Sandy Fielding-Jones and the warring factions opposite each other. She feared the worst.

'She wants me at the head of the table, as the host,' he said when he came back, all smiles. 'I have to introduce everyone to her and Jasper when they arrive. Then she said she wants me at one end of the table and she will be at the other.'

'Where've you put me?'

'Between Jasper and Jim the gyppo.'

'Oh, thank *you*! And who is sitting next to you? Sandy Fielding-Jones, no doubt.'

George looked surprised.

'I can't spend all night with some dumbo, can I? We have a lot in common, Sandy and I.'

'Dumbos? I thought a mix of the intelligentsia was what was required? You chose them.'

'A general mix. Not many of us are intelligentsia, let's face it. She wants to meet the country people. I chose mainly the rich ones, give 'em some common ground.'

'Talk about our investments all night.'

'You're being bloody difficult about this, Miranda.'

Miranda thought she had good cause. She feared George would drink too much, when anything might happen. He was apt to get either belligerent or morose with too much drink, not happily stupid like most. She took his best suit down to the cleaners and called on Ianthe to see if there was anything she could help with.

'Your husband has been marvellous. I'm sure it's going to be great fun.'

'Well, I hope so.'

Ianthe had a numbing effect on Miranda: there was so little Miranda could find to relate to. Ianthe had a hard shell which showed no cracks: all her remarks were completely impersonal; she showed no curiosity, no interest in relationships. She spoke only of her house, her few problems, never of her feelings, her ambitions, her past. She was still faultlessly coiffed and dressed, no slackening into country ways: immaculately pressed white trousers for leisure wear, no sign of jeans or wellies, no gardening grime under her fingernails. She seemed to spend all day polishing her silver, washing her vases and arranging flowers that arrived in a van. She seemed to Miranda a total nonentity, with a watertight self-assurance and no communication lines open for business.

Miranda, having had a vague idea of issuing a warning as to the heavy content of Ianthe's guest list, decided to let nature take its course. She admired the dining room with its amazing polished table to seat nearly thirty and the new curtains, draped with enough swags and frills to fit out a dancing troupe – however did one wash such things? – and went home to ponder over what to wear. Everyone had seen her only decent evening dress quite recently at the Hunt Ball, and many times previously. She went through Alice's stuff, nostalgically packed in a large tin trunk in the spare bedroom and wondered if she dared, wear a ruby velvet creation with long tight sleeves and a stunningly cut skirt, several inches too long. She played about with it and decided to take the risk: no one ever noticed her anyway and it was dark and discreet in colour. She shortened the skirt and tried the dress on with the ruby ear-rings which she had tried to give to Philippa. The effect was pretty good. The crimson actually gave her rusty hair an impressive backdrop and the rubies were pure class.

Felix moaned about being on the guest list but George said he had invited Ellie Beenbeg, especially for him, a girl who rode point-to-point and was dashing company, so he stopped complaining. On the night he dressed with great care. Miranda wondered if George had noticed how his younger son was now a far greater attraction to the ladies than he was; she had noticed that Sandy liked Felix, when she could get away from George. The nice thing about Felix was that he lacked any sort of conceit and would have been surprised if anyone had told him he was attractive. He had had plenty of girlfriends but none had meant much to him so far.

George found the car wouldn't start.

It was a cold clear night a few days before Christmas. Miranda stood at the door with her coat clutched around her waiting while George crashed around in the yard. He was muttering about jump-leads.

'Jack's got them,' Felix said.

Miranda's car had a puncture and Felix's car had been borrowed for the night by some buddy of his.

'We can walk down,' Miranda snapped. 'I told you about my puncture three days ago.'

George had already had two slugs of whisky to put him in the mood and was in a cavalier frame of mind. He came to the door in the tractor.

'Get in!'

'God in heaven!'

Felix and Sally were laughing. George moved his shotgun over so that she could climb up.

Miranda wished she had taken to strong drink too. She sat scowling as the tractor moved off down the drive.

'Remember her name's Ianthe,' she hissed, 'when you're introducing. Not all those other concoctions you keep coming up with.'

'You can do all that,' George said, 'if you're so good at it.'

George parked the tractor right in the middle of the drive, as close to the door as possible. Miranda got down, seething. George went in, yoo-hooing through the kitchen, all smiles again.

'Hullo, darling! We're the first, like you said. My God, you look smashing!'

Miranda thought Ianthe looked like one of her own

curtain designs, all frills and swags. The crimson skirt was flamenco style and a white blouse frothed down the front, laced with gold chains and black bows. Huge diamond ear-rings swung round her head. Alice's rubies were chaste by comparison and Alice's velvet faded into the dimmed shadows of the kitchen.

They went through to the drawing room. The huge space was made intimate by pools of light picking out the groups of chairs and sofas cunningly arranged; the upholstery was all palest cream, the carpet the same, and the lights gave the effect of gold and silver, picking out cushions of gold and silver and the occasional puce and flame. On a low silver and glass table Jasper was presiding over a huge silver bowl of steaming punch. He was all smooth smiles, smelling strongly of Paco Rabanne, dressed in a white jacket and tight silky black trousers. Unlike the tense, hard Ianthe, he had all the right words and sympathetic expressions. Miranda wondered suddenly if he was a salesman. They had never found out what he did in order to be able to spend so lavishly, calling him insolently the Lilyshine yuppie.

Recalling the chintzy brown, dog-worn, largely decaying interiors of the people about to arrive, Miranda saw the place as they would see it, more a film set than a home. She thought Ianthe would be pleased at the astonishment she was going to provoke. Felix was pole-axed.

'Bloody hell, was this the old study?'

'This end, yes.' Ianthe smiled at him and Miranda saw that she was one of those women who naturally turned on for a handsome young man. Her hard-stone eyes sparkled beneath her perfectly plucked eyebrows. Miranda remembered old Alice's funeral reception, and she behind the curtains being every bit as catty as she was feeling now, watching Ianthe. Dear Meg hadn't been asked because she wasn't rich enough, George said, and had a habit of making everyone feel good. It wasn't what he wanted. And a pity about Tom the vicar.

In the kitchen some functionaries in uniforms were working at the drinks trays and at the dinner, presumably. Miranda didn't know any of them; they were obviously imported. Most people had the same old couple if they needed any help, and parties at Christmas were staggered according to Ted and Ena's engagement book.

The punch was fairly lethal, Miranda discovered by the first sip. George was on his second glassful before the firstcomers arrived, Major Parmenter and his wife Marjorie. Major Parmenter was a shooting man and Marjorie the chairman of the local Conservative party, a booming lady with much to say, even before the punch. She wore Thatcher blue, with draperies across her stomach, and pearls. At dinner she was to sit opposite Napoleon's wife Eleanor, a sweet quiet Friend of the Earth. Because Napoleon was a prairie farmer, Eleanor had given a good deal of his hard-won profits to Green causes, but he did not complain. Miranda thought he admired her for it, and in the aftermath of grain surpluses Eleanor had won ten acres off him for a new wood.

'I do so envy you your woods at Violets,' Eleanor said to Miranda, soon after arriving. 'A new one is so frustrating, so slow – one's plans all in the head. And you've already got those wonderful oaks. What a terrible thing this woman has done to your lovely house. Poor old Alice will be turning in her grave.'

But Marjorie was loud in her praises. While Miranda was wondering why she had never had time to walk yet in her lovely woods, May Bloom arrived with her father Percy, aged ninety-five, frail as gossamer and stone-deaf. He was wearing what looked like a hand-knitted suit, and May Bloom was in tweeds and boots, the same outfit she would wear for her Christmas shopping: 'It was always so bloody cold in this house, Mrs Pertwee, I can tell you!'

'Do call me Ianthe.'

'Ianthe! What sort of name is that, my dear? Are you a foreigner?'

'It's Greek, May, you old fool, like Penelope,' George said.

'Are you Greek, dear?'

'No more than you are,' Ianthe said sweetly.

May chortled appreciatively. 'Well, you've got the pipes going at last. Poor George never could make them work. I might have to take my jacket off. Have you knocked some walls down or something? It used to be like a row of dog kennels in here.'

The rooms started to fill up. Felix was plainly bowled over by Ellie Beenbeg whom he had only seen before in crash hat and racing jersey, mainly from behind, and who now revealed herself as a longlegged enchantress only too relieved to find someone her own age; her brother Henry, a plausible old Etonian known as an 'entrepreneur' (in and out of work was Miranda's translation) was laying it on thick to a goggle-eyed Sally, and George was already waylaid by the shameless Sandy who looked stunning in a very simple dress of ivory satin, hung from her shoulders by the slimmest of straps. Ianthe's eyes narrowed as she took her in. Miranda moved over to help with the late entries, George being too feeble to resist Sandy's, 'Come and show me what's different.' Miranda fizzed with jealousy. Who was there for her amongst this motley crew? She knew she would gravitate presently to poor old Percy Bloom, bewildered on the white sofa, so large and squishy his poor little sticklike legs would not reach the ground. Momentarily she remembered dear Martin coming to her with a drink on the day of the funeral . . . now there was a sweet and genuine man. He would be taking care of Percy if George had bothered to invite him.

'Jim and Cissie,' she murmured, as the millionaire gypsies arrived. Nobody knew their surname, did they have one? Jim bowed deeply to Ianthe.

'My great pleasure, ma'am.'

He wore a bottle green cravat tied in a big bow under his chin, and a suit of very fine tweed. Gold teeth, gold cufflinks and an ear-ring glittered. His hair was luxuriantly black and shiny, curling grandly over his ears and collar. Ianthe gaped. There was nothing Jim did not know about catching a trout or a rabbit with his bare hands. He still went poaching on moonlit nights, letting himself out the back way in his poacher's coat, lurcher at his heels. He could not live without the sky and the moonlight, for all his grand house with electronic gates.

'How kind of you to invite us,' Cissie said warmly. 'Not everyone takes us in, you know.'

Ianthe was at a loss, not knowing who they were, and Miranda forebore to explain in their presence.

'Jim and Cissie live at Gold Arbor – the big house above the green, with the – the gates.'

No one could say Ianthe wasn't learning a thing or two. She was beginning to look quite animated.

Miranda said to Jasper, 'I think George has chosen a rather colourful cross-section of our friends. He thought you would enjoy it more.'

'It's lovely, my dear, so kind of him to go to so much trouble.'

Jasper had a spaniel way of looking, large brown eyes very honest and sympathetic. He seemed professionally soothing. His face was broad, bland, scrupulously shaved, his hair smoothed back. For a yuppie, he hadn't the shark's touch, the gleam of avarice. Miranda found the two of them hard to assess. She felt they knew quite well where they were with her: the drab lady from up the farm.

'You look lovely tonight, Miranda. Are you glad to be freed of this white elephant of a house at last?'

This was Napoleon, Arthur Martindale, dapper and smiling. His remark was just what Miranda needed. With another glass of punch in her hand she began to warm to the proceedings.

He went on, 'I always thought Violets a very desirable residence, even when it was in ruins. Such a fine position up on the ridge, not squashed down on the road like this one. George wasn't stupid to sell.'

'It was always such a mess when we had it. I could

137

never have conceived of doing this to it – I don't think big, I'm afraid.'

'Well, it's just another house now, isn't it? It's lost all its character. How's the horse coming along?'

'They've backed him, I believe. Felix has ridden him round the yard. He seems quite amenable, but heaven knows when he's going to get the schooling he deserves. We're so short-handed now Jack's gone.'

'He's not coming back? I thought perhaps it was just a row – you know . . .'

'He's setting up a woolshop in town with his girlfriend Carol. Please don't talk to George about it. He goes off the deep end in a big way. A *woolshop*! he says in a voice like thunder, and that's it for the rest of the day, black looks and heavy groans. "*The ingratitude!*" – all that sort of stuff.'

'Farms can't support families like they used to. Times change. A woolshop is probably a far better bet.'

What a nice man Napoleon was, Miranda was thinking: so sensible and calm, intelligent, patient, shrewd, kindly. All the virtues. His farm was a model of good husbandry, in spite of being markedly unGreen. Rumour had it that Napoleon was putting in for a golf course. He did all the things a nice man shouldn't, but remained unequivocally nice. If one had a husband like Napoleon, Miranda thought, one could relax and get on with one's own life, instead of forever being on tenterhooks. He was unassuming in manner, quietly spoken, and looked nothing like as rapacious as his nickname would give one to believe.

'Your mother used to tell me what a fine rider you were as a girl. Why don't you school The Druid? You have the patience, the right attitude. You could give him the right start.'

Miranda was startled.

'I always hated riding! When did she tell you that?'

'More than once, as I recall. Beautiful hands, she used to say, and shake her head – "A terrible waste. . ."'

Miranda didn't know what to say. She had never ridden for pleasure, only under duress. As a child she had had to show ponies for her mother's friends the whole summer through, because she was small and light and could make them do all the right things. They had taken the rosettes and silver cups and chucked her under the chin. 'Good gel, that's the ticket!'

'He's too good a horse not to have the best.'

'George should employ someone, a good girl, I've told him. But you might as well talk to the wall.'

'You're a good girl,' said Napoleon and smiled. 'It's time you looked about you, now your mother's gone.'

Eleanor claimed him to go and talk to Cissie and Jim, and Miranda was left turning over Napoleon's ambiguous and rather personal remark. Now Alice had departed there was, actually, no reason why she shouldn't go hunting if she wanted, and join in the fun and games of the outdoor set, yet the idea had never crossed her mind. Riding cross-country was, after all, a great lark, especially if there was only oneself to please. The idea was not entirely ridiculous.

Now slightly lightheaded, Miranda went off to console Percy Bloom, stranded on the sofa. The party was well under way, everyone talking very loudly, the laughter braying out, Jasper's punch doing its duty. George was breathing heavily down Sandy's décolletage in the hall and Henry Beenbeg had his hand on Sally's thigh on another sofa. Sally was showing a lot of thigh, asking for it, Miranda would have said, but Percy, for a nonagenarion, was not too far gone to let his blue-veined hand stray in a surprising direction. Miranda was glad when May came to scoop him up and take him in to dinner.

George's seating arrangements had at least spared her too much hardship. She was between Jasper and Jim the gypsy, opposite old Windy and Marjorie Parmenter. George had Sandy next to him on one side, pretty Ellie Beenbeg on the other. Felix was next to Ianthe herself at the other end. Miranda could see that George had already had too much to drink; this was their usual predicament. She would warn him to go steady, he would lay off and become sober and bad-tempered and want to go home. She decided to say nothing. Ianthe's marvellous cooking would, with luck, line his stomach and all would be well. The wines being served were of the highest quality, none of the usual country plonk, and everyone was into the second glass before the delicious stilton and celery soup was finished. Voices were loud and opinionated. Jasper drank heavily but seemed to be completely unaffected.

'What a delightful occasion this is,' he said to Miranda. 'A real house warming! Next week, over Christmas, our old friends will be coming up from London, but this makes me feel I have really moved in, become a part of the countryside, so to speak.'

As he was so rarely in it, commuting daily early and late, Miranda asked him what he did for a living, the wine loosening her tongue.

'I'm a funeral director,' he said.

'An undertaker!'

'That's right. By appointment to the very best people, you understand, royalty included.'

'Oh!'

His steadying smile over the rim of the crystal glass transfixed her. It was one step away from unctuousness, she saw now, soothing to the point of being hypnotic.

What did they talk about, he and Ianthe, when he came home to dinner? . . . 'Did you embalm the ambassador satisfactorily, darling?' 'Yes, and the princess looked very sweet when we'd finished with her.' Miranda found she had no undertaking conversation. Only crude questions came into her mind. It was as much a conversation stopper as if he'd said he was in computers.

'One is never out of work. There are no recessions. A very sound profession, and not overcrowded. The young rarely take to it.'

'No, it wouldn't appeal, would it?' Miranda thought George would have likened it to Jack's new job.

'But it's a breath of fresh air, coming out here. I love it. I used to ride, you know – Richmond Park and Wimbledon Common. I was wondering, if I were to take the odd day off, if I might try hunting myself sometime?'

'Really?' Miranda tried not to sound too amazed. 'Well, I'm sure we could fix you up with a horse between us, if you want to try it. Ask Billy Beenbeg – he's one of the Joint Masters. And Boxing Day – why don't you come to the meet anyway? That's always a bit of a lark, unless there are too many "antis" about.' It was actually more of a lark if the antis came, but she didn't say that. 'You can come with me.'

'That would be delightful. Certainly I'll come.'

Miranda was always suspicious of people who used

the word delightful. Delight was such a rare occurrence, in its true sense.

Smoked haddock in a delicious sauce was followed by an enormous joint of rare Scotch beef. The farmers took several portions and the silk red claret flowed. George took his tie off. Salacious gossip began to ripple round the table, and after the pudding the subject got on to artificial insemination of broodmares.

'It's got to be fresh – they deliver it by motor cycle carrier.'

'How in God's name do they masturbate a stallion?'

'They have this contraption, a sort of false mare, and they tease him—'

At the far end of the table Percy was riveting his group with the battle of Ypres, and had all the spare cutlery, cruets and glasses marking out the divisions. The flunkies hastily gathered up the debris. Miranda had heard all this stuff before, many times. She noticed it was gone two o'clock and that George was very drunk and hadn't spoken for some time. Sally had her head on Henry's shoulder. So much for Sam, whom Miranda had become fond of.

George suddenly said, 'I think it's bloody bedtime. Time to go home. I'm going home.'

He got up from the table and lurched out into the kitchen. Everyone laughed and hooted.

'Party's only just starting, George!' they shouted.

The port was going round; a second and a third decanter were produced and cigar smoke wreathed the air. Sally went to sleep. Felix took a cigar, which Miranda knew would make him sick.

George could not get the tractor out as it was hemmed in by cars and came back annoyed.

'Bloody bedtime everybody!' he shouted.

They all booed and jeered. He lurched out of the room again into the hall and was heard going up the stairs. Miranda assumed he would flake out in his old bedroom and was relieved, but shortly he came downstairs again carrying a pair of very smart silk pyjamas, presumably Jasper's.

'I'm going to bed, and so should – so you – all – should—'

He started to undress. Everyone started to cheer.

'Bloody go home!' George shouted, struggling out of his shirt.

'I'm terribly sorry,' Miranda whispered to Jasper.

But Jasper was entranced. 'I say, what fun!' He got up from the table and went out, to return carrying a guitar. He came back to his seat and started to strum goodbye tunes, very professionally. Everyone cheered and the attention shifted to Jasper.

George started to struggle out of his trousers.

Miranda's heart sank deeply within her gorged torso, and she began to feel sick.

When George was naked save for his emerald green Y-fronts, everyone started banging their spoons on the table, shouting, 'Strip 'em off! Strip 'em off!'

Jasper's music changed tempo, became faster and more Hispanic.

'Come along, darling!' he shouted to Ianthe, 'let's have a dance! Clear the table! Clear the table, everybody!'

'Clear the table! Clear the table!'

In a flash the guests had deposited all the china and glass on to the white carpet. Miranda saw red and excited faces swirling through her alcoholic haze. Ianthe leapt on to the table and started to strip off her white blouse, her heels already moving in time to Jasper's heady music. Jasper started to emit flamenco cries. Ianthe's face was alight; the diamonds whirled as she tossed her head and the blouse flew across the table. Gold chains and baubles bounced on her bare breasts. Head up and laughing she danced like a dervish the length of the table. Percy's last Ypres outpost went flying and the old man's face was red as the port, the rheumy eyes popping with lust; Miranda saw Felix transfixed. May Bloom started shouting hunting cries, struggling out of her jacket.

Jasper the undertaker stood up and began to sing, and everyone banged on the table in time to the Spanish rhythm and let out yelps and cries as Ianthe banged her heels triumphantly. The room was in uproar.

Through it all George's voice could be heard, 'Bloody bedtime I said!'

Still in his green Y-fronts he stood at the head of the table with his shotgun.

'Get out of my house! Get out of my bloody house!' he roared, and let off the shotgun. All the lights went out.

Miranda wanted to die.

CHAPTER SIX

EVERYONE AGREED THAT it was a very good party, one of the best. Jasper and Ianthe received invitations all round. 'Bring your guitar, Jasper!' Felix, transfixed by the glorious sight of the bare-breasted Ianthe dancing on the table, could not get the vision out of his head. He made excuses to go down to Lilyshine, looking for the flamenco dancer behind the hard-edged eyes. Sally spent the whole Christmas week 'out with Henry'.

'Henry is frightful, far worse than poor Sam!' Miranda complained to Meg.

'You got Sally weaned off Sam exactly as you intended, you can hardly complain,' Meg pointed out. 'You are a whinger, Miranda.'

Miranda was very put out by this remark. She knew Meg was quite understandably annoyed by not being asked to the now famous dinner – 'But it was all the same old thing until Ianthe unleashed herself – Percy at Ypres and hot semen on motor bikes – you've heard it

147

all before. George was letting you off lightly not asking you, or so we all thought.'

She remembered Napoleon saying, more or less, that she should get off her backside, and pondered the remark. Now that Violets was more or less in working order, it was quite true that she had time to walk round her woods and take an interest in the social scene. Jack having left home made a big difference. Sally was hardly ever in. Miranda decided to take Jasper to the Boxing Day meet and think hard about Napoleon's remark. She asked Jasper and Ianthe up for a drink before they set off.

'I used to hunt, but gave it up when the children were small.' That was twenty-five years ago: had she really spent half her life doing nothing but look after other people? The answer was yes. The thought actually made her feel guilty, when there were women about who sailed round the world singlehanded, trained Grand National winners and ran the country.

She served hot toddies in the kitchen when Jasper and Ianthe arrived. George and Felix were still crashing about upstairs tying stocks and arguing over three lefthanded gloves and only one righthanded one.

'Do sit down, there's no hurry. George and Felix will be down in a minute.'

The steadfast Sam was getting the horses ready –

what a brilliant idea that had proved . . . Felix was eternally grateful. When he came down Miranda noticed with amusement that Ianthe's eyes flickered instinctively, showing astonishment and a hint of excitement. She had never seen him in hunting gear, the immaculate black jacket and white stock and hint of a mustard waistcoat. The dark chestnut curls lay closely against his skull and Alice's glowing-coal eyes reciprocated Ianthe's appreciation. To her amazement, Miranda noticed that a blush crept over his splendid cheekbones. He was remembering Ianthe's wonderful bare bosom dancing the flamenco.

'Do – do you ride?'

'No,' Ianthe said.

'Jasper's thinking of having a day out,' Miranda said. 'I said we'd fix him up if he's serious.'

'Why not? Great.'

'Find him a steady horse.'

Felix laughed. 'Not one of ours, I'm afraid.'

'What's wrong with yours?' Ianthe asked.

'Anything Dad has to do with – a bit crazy. Harry pulls your arms out and doesn't look where he's going, and Maureen stands on her rear end if she can't get a move on. We're not very popular.'

'I don't believe that.' Ianthe batted her eyelids.

George did not hold Ianthe's attention as did Felix,

Miranda noticed. But George cut Felix out of the conversation and told Ianthe all the things she didn't want to know about hunting until he noticed the time. He hastily gathered up his whip and hat and the two left gloves Felix had carefully left for him.

'See you up there then!'

They departed noisily.

The three of them followed when the horsebox had got clear, and drove in a leisurely fashion the five miles or so to the Boxing Day meet, which was taking place as it always did outside the Horse and Groom in the small town square of the local market town. It was a cold bright day, an encouraging day for the spectators, and the huntsman had had the hounds unboxed in plenty of time so that they could demonstrate their innate good nature by licking children's faces and accepting cold mince pies and squashed turkey sandwiches in their gentle mouths. It confused the picture the anti bloodsports people wanted to propagate, of gnashing jaws and bloodlusting eyes. They were out in force with their banners, but did not seem particularly militant, the little bearded men in drab anoraks rather outnumbering the skinhead and leather-jacket brigade with their aerosol cans of antimate. The sheer presence of some fifty or so shining hunters with their immaculately turned out riders was impressive and the crowd was all in favour, which kept the antis quiet.

Miranda, feeling like a mole come up into daylight after a long sojourn underground, noticed that her menfolk looked magnificent on the two difficult but gleaming and impressive horses, and could not help picturing herself in the same setting next year on the even more impressive Druid. George was forever nagging her to 'give 'im a bit of a school'. Now Alice had gone, there was really no need for her to stay under her stone any more. An unexpected little surge of wellbeing and excitement jumped inside the depths of her anorak.

'Don't they look marvellous!' She meant the whole scene, of course, but was not unaware that Ianthe's eyes were still all for Felix. He rode over and looked down on them, smiling.

'Might have a bit of fun when we move off, with that lot.' He nodded towards the banners.

'Now, Felix!'

They were under strict instructions not to retaliate, use bad language or be anything but civil to their tormentors. In deep cover and out of sight the instructions were sometimes forgotten, usually when hounds or horses were distressed or frightened by the antics.

'They don't know anything about it, that's the trouble.'

'Some of them do, some of them are very sincere,' Miranda said.

'Not the rent-a-mob lot. They cause more mayhem to wildlife with their chemical sprays in ten minutes than we do the whole year round.'

'You'll soon leave them behind.'

'Yes. Billy goes off like the clappers when they're around.'

He grinned, the cold whipping up his colour. He always professed to find the compulsory riding a great bore but he did actually love the hunting and the race-riding once he was on board and free of all the chores which accompanied the sport.

A large hound lolloped over to Ianthe and stood up with its paws on her shoulders, all affection. She shrieked and pushed at it disgustedly.

'Leave it, leave it, Proudly!' Felix said sharply.

The hound dropped down and gave Felix a sad look and disappeared to look for a more discerning friend.

'Do you know all their names?' Jasper asked, surprised.

'Most of them, yes.'

It wasn't difficult, but Jasper was impressed. A hunting undertaker, Miranda thought, would be quite a cachet, almost in the league of the now extremely rare hunting parson. What a lot of good a day out would do

Tom the vicar, free him from his niggling concerns! There was nothing like a day's hunting to wash away clutter in the brain, set one up for the week ahead.

'You must try it, Jasper! Say the word and we'll arrange it for you.'

'My word, yes, it's tempting!'

He moved back as the huntsman, a weathered, bandy-legged professional known as Jock (in spite of being Irish) blew his horn to gather hounds together. The square echoed to the clatter of hooves as the horses were drawn back to let them through. Miranda saw May Bloom on her heavyweight grey, in her jodhpurs of astounding cut, half a century out of date, still eating a mince pie and talking through a spew of flaky pastry to Ellie Beenbeg, and George manouevring Harry smartly round several hindquarters to come alongside Sandy on a flashy chestnut especially chosen to impress the crowd. As they moved off the square was a riot of glorious horseflesh, impeccably drilled hounds and ultra-smart riders whose uniforms hid a multitude of eccentricity, prejudice, kindness, selfishness and warmheartedness that had nothing at all to do with what the banner-bearers were trying to proclaim, that they were blood-crazed killers.

'It's the galloping cross-country in a great throng, being so exhilarated, so scared – it's wonderful . . .'

Miranda, remembering, tried to explain the attraction.

'Bloody killers!' chanted the banner-bearers. The younger members were scurrying now to take to their battered vehicles to pursue. The police cars moved smoothly forward to cut them off. The crowd jeered.

'It looks like a sport on its own, saboteuring,' Ianthe said.

'Oh, it is, a grand day out for them.'

And then, seeing the mild-mannered local school-teacher dismantling his banner until next year, she felt forced to add: 'But one has to respect . . . all sorts . . .'

Jasper drove back, and Miranda refused the request to stay to lunch at Lilyshine and went back to Violets. The weather had clouded over and a bitter wind blew across the ridge. The bare branches of her envied oaks fretted against the sky and the rooks were shaken about, rags and tatters above their broken nests. She had never known anything else, Miranda realised, never looked around, never thought for herself. It had taken all this time, nearly a year, to wean herself off Alice's domination. She called the two dogs, Rough and Carstairs, and crossed the small paddock that divided Violets and its drive from the wood. It was hard to find a gap in the ancient hedgerow thin enough to scramble through. She was agile enough, unafraid of brambles and nettles and the traps offered by fallen boughs and uprooted trunks, but she had to confess that her wood was sorely overgrown. She could make no headway. Eleanor's new woods had been designed with rides and glades, and once the Violets woods – she remembered from her childhood – had been a place for walks and picnics. A small tributary of the stream wound through its heart and the banks had been carpeted with bluebells. Perhaps they were now all vanquished by the encroaching undergrowth. It might be worth following the stream up, and finding out if there was still a way through. She would make a way, get Felix to take the tractor in. Or take the tractor in herself, she wasn't incapable.

After struggling some way, she stopped and leaned against a tree, listening to the wind in its top. Fine needles of rain pricked her upturned face. She felt an astonishing sense of release, the first time she could remember for years doing something useless, time-wasting, completely self-indulgent. The excitement stirred again, and something very like pure happiness momentarily touched her senses.

A pair of pheasants whirred up, disturbed by the dogs, and their startled croaks echoed in the hollows below her. Spurred by her unexpected sense of freshness, of rebirth, she retraced her beaten track through the covert and made her way back across the field and down the drive to the old stableyard. She hadn't visited it since she had moved up to Violets. It lay behind Lilyshine, on a level with the bedroom windows; Lilyshine's garden plunged down to the road, and a band of cupressus planted by Alice long ago hid the view of the manure heap from the deckchairs on the lawn.

Miranda went into the old barn and down to the looseboxes at the end. The Druid was there alone, dozing in his box. He jumped round at the sound of Miranda's approach and let out a piercing whinny.

'Are you lonely, old fellow? Have they all gone out without you?'

He came to the door of his box, all ears and eyes, a very positive presence. Miranda leaned her arms over the door and spoke to him, while the dogs rooted joyously in the old straw heap, sniffing rats.

'Shall I ride you then, Druid? What a terrible name that is – I can't ride a horse called Druid . . . I'll call you something else. Jasper, perhaps, after our friend down there. Jasper is a horse's name anyway, not a person's. What do you think to Jasper?'

He was probably much too strong to be a lady's horse, but Miranda knew she had the knack of calming keen horses; it was in her nature, to calm, just as it was in George's nature to excite. She would not be frightened of him. Tomorrow, when Sam was down in the morning, she would school Jasper and see what he was made of.

Not to please George, but to please herself.

Miranda took to riding. George was enthusiastic, seeing all the hard work which he so much hated being done for nothing; Felix was impressed – 'God, Mother, I never knew you could ride like that!' – and Meg cynical.

'Charge George by the hour! As soon as you've got the beast going well and got fond of him, George will have him off you.'

Miranda laughed. 'Funny, isn't it, now Alice has gone I'm doing what she was always trying to force me to do, off my own bat. I must say it takes my mind off things.'

'What are you worrying about now?'

'Sally. Jack. Felix. And always Philippa, I suppose.'

'That only leaves George.'

'Well, I'm used to George, aren't I? I've given up on George.'

'So, why the others? Sally? You don't like Henry Beenbeg?'

'How could any mother like Henry Beenbeg. He's a crook.'

'An Etonian crook.'

'That makes it worse! And so charming and plausible, weak, just after all he can get. And Sally – still at school! And poor Sam seeing Henry's car whizz up the drive every evening . . . he's heartbroken.'

Meg laughed.

'Rubbish, Miranda! Peanuts. It'll be someone else in no time, as well you know. Case dismissed. Jack? I'd have thought that was a move for the better.'

'Well, yes, perhaps. It's just the woolshop that George goes on about so, so unmasculine – although he's only fitting out the interior and the flat, getting it straight, then Carol's going to run it.'

'Highly satisfactory I would have said. Jack's not a driver, is he? And if he's found a driving partner and can go along with her, that's the basis for a good partnership. Better than getting walked all over by George. What's wrong with Felix?'

'Restless, moody – he riles George a lot. I keep thinking it's because Jack has gone, and he's wondering whether he ought to do a runner too. George offers him no sort of a future.'

'There's nothing new there. It's up to him, to tackle George, nothing for you to do at all.'

'And Philippa never came home for Christmas, said Paul had engagements. No one ever played concerts on Christmas Day as far as I know. It's only a couple of hours' drive, after all. She usually manages to get up here for a day or two . . . I worry about that marriage.'

'Yes, well, she's too nice. She should leave him if he bullies her. There's no children, no ties. Martin says he's a demanding sod, but you give in to him because he's a genius.'

'Rather how Geroge sees himself.'

'Well, there you are. Philippa's learned to put up with hard cheese in her marriage, and who did she learn it from? You, dear.'

Miranda was used to Meg's chiding. She knew it was good for her, but one could not change one's nature. Meg worked so hard, with her Bed and Breakfast, her house-cow, her egg-round, her vegetable garden and the Women's Institute that she never had time to sit and worry. She was immensely tough and the physical life suited her. Miranda, thin as a stick but hard and wiry, decided that the physical life would take her mind off her groundless fears.

'I'll aim at hunting Jasper next year. Stop being a bloody housewife day and night. George can do his own cooking and washing.'

'Put that in writing! Well done, Miranda! I'm with you all the way.' Meg's enthusiasm was cheering. 'Be your own person!'

Miranda did not know what her own person was

but presumed she would find out eventually. She was only a bare year out from under her mother. The riding was the only thing she could grasp at for the moment, and it served her purpose well. The big grey horse was worthy of one's best efforts, and after her first few tentative forays up and down the drive and a cautious trot round the confines of the orchard, Miranda found her confidence. Jasper was kind and willing to please, and the formidable strength apparent in his magnificent bearing and outlook was not pitted against her. He responded to her gentle touch, whereas George's dominating attitude had riled and upset him.

'Bloody animal never settled for me like that!'

'Mum can ride, that's the difference,' Felix said. 'Kindness is all. You wouldn't know.'

George was torn between being jealous, infuriated by Felix's put-down, and relieved that the great worry over training his expensive purchase might be resolved. He would not admit that Miranda was better than he was. He said, 'Some horses go better for women.'

'They all go better for good riders,' Felix said.

Felix was needling George again, asserting his growing confidence and independence. George didn't know how to react. He had always put Jack down successfully because Jack was a less aggressive character, but Felix was more difficult to handle.

'There's no need to be insulting, Felix,' Miranda said coldly. 'Schooling was always my province. Racing is something else. Count me out there.'

Felix laughed.

'I don't know what's got into that young puppy,' George said later.

'He isn't a young puppy any more. But you treat him like one. If he goes, like Jack, you'll be in real trouble. You ought to be careful.'

'Doesn't know he's born, working for me! Any day off he wants, no trouble! Hunting for free, racing – other boys would give their eye teeth for it. How am I supposed to treat him?'

'As one adult to another.'

But George was more a child than Felix. Miranda fixed her mind on Jasper, working out how best to advance his education. She thought she liked him better than her family. He was much less trouble.

CHAPTER SEVEN

'FELIX!'

'For Christ's sake, Ianthe!'

'Come down to the house! We've got an hour before he gets in . . .'

She came up to him and put her arms round his neck and pressed herself against him, so that he could feel her breasts hard against his chest. Her fingers touched the top of his spine and wound in his hair. He was helpless, spinning.

He was feeding the horses at the time, it being Sam's afternoon off. Maureen was kicking her door at the delay and his hands were sticky with molassed chop.

'You're driving me crazy, doing this! I've got to feed them, for God's sake—'

'Give me the bucket. I'll help. Quickly!'

Even the sex-crazed Ianthe could see that one could not leave the horses at such a critical moment. She scurried off with the buckets to the appropriate boxes as

Felix mixed the feed, stumbling on her high heels, laughing, excited.

'You will come? Hurry! Quickly!'

There was no way he could resist. His dinner would be on the table at home, Jasper was already folding the evening paper back into his briefcase on his homecoming train, yet the dangers only added spice to the crazy longing that Ianthe knew she could arouse in him. Hand in hand across the yard, ducking through the hole in Alice's cupressus, they ran across the frosty lawn and into the humming bright warmth of old Lilyshine. Up the stairs two by two . . . 'The guest room, quick it's best—'

'Ianthe, you're wonderful!'

'Darling – darling Felix!'

With a quick whip of her arms she had flung off her sweater, then in one bound out of her jeans and tights . . . she jumped up on to the bed and stood with her arms flung out, stark naked, laughing. She was magnificent, creamy white, curved and triumphant in the pink-fondant setting of her best guest room. Her diamond eyes shot sparks. Bloody gumboots, bloody dung-spattered cords . . . his grained and stinking hands fumbled and tore.

'Oh, God! Oh, Jesus!'

And then he leapt on her and tumbled her back into

the warm nest of the bed and they threshed and laughed and came together in a clashing upheaval of pure lust, given and taken, magnificent, coarse and heavenly.

Felix flung back, panting. His head whirled. He wanted to laugh and sing and cheer; he had never been so bowled over, brainstormed . . . not even when he won his first Open on Carnival Boy as a boy of seventeen.

'You are stunning, Ianthe!'

Five minutes ago he had been mixing feeds. He felt as if he were on another planet. She had planned it, waiting for his van in the yard, coming to feed . . . turning on the electric blanket. Soft lights illuminated rose-trellis wallpaper, stars on the ceiling . . . stars in his eyes. The pure luxury of his feelings washed him with delight. His life had never exploded stars before, keeled him over on a big crashing wave of pure heaven. He wanted to breathe it all in, treasure it like a best cigar, not waste a jot of this amazing feeling.

She stroked his damp hair, curling close to the sweaty farmer's skin.

'You are lovely, Felix, so real. So outdoor.'

'Smelly?'

'Wonderful!'

'This is bloody crazy, Ianthe!'

His dinner would be on the table now, his mother wondering what had kept him.

'What time does Jasper get in?'

Ianthe glanced at her tiny gold watch, the only thing she wore.

'Twenty-five minutes.' She laughed. 'Darling, darling Felix!'

He groaned. In films they played in bed all night. You were supposed to spin it out, coming and going, lots of finesse. He had no finesse and she seemed not to want it. She came like a flame struck by a match, just like he did. Was this what they called an affair?

'Haven't you got a girlfriend?'

'No. No one in particular. I go out with a few.'

'Haven't you ever been in love before?'

He considered.

'Not like this.' He turned and looked into her face. She was almost another person, not hard-edged at all, not cold and bored as she had always struck him before the party, but glittering with warm blood and flowing life, her eyes enlarged like a cat's in the dark. She smelled musky and alive.

'How then?'

'Oh, just kissing and . . . you know . . . in the car, playing about. I'd like them for a week or two, then get bored.' He paused, thinking way back, about the first. Something he had never told anyone, ever. At school.

'There was a girl, when I was sixteen. She had a

baby. I never saw it, never saw her again. I never went with girls after that, not for a long time. It made it—'

There was no word for what it made it. He had a daughter of ten somewhere, his mother Miranda was a grandmother, but she would never know, he would never tell her. The adolescent feelings had been almost uncontainable, sent him round the bend. The school thought it was the pressure of exams. What a laugh! Work was one thing that had never worried him.

'Felix!' Ianthe was impressed, excited. 'Really?'

'Yes. But no one knows.' He felt a sudden qualm. 'You'll never say – don't tell Jasper, for God's sake! Promise!'

'No, of course.'

'My parents would die of shock. My mother, at least. I suppose my father would laugh.'

'Your father's got quite a reputation, from what I hear.'

'Oh Lord, yes, he's hopeless. Poor old Ma.'

'She should take a lover!'

'What, my mother?' Felix laughed. 'She's so pure – pure in thought, word and deed, like an angel.'

'How boring!'

'Yes, it doesn't make her happy, being so selfless.'

'Oh, I don't know. I think she's happy.'

'Not unhappy, more. Sort of negative. Being happy is this!'

'Is it?' Ianthe laughed. She flung her arms round him and kissed him and licked him and bit him until he had to shove her away.

'Ten minutes, for God's sake! Get dressed, Ianthe!'

He leapt out of bed and scrambled into his clothes. There were bits of chop and bran scattered over the cream carpet and gumboot prints up the stairs. He pulled on his anorak as he went.

He fled.

His head was still whirling when he reached Violets. He got out of his van, stood for a moment, taking long breaths of the icy night air. It was very still, and from far in the distance he could hear the faint echo of Jasper's commuter train homing into the station. Violets' lights splashed out on the rutted drive. The difficulties of having an affair with Ianthe possessed his mind, the mightiness of the whole business making it imperative to continue. But there was no hour of the night when she wasn't with Jasper and no hour of the day when he could convincingly disappear from the farm unless on business. Sam did evening feeds six days out of seven – and even now, there would be excuses to make.

His dinner was in the oven. George and Miranda had finished. Sally was still at the table, drinking coffee.

'What kept you? Horses okay?'

'Bloody van wouldn't start. I nearly left it down there.'

He kept his head down, feeling that his face, his eyes, would show all. His blood was still jumping, pounding with joy. Her body, arched beneath him, filled his vision. He almost felt his teeth would chatter with excitement if he left off holding himself in check, head-down to the shepherds pie. He tried to eat very calmly. Sally stared at him.

'You do look odd,' she said.

'Hark who's talking!' Sarcasm came easily, but he trembled. 'Where's the famous Henry tonight? Got tired of you?'

'No. He wants us to be engaged.'

'Oh, my God, he must be off his rocker! Mrs Beenbeg! Pull the other one!'

'Honestly, Sally, don't talk such nonsense,' Miranda said sharply. 'You're under age and he's no right to talk like that.'

'I wouldn't mind young Ellie in the family!' George laughed. 'There's money in the Beenbegs – the old boy's got plenty.'

'Yes, and he's making sure Henry doesn't get his hands on it. You must have heard the talk? They say he's cutting Henry out of his will in favour of that egg-headed nephew in genetic engineering, the one that's trying to give pigs fur coats.'

'Who tells you these stories? You're making it up!'

'Something unnatural. Meg told me. Find some one round here who Henry doesn't owe money to, that'll be a good start. How does he pay when he takes you out to dinner? Not with a cheque, I'll be bound. No one will take a cheque from Henry any more. Even you, George.'

George looked shifty, having insisted on cash for Alice's best pair of binoculars that Henry had coveted.

'Well, he's young. He'll learn sense.'

'He's nearer thirty than twenty. He's the same age as Jack. He's thoroughly lazy and not entirely honest, put it that way.'

'You don't like *anyone*!' Sally accused her mother. 'Not Paul, not Carol, not any of my boyfriends. And yet look who you married!'

'What do you mean by that?' George sent her an amazed, but sharp, look.

'*Touché*,' Miranda said, and laughed. 'At least my mother approved of him. Didn't she, dear?'

'Alice had an eye for form, good old Alice!'

Felix relaxed as the conversation turned away from sexual partners. Sally was a goer, and her entanglement with the unsuitable Henry would preoccupy Miranda nicely. Felix wondered how many men his sister had had already . . . Miranda was surely fighting a losing battle there? Sally exuded an air of sexual excitement even when she was only drinking coffee. She had a way of looking not unlike Ianthe, a look used to signalling sexual appetite. Restless and unhappy with school and home, she seemed to smoulder in her chair, all long legs and slender neck, touchingly young and ripe and primed for disaster. Biology was cruel, pushing and unrelenting. He was now pushed himself but at least was going into it with his eyes wide open. An affair with Ianthe was a fox stealing chickens in his home yard: it didn't make sense and could only end in tears. Time would tell. He was game, if she was. An intense happiness seized him; he could hardly eat.

'Is there a beer?'

His mother fetched him a can from the fridge.

Sally kept looking at him suspiciously, her wavelength homing to the vibrations she sensed and was familiar with.

George said, 'Only three weeks to the first point-to-point. Hope you're fit, Felix, you don't want to be letting me down. Maureen's just about wound up and the ground's a treat for her. By gum, to think – this time next year it'll be The Druid! With luck we'll get two winners a meeting! Old Alice'll be dancing on her grave.'

On the surface nothing was changed, yet Felix knew that life had taken on a new dimension.

Felix went to meet Jack and Carol in a pub near their woolshop one lunchtime when he was in town to visit the dentist.

'It's time you surfaced. Dad's over the worst, all wrapped up in racing now, and Sam's doing the horses – I don't think he'll give you too much stick.'

'Funny thing, I haven't really had the time.'

Even to the unobservant Felix, Jack seemed a different person, relaxed and forthcoming, even enthusiastic.

'It's going well then?'

Carol said, 'He's made a super job of the shop. He's a real carpenter, not a bodger like Dad. You must come and have a look. We're just about to restock it – it'll be open for business next week.'

'You're not going to run it?' George's scorn had rubbed off on Felix.

'No. It's Carol's. I might stand in if she's in the hairdresser's sometimes, but mostly I'll be working upstairs getting the flat straight. We want to move into that as soon as we can. And after that – well, there's quite a few things come up—'

'His work's so good – Lennie in the grocer's wants him to do the shelving in his stockroom, and the solicitors, you know, Burnham and Greaves, Mr Greaves wants him to put new windows in their office – he's got plenty lined up.'

Carol was like quicksilver, eating her sandwich, drinking, glancing at her watch. She didn't believe in sitting still.

'Lovely to see you, Felix. Honest, we'll visit soon – we're not being funny about it. I reckon I can stand up to your dad, whatever he thinks, and I'm sure your mother is a sweetie.'

'You'll be a match for Dad. It's all bluster with him. He's a bully. But you've only got to bat your eyelashes – he's a sucker for a blonde, isn't he, Jack?'

'Yes, I've told Carol. He'll be eating out of her hand.'

'We'll do that then, one Sunday, as soon as we get a minute.' Carol looked at her watch again. 'I must dash now. There's no hurry for you, Jack, you stay. I want to see Polly in the salon before she goes for lunch. Lovely to see you, Felix. Cheerio!'

She was gone in a whirl of scent, very positive. Felix was impressed.

'She's quite a girl, your Carol.'

'God, she's a worker! She's marvellous.' Jack's expression was warm and glowing. 'You know, when I first set up with her, I thought it could be out of the frying pan into the fire. But I was so mad at Dad buying that horse – you know, everything – it seemed worth the risk. I'd been miserable for such ages, under his thumb – I don't have to tell you. And yet I didn't realise it, not till she told me what a fool I was. She seemed to have it summed up in a flash. And that's what she's like, she sees a situation and gets it sorted out, no messing. And yet she's not bossy, not if you go along with her. You seem to get carried along. I've never worked so hard in my life, and yet I enjoy every minute. It's a laugh with her, it's great. Can I get you another? You're not in a hurry, are you?'

'No. I'll have another, thanks.'

The town bar was busy and, unlike the Red Lion in the village, its clientele were all strangers. Felix moved into a corner where a table stood empty and sat back against the fumed oak and chintz, glad to let himself down, see things straight perhaps. Life at Violets, he saw now, was stultifyingly constricting. One could easily become a clod. All right for the old folks, but he was only twenty-six. If it wasn't for the hunting and racing, he might as well not be alive at all. And Ianthe. God, *Ianthe*! A sweat came up on his brow.

'Hot in here, isn't it?' Jack came back with the drinks.

'You living with Carol – you know—?'

'Yeah! I've been promoted from the spare room,

moved in with her. Permission granted from Ma and Pa. Mind you, that's why I want to get the flat ready as soon as I can – it's no go in that little house. They're nice enough, but it's television on all night, like sitting in a rabbit hutch, can't talk. We come back after tea and work again, it's more fun. Then an hour here before closing time. It's great. It's really good.'

'Amazing – you're a different man.'

'I left you in the lurch, I realise that. Don't think I haven't thought about it from your point of view.'

'Oh, I don't know. The chance was there. There's nothing to stop me doing the same thing.'

'That would put Dad in the soup good and proper.'

'I like farming. I could make a go of it if I put my mind to it. Make him get off my back. If I really wanted . . .' Felix shrugged. 'But now racing's started, you know how it is – all that side of it – you get hooked, and no decisions are made.'

'What's bugging you? There's something else.'

'There's no private life. It's impossible—'

Felix, with two pints inside him, felt his frustrations rising.

'Bloody hell, Jack, I've got myself into a crazy – God, you'll never believe this—'

He had to tell somebody, and Jack, above everyone, would appreciate the problems he faced in wooing

Ianthe. 'Out of the blue – she came – it was incredible! You know what she's like, what we've always thought – cold and calculating . . .'

Jack was satisfyingly amazed and impressed. Half amused, half admiring, he bent to Felix's slightly incoherent tale, cataloguing his astonishment, turmoil and delirious excitement over the turn of events.

'She takes the most incredible risks! I beat meeting Jasper by all of two minutes sometimes, and she comes into the stable when I'm feeding, misses Ma by seconds – she watches for her leaving . . . leaves a curtain half-pulled to tell me the coast's clear, but what the hell do I do with the van? I can't park it in the drive or leave it in the stableyard if I've told Dad I'm going to see someone – I have to drive up the gateway into the Long Pond field and hide it behind the old straw stack, and even then you can see it quite well from the road. Meg walks the dogs up there – if she says something to Ma – the mind boggles! Sometimes she goes out in her car and I meet her – we go up that dead-end lane by Marstons, but last time some idiot woman came past on a horse, stared in and we were upended on the back seat, windows all steamed up – I bet she couldn't make anything out, but you never know, she might recognise the car. It's crazy – I keep telling her that, but I can't stop it any more than she can! She's fantastic, I'm absolutely off my nut — the lies I tell Dad — been down to the forge, been to see Napoleon's new horse, had to call in the bank — it's bound to catch up with me before long . . .'

'So what? If she's so keen — make the most of it! We're bloody slow starters, Felix, you and me — got a lot to make up.'

'It's bloody fantastic, I'm not denying. But getting a clear coast — that's something else. That's what makes me see — if I had a place of my own, a bit of independence—'

'But what's in it for the future? Does she want to leave Jasper?'

'Christ, no! I think it's just her style, not the first time she's done it, I'm sure. And I wouldn't be surprised if he was the same — he's a funny blighter, isn't he? I don't think of the future at all, only the now! And it's absolutely bloody crazy. What if Ma finds out? And Dad?'

'He can't talk. I've seen him in here with Sandy a few times. I make sure he doesn't see me. If Ianthe gave him half a chance — well, he'd be there, wouldn't he? Make the most of it, you idiot. If you want to use our place. The flat, I mean. Give me a bit of warning. Carol would think it a good joke.'

'Yes, I might take you up on that. Great.'

Felix drove home feeling comforted by his confession to Jack. Jack seemed to have made out, and his content and his new future made Felix realise how fraught was his own. He turned off on the minor road that led to Lilyshine and crossed the canal bridge. Although it was February, a narrowboat was chugging along towards the next lock two fields away, and a man and a woman stood by the tiller. They were young, and laughing, and as Felix glanced down they kissed each other. Another happy couple! Where am I going, he wondered? There was a bloody great lock gate for him not far ahead and he was making for it at a rate of knots and as far as he could see there was no way of stopping.

Ianthe came to the point-to-point with Jasper and gazed at Felix with pure lust glittering behind her false eyelashes. Miranda recognised it and was impressed, but Felix when racing had too much on his mind to notice, and Miranda assumed it was always so. Felix, she thought, was not obsessed by sex like his father. She met Billy Beenbeg, Henry's father, and he insisted she come back to his Range Rover and have a drink. Henry was already standing by the opened back, dispensing his father's champagne to a group of his friends, including Sally.

'Steady on, Henry! I've some friends to entertain

too, you know. The farmers' bar is open, in case you haven't noticed.'

'Yeah, great, Dad, just a starter. You won't get through that lot on your own and still be fit to drive home. Like to help you out, eh? Nice to see you, Mrs Fairweather. Your horse going to make it today? Sally says it's worth putting a fiver on.'

'You could do worse, I think.'

'Have you met James? James Kennington, Sally's mother Mrs Fairweather. And this is Chris Hall . . . Peter Strawbridge . . .' He introduced his handsome, drunken, well-bred friends, and Miranda wondered why her heart sank so deeply when they were all exactly what she had wished for Sally when she was going out with poor Sam, a bit of class. Their glazed eyes focused with difficulty as they shook hands, and they said all the right things without stammering or mumbling, so smooth and well-versed that they could get it right even when their brains were paralysed; it depressed her deeply. Henry was tall and fair and undeniably handsome, and his slightly familiar bonhomie made him good company; he was never short of hangers-on. She could quite see why Sally found him so attractive. But honesty, a characteristic so infinitely desirable that one tended to take it for granted, loomed small in Henry's reckoning. He 'moved on' in life, usually because it was imperative.

On was not necessarily up and whether he was clever enough to survive unscathed Miranda rather doubted, although there was evidence enough to prove that a crook could prosper.

As he moved off with his crowd and her own delectable daughter, Miranda glimpsed the anguished Sam in the doorway of the beer-tent seeing their approach and panicking, backing down between the hotdog stall and the jacket potatoes and getting lost. In half an hour he would come and help get Maureen ready and lead her round the paddock, and Sally would pretend not to see him and he would be humiliated afresh.

Miranda sighed.

Billy gave her a glass of champagne and said gruffly, 'Hope my lad's not leading your girl astray. She's a shade young, I would have thought.'

'Our parental discipline is rather ineffective, I'm afraid. Don't worry about it.'

'Henry doesn't take advice, never did. We failed there, I think. But if there's anything I—'

Miranda wondered if Billy had asked her for a drink in order to reveal his concern. She was touched, but laughed off his doubt; it would be too painful to discuss seriously.

'No, honestly – we all worry, don't we? But they

have to work it out their own way. Something we all have to endure.'

Making light of it, she reassured him. He was a nice man. He had made a fortune out of building, but had lost his wife from cancer when the children were still at school. He still missed her badly and had never looked for anyone else. Miranda changed the conversation to the racing, and Billy's champagne made her feel nicely optimistic about the afternoon. But as is the way with horses, nothing went according to plan. Maureen was brought down at the fifth fence and Felix broke his collarbone. George went berserk – 'No rider for a month, after all the work I've done to get her fit!'

'There'll be riders queueing up for her, idiot! She's a good mare!'

'I like to keep it in the family.'

'Lose your beer-gut then, and get up yourself!'

'Do you think I could?' He was serious. Point-to-point riders had to ride at twelve stone seven, and George was over thirteen stone. He went and weighed himself in the weighing room while Ianthe and Jasper took Felix to hospital. Miranda, champagne woozled, was trying to work out why Ianthe was so willing to forego what any normal person would have considered a jolly afternoon.

'It's three years since I raced,' George told Meg. 'I

reckon I could lose that weight without much trouble.'

'What, by next week?'

'I wouldn't be racing fit, that's the trouble. Even the lad – takes a few races to get the body tuned.'

'Let's face it, George, your body will never be tuned again, not to that extent.'

'Saunders won the Grand National at – what was he?'

'Very bad-tempered, I heard, from getting the weight down.'

'By gum, I wouldn't mind riding The Druid when we get him here! It's an idea, eh Meg?'

'You're never short of ideas, I'll give you that, George.'

Miranda was with Sam by the horsebox, looking the mare over for damage. George rarely bothered himself with after-race care, having always left it to Jack. Miranda wondered what he would do if she hadn't employed the loyal Sam. Maureen was distressed by the fall, although not hurt. She had run loose round the course and been caught by a steward just before taking to the main road.

'Lead her round for a while, settle her,' Miranda advised. 'Poor old girl!'

Sam buckled her rug and took the bridle from Miranda. His pimples looked raw in the cold wind; his ears stuck out from his cap and his black leather gear, in fact severely practical, looked out of place amongst the waxed and quilted jackets of the other grooms. Miranda wanted to hug him, understanding his misery. He was so genuinely reliable and helpful; the really basic qualities lacking in Henry were instinctive in Sam, yet Sam could scarcely articulate, even when sober.

When she got home she was just in time to catch a telephone call. It was Philippa.

'Hey, Mum, you'll never believe this, but we're coming up next weekend, both of us. If it suits you, that is.'

Her voice was strained, with a false cheerfulness, and Miranda wondered if Paul was listening.

'Why, that's wonderful!' she answered, at the same time feeling her heart sinking deep into her stomach. 'What's happening?' Perhaps Philippa was pregnant: this thought caused even more stomach-churning. 'Is everything all right?'

'Yes, of course! It's just that Paul's got a concert at Cambridge on Saturday night, and he's got to be back there in the morning for a sort of lecture-cum-coffee-morning at one of the churches, and I pointed out how handy it would be if we stayed the night at Violets, and he agreed. You won't see much of him, I'm afraid.'

'That's all right, fine, wonderful. I suppose we'll be racing but I'll make sure I'm back early. I have to help out a bit now Jack's gone, and Felix has just cracked his collarbone.'

'Oh, Mum, you're not getting horsey, are you?'

'Well – we're a bit short of hands these days.'

'It's better than looking after Alice, I suppose.'

'Oh, Lord, yes, they're not nearly so demanding! It'll be lovely to see you, darling.'

'I'll ring on Friday and let you know what time and everything.'

Miranda put the phone down and sank wearily into the nearest armchair. She longed to see Philippa, but the thought of Paul was grim. With luck he would be at Cambridge nearly the whole time. Paul brought out the worst in George, who played the yokel with all the stops out. Paul had that effect: he seemed unable to relax and relate to anything outside his work. If one made intelligent conversation about music he was fine, but nobody in the family was capable. Miranda remembered her fine ideas about becoming an intellectual. Looking after horses, not to mention Alice, had a very stultifying effect on the intellect. She had made no effort to read Thomas Hardy or start an embroidery or learn Spanish; her mind remained unimproved. The thought of conversing with Paul terrified her. She wondered if

Martin might be around next weekend, and if she might invite him over with Meg. Meg was wonderful, even with the likes of Paul. She could draw people out, relate in her thoroughly sensible and intelligent way, without fooling like George or drying up like herself. It was sad how the joy of knowing Philippa was coming was so sadly tempered by thoughts of Paul.

Felix came in shortly afterwards.

'Did they keep you all this time? How is it?'

'I've been down at Lilyshine, stayed for a drink. It's okay, I'll get by with a bit of bute.'

'Don't take too much – remember it's meant for horses. You won't be riding next weekend, surely? Philippa and Paul are coming down.'

'Paul! Blimey, what have we done to deserve that? I'll try and be out.'

'Oh, don't be so unhelpful. For Philippa's sake – it hasn't got to be such an ordeal, if we all try.'

'We shouldn't have to try, Mum. Paul should try, for God's sake.'

Miranda sighed. Felix was quite right. 'All the same, Felix, make it all right for me. That's not asking too much, is it?'

'For you, Ma darling, anything you ask.'

He bent down and kissed the top of her head. He smelled not of hospitals but of scent, which Miranda thought strange. What an odd mood he was in these days . . .

Her thoughts turned back to Paul. Oh God, she remembered he was vegetarian. What on earth could they eat that George wouldn't make remarks about?

CHAPTER EIGHT

THE CRACKED COLLARBONE, even after a dose of bute, caused difficulties in the abandoned love-making that Felix had become accustomed to. However, Ianthe could do it all ways up and found several ingenious solutions to the problem which seemed to excite the relationship still further. Felix suspected that boredom lay at the root of Ianthe's promiscuity. He suggested she learned race-riding – 'That gets the old adrenalin running,' – but Ianthe's answer was to increase the risk in both the timing and the placing of their meetings. In the Lilyshine guest room Felix's escape grew ever closer to Jasper's estimated time of arrival, and outside Lilyshine Ianthe suggested crazily dangerous rendezvous, like Meg's cowshed, the vestry, and The Druid's loosebox. Such was her attraction, Felix agreed to some of these against his better judgement. Drawing the line at The Druid's loosebox, he found himself powerless to dissuade her from choosing the hay pile in the middle of the barn. It was high, and the top above eye-level, and there was a ladder up it so that the hay bales could be pulled down from the top. It was in fact very comfortable, especially with a rug beneath them that Ianthe supplied. The drawback was that now Miranda took an interest in the horses, there was no certainty of being undisturbed, as she had no fixed routine, like Sam. She tended to drop in, exercising The Druid at different hours, or spending a quarter of an hour cleaning tack or putting something to rights.

'The plumber's in all afternoon,' Ianthe sighed. 'It's no go at home and this is super. No car to hide, and you know I hate walking far.'

'Those idiot shoes you wear, how can you? You're useless, Ianthe – you should be a country girl by now – a pair of wellies—'

'Oh God, that point-to-point – did you ever see such frights!'

They had made love (it never took long with Ianthe; Felix worried about whether he was getting into bad habits) and were lying on their backs looking up at the amazing crucks of the old barn timbers above them. George had gone to see a contractor and Miranda had driven off to do some shopping.

'You're a real townie, aren't you? My poor sister's coming this weekend – she lives in town and hates it.'

'Why does she then?'

'She's married to a bloody townie, that's why. A pianist.'

'What's he called?'

'Paul Farringdon.'

'Really? But he's famous!'

'Is he?' Felix was surprised. 'How do you know?'

'Because I know those sort of things, you clod. Who's who and what's what. Can I meet him?'

'None of us want to, that's for sure. He's a pain. Yes, come up with pleasure. You can say all the right things. Talk about culture and stuff.'

'He's terrifically attractive. Women swoon over him, you know.'

'You're joking!'

'No. Honest. I bet your sister has her hands full.'

'What, old Philippa? But she – she—'

Felix couldn't follow this new train of thought. Philippa, nice though she was, was certainly no sexpot, in fact nearly a frump, so how could she compete with swooning multitudes? Is that why she always looked so worried? Felix tried hard to remember what Paul looked like. Dark and gloomy, as he remembered, tense, vulnerable . . . is that what the females liked, perhaps? For himself, he had never thought Paul was Philippa's type at all. She too must have fallen for the physical – just like himself. Ianthe wasn't his sort of person at all, yet he was totally entranced by her and fell hopelessly for her every crazy suggestion, however dangerous.

As if to emphasise the point, he heard Miranda's car come in off the road. Instead of continuing up to Violets it turned into the stableyard and the engine was turned off. Ianthe froze beside him.

'Oh, Gawd!' She giggled deliciously.

'Keep quiet. She'll never see us up here.'

Felix felt like a schoolboy again, up to tricks in the dorm. He was desperately afraid of being discovered, far more than Ianthe seemed to be. There was this pure and innocent aura about Miranda that gave him a far deeper sense of guilt when found out by her than anyone had a right to suffer; if it had been George in the yard he would have been embarrassed but not aware of this deep, hurtful anxiety. It was agony, waiting.

Miranda came in and walked up the length of the barn past the haystack towards the looseboxes. From the sounds, Felix knew that she had Carstairs and Rough with her. They were casting around in the loose straw, snuffling and excited.

'Oh, God!' he breathed in Ianthe's ear. 'The dogs! Don't breathe!'

'I'll lie doggo,' she promised wittily, and giggled.

The snuffling below stopped. Felix could picture the dogs' noses lifted, their ears pricked. What an idiot the woman was!

'Hullo, Jasper darling!'

'*Jasper?*' Ianthe nearly choked. She turned her head into Felix's shoulder to smother her laughter. The pain in his collarbone nearly made Felix cry out.

'For God's sake!' he hissed.

Rough barked.

'Shut up, Rough. It's only rats,' Miranda called.

'You rat!' Ianthe whispered.

Felix elbowed her angrily in the ribs. The dogs were below the hay bales. He could hear them snuffling and sniffing. The Druid gave a little whicker of the nostrils as Miranda went into his box, and they could hear her talking to him.

'Are you my lovely boy, Jasper? My old sweetie.'

The Druid's new name unfortunately seemed to give Ianthe hysterics, for she started to make long gasps of laughter into Felix's shirt front, so that Rough barked again. Carstairs, the terrier, scrabbled on the ladder. Felix knew he could climb ladders. He clamped his hand over Ianthe's mouth. She bit him. He gasped. Rough barked again and Carstairs came scrabbling up the ladder. Felix saw his eager little face appear over the top. When he saw Felix he leapt on him with shrill barks of excitement, thinking some extraordinary game was up.

Miranda came out of the stable and shouted.

'Carstairs! What've you found?'

'You'll never guess,' said Ianthe.

She was not at all put out, still heaving with laughter. Felix turned on her furiously.

'You're an absolute idiot! If you'd kept quiet . . . Get off, Carstairs!'

He fought himself into a sitting position. His shoulder was agony. He felt himself sweating with embarrassment and misery. He turned to Ianthe and hissed at her, 'Keep your head down and *shut up*! There's no need for her to know who it is, if you shut up.'

'I don't care!'

'Well, I do. For God's sake, Ianthe! See sense – please!'

Her diamond-spark eyes glittered in the hay. Felix had a sudden vision of her leaping to her feet and flinging her remaining clothes off, dancing a flamenco naked on the top of the hay. He knew that was exactly what she would have liked to do.

'For me, please, idiot!'

'For you, darling!'

She bit him sharply on his naked thigh as he struggled to pull up his jeans. Carstairs licked his face.

'Carstairs!'

Miranda's voice was sharp at the foot of the ladder.

'Who's up there? What's going on?'

Felix crawled miserably to the top of the haystack and peered over the top.

'It's only me, Mum.'

Afterwards, remembering the look on her face, he supposed she thought it was George.

'Felix! What on earth—!'

As he was half-undressed she could not fail to understand the situation. She looked stunned, then as embarrassed as he did.

'For heaven's sake! Carstairs, heel!' Very sharp. Carstairs bounded down the ladder. Miranda turned and walked out, the dogs obedient at her heels. The next moment her car started up and she drove away towards Violets.

Felix stood up, gathering his clothes together.

'Oh God, that's all I needed!'

Ianthe lay very relaxed, curled on the rug, laughing.

'You're a big boy now, darling. What does it matter?'

She was quite right, but Felix could not accept it. The lovely adventure had become grubby. Yet when he looked down at the gorgeous creamy breasts that Ianthe so delighted in baring he knew that he could not give up this wonderful game, not when her invitation was so warm, her body so seductive. She stretched her arms out to him.

'She won't come back now. We've got ages, till Sam comes. Darling Felix, you only live once!'

'Oh God, Ianthe, you're wonderful!'

And he tumbled back into the warm nest they had made, putting off the hour of retribution.

All Miranda said to him, later, was, 'Not on your doorstep, Felix, it's really very silly.'

'No, Mum, sorry. It won't happen again.'

No more.

Miranda longed to ask if it was Ianthe, but didn't. It was none of her business, although Felix cuckolding Jasper could make for terrible embarrassment. But if Jasper didn't mind Ianthe dancing naked on her own dinner table perhaps he turned a blind eye to her affairs? Perhaps he had affairs of his own. For the time being she had enough to think about with the impending visit of Philippa and Paul.

George decided he would be out.

'All the time?'

'As much of the time as Paul is around.'

'George, for God's sake! Can't you be remotely civilised for once? For Philippa's sake? You must be in for Sunday lunch, at least. As far as I can see, that's the only time he'll be here for a meal, and you never miss that.'

'Well, I'll be racing on Saturday.'

'Who's going to ride Maureen?'

George looked offhand and mumbled an answer.

'Who?'

'Sandy said she'll ride.'

'Oh, George, surely you should have got someone more experienced? A man – Maureen needs a man. She's not easy.'

'Sandy offered.'

'Well, she would, wouldn't she? But any of the boys would take her on—'

Seeing George's expression, she realised she might as well save her breath. George would be able to put his hand on Sandy's lovely thigh as he tightened the girths, and kiss her if she won. Anger blazed momentarily in Miranda's patient soul. Felix, George, Sally . . . they were all at it, sweet Jack too . . . She alone ploughed her loveless furrow, spending her life worrying about things that didn't matter and were none of her business if they did. Thank God for Jasper the horse, her only comfort in life. And dear old Meg: she asked Meg to Sunday lunch.

'Martin's coming that weekend. Can he come too?'

'Oh, splendid! He can talk to Paul! Brilliant! That'll get us all off the hook.'

The arrangement put the weekend in a much happier light. She made an extra effort cleaning the house and getting ahead with some cooking: cake, soup and a couple of apple pies.

Philippa rang up on Friday.

'We'll be with you about teatime tomorrow. Paul will just come in for a cup of tea then he'll be off to Cambridge. I'll stay with you, Mum. I thought perhaps – later – if you want –'

She hesitated.

'What might I want?'

'To hear Paul play? You might enjoy it. We could go in your car and come back together.'

'I would like that, yes. I really would.' Without Paul, just Philippa, the two of them doing something intelligent, talking . . . a concert. Miranda's spirits soared. Dear Philippa. George could get his own supper, home from his pawing of the lovely Sandy.

'Oh, good!' Philippa sounded strangely relieved. 'That'll be lovely, Mum. See you tomorrow then.'

'Goodbye, darling.'

Miranda now found she was looking forward to the visit, instead of dreading it – nearly all Philippa and not much of Paul, with luck. Felix seemed to be keeping out of her way; George went early to the point-to-point, driving the horsebox, and Felix and Sam went with him.

It was a cold March afternoon, but with a glimmer of spring in the smell of it which made Miranda feel optimistic. She took the dogs down the drive to the road and back, everything ready in plenty of time. She felt itchy. Lilyshine was deserted, manicured and gleaming in the fitful bursts of sun between huge, full-bellied clouds. Professional gardeners had extended the garden and the sweeping drives at the front of the house had been dug up and turned into lawns and flowerbeds. The Lilyshine cars were now kept out of sight round the back of the house and came out via the farm drive. Miranda wondered vaguely where the actual boundary of their land now lay; presumably George had drawn the lines when selling the property, and given the house access from the Violets drive. The part of the drive the Pertwees now used had been resurfaced and was smooth and firm, which showed up the bad condition of their section up to the farmhouse. It was always so: Miranda was used to everything George had charge of looking dishevelled and down-at-heel, from his cars and his barns to his drive, his horsebox and, possibly, his wife. The only high-class possession he could boast was his horse, The Druid. Miranda called in and chatted up the lovely horse while the dogs sniffed round the haystack and Carstairs decided that there was nothing doing up the ladder.

'This time next year, old boy, and you'll be racing . . . What will you make of that, my old darling boy?'

He was so kind, so generous. Next year racing would

take on a different dimension for her. She would be totally involved, and would suffer, knowing the dangers. It would no longer be just for Felix, but for the horse too, so much more vulnerable than the rider. Riders' bones could be mended, but horses' could not. Point-to-point was a rough and cruel game in many respects, its amateur status making it more of a risk than the professional game. But it was addictive and glorious. At least The Druid would have the best when it came to jockeys, for Felix never won at the expense of the horse: he had more sense and consideration. The Druid would be in good hands. George had never had as much sense when he had ridden. Thank God those days were over! Miranda remembered how she had suffered when the children were small, seeing the idiot risks the hairbrained George had taken with any young horse offered him as a ride. The line between bravery and lunacy was a fine one, and Miranda had considered George more lunatic than brave. As a father of four small children, he had ridden like a careless boy, egged on by the eager, sparking figure of his mother-in-law. Not for Alice the granny's role of looking after the children while Miranda helped George – Miranda was alone with her push-chairs and picnics while Alice shared in the glory of the winners' enclosure.

Miranda sighed. She was getting old and nothing

had happened to her of any great interest. People generated their own excitement if it was in them. There was nothing in her.

She went back to the house and shortly afterwards Paul and Philippa arrived. Seeing the car, Miranda felt herself stiffen with reluctance. She reminded herself not to be childish, and went to the door. When she opened it she could see that Paul and Philippa had not moved and were obviously having a quarrel. She knew then that Paul was hating coming just as much as she was hating receiving him, and she felt a lot better about the whole thing, even sympathetic towards Paul, so went forwards with a smile. Their bitter faces readjusted and they got out. Paul said nothing, just stood fidgeting with the door handle.

Philippa smiled and said rapidly, 'Hullo, Mummy darling! Paul is just dropping me – he's going on to Cambridge.'

'He can have a cup of coffee first, even if he doesn't want lunch – come in, Paul. It's so long since we've seen you.'

She saw the two of them exchange glances. It struck her then that Paul was like a child; he needed Philippa to intercede for him.

'Yes, Paul, I'm dying for a coffee and you must be too. You've plenty of time.' She glanced at her watch. 'It's not an hour from here to Cambridge.'

'Very well.'

'There's only myself,' Miranda assured him. 'George and Felix have gone racing.'

Philippa had put on weight and looked tired and harassed. By contrast Paul was slender and elegant, dressed in a dark suit, a cream shirt and a crimson silk tie. He had a pale, fine-boned face and rather long dark hair, and a naturally austere, almost haunted, expression. Even Miranda had a pang of maternal concern for him, seeing him standing there in the cold. He looked every inch a concert pianist, his beautiful, long-fingered hands nervously turning over his car key, his Lisztian hair lifting in the breeze.

'Do come in. You must be frozen.'

She had forgotten people like Paul had heaters in their expensive cars; she hadn't had one working in hers for years. But Paul followed her into the kitchen where the coffee was ready on the stove.

'Oh, Mum, you have made it nice!' Philippa said appreciatively. 'And as for Lilyshine –!'

'You wouldn't recognise it, would you?'

'It's great, coming back!'

Philippa couldn't hide her joy, while Paul frowned and fidgeted.

'It's not Australia,' Miranda said, and wished she hadn't. It wasn't distance that kept Philippa away, only the silent Paul. Damn him! Miranda thought. His mother must have taught him some manners once.

'What's this concert you're playing tonight?' She turned to him. 'Is it just you, or is there an orchestra?'

He glanced at Philippa.

'It's a solo recital,' she said.

'And what are you playing?'

'Chopin studies,' Philippa said.

'Milk in your coffee?'

'Please.'

He actually spoke. If it hadn't been for Philippa's feelings Miranda would have made a comment, but she curbed her tongue. She passed him his coffee.

'Who's riding for Dad today?' Philippa asked.

Miranda launched on a description of the racing situation to fill in the time while Paul drank his coffee. Philippa asked leading questions, and they both knew they were spinning out the moments, waiting. Then Paul put his cup down and stood up. Philippa sprang to her feet.

'You know the road? Up out of the village and turn right at the first junction. Then it's signed from there – you can't go wrong.'

She went out with him.

Miranda watched her fuss him into the car. The car turned round in front of the house and disappeared down the drive. Philippa came back into the house.

'What's wrong with him. Can't he make conversation?' Miranda couldn't help the irritation spilling into her voice.

Philippa sat down at the table.

'Oh, don't, Mum. Please.'

'It's not – it's just that – that I can't bear him keeping you away from us.'

Philippa didn't say anything, but the tears ran silently down her cheeks. Miranda was appalled.

'Please don't – oh, don't!'

But Philippa put her head down on the table and started to sob. Miranda went to her and put her arm round her shoulders, hugging her. She was close to tears herself.

'Please don't! Philippa, they aren't worth it! Don't cry!'

Philippa turned her head and Miranda took her into her arms and held her.

'I do love you! I can't bear for you to be unhappy!'

It was almost as if Philippa had come home to cry, saving it up for this moment when she was alone at last with her mother. The years of her tight-lipped silence about her life with Paul gave way to uncontrolled tears which soaked into Miranda's cardigan until she was crying too. Miranda's tears were all for Philippa, yet they could have been for herself, equally disappointed in the aftermath of passionate love. But she did not think Philippa's tears were caused by Paul's infidelity, as hers would have been for George: rather the opposite.

'I can't go on living with him, Mum, honestly, I shall go mad.'

When Philippa surfaced, she was ready to talk.

'I didn't mean to do this, I'm sorry – I didn't mean to break down—' Her face was blotched and red and the tears still tipped over her pink lower lids and slipped copiously down her cheeks. There were threads of grey in her dull brown hair. She was only thirty but looked nearer forty.

'Don't be sorry – I've seen for ages that you weren't happy.'

'Coming here – it's set me off. The row in the car was nothing new, but seeing you, and Violets – this place . . . Funny, it's not Lilyshine, but it's home just the same . . . As soon as I came in I just felt – oh, hopeless, Mum – really so useless . . .'

Miranda carefully asked no questions, but Philippa could scarcely cover up any longer.

'I don't know why he chose me to marry, it was a terrible mistake. I don't know a thing about music, even now, and yet it's his whole life. But if I suggest it's a mistake, he goes crazy – he says he can't live without me. But it's not for love of me, it's for what I do for him.'

Miranda thought, another doormat. She's got it from her mother.

'I've no life of my own at all.'

'I've noticed.'

'He's like a child about ordinary living. He can't cope at all. I have to do it all for him. Everything but the music, and that's a world I can't enter, and that's all that matters to him.'

A less inhibited, more glib person than Philippa could have taken the music aboard, Miranda suspected; with more self-confidence she could have made the right sort of noises. But modest, honest Philippa was not that sort of person. Having kept reverently in the background in the early days of adoration, she was now lumbered.

'Sometimes he doesn't talk for days. Even when people come, he doesn't say a word. And other times he'll stay up all night, after a concert usually, and want a meal in the small hours and want to chat. If ever I'm not there when he comes home, he goes absolutely potty, and yet he can go away playing for days at a time. And while he's away he rings up all the time to see I'm home, or he'll leave me lots of jobs to do: get the car serviced, buy some new shirts, see so-and-so about an engagement. I have to do everything, arrange all his travelling, get his tickets, make all the arrangements on the phone, keep his appointments in order, see his agent . . . I have to cook for him, keep his clothes nice, keep his music from falling apart, get the piano tuner, keep the accounts, answer the phone, pay his parking summonses . . . you name it, I do it. I can never have friends in – that sends him berserk! Sometimes I think he's mad. But his agent and his music lot say he's a genius.'

Miranda couldn't resist a sort of snort.

'He is, at keeping a slave.'

'Well, yes, that' how it's become. I see it now. I've spoiled him so utterly he now relies on me for everything. But there is no love or thanks in return. So I feel I've come to the end – I really do, at last.'

The tears had dried up. Philippa looked as if she had made a decision, but Miranda was doubtful.

'I suppose his mother did all this for him before you?'

'Yes. She's dreadful. She thinks it's my duty to carry on the same way. She thinks he's so talented that I should be happy to support him, to help him give his genius to the world.'

'Hmm.'

'I would, if it made me happy.'

'No one could be happy, getting nothing in return. Is there nothing – physical? There was, surely?'

'Yes. Yes – oh, yes!'

At this Philippa's tears welled up again.

'That's the trouble! Why I stay!'

Miranda sat back helplessly. Felix had told her that Ianthe had told him (when? In the haystack? She had not enquired) that Paul had a devoted following of female admirers like a pop idol. And yet he expended his physical desires on frumpy enslaved Philippa. He never looked at his adoring public. What a stupid tangle! A quite normal infidelity on his part would have severed Philippa's sense of loyalty nicely, yet he perversely chose to ignore what ninety-nine men in a hundred would take advantage of. (Her figures were coloured by her experience of George.)

She said, more briskly, 'Thank goodness you haven't any children, at least.'

'Oh, Mum, he refuses point-blank! And I do so want – oh, I want –' Tears engulfed her again. 'I would be happy if – I would—'

She wept.

Miranda embraced her again, feeling tired and bitter. People got themselves in such a mess, even when they had intelligence, money, a home, friends and good things going for them. Sometimes she lay in bed at night and thought of all the people who had nothing. When she was depressed with her lot she reminded herself how lucky she was, and it made no difference at all.

'You have more than enough justification for leaving him, I would have thought. If you can bring yourself to do it.'

'If only I had the – the courage, Mum—'

'You could come home for a while, think about it.'

'I'm just nothing.'

Miranda knew she would love Philippa to come back and live at Violets. Philippa was the one she truly loved, the one she understood. Philippa needed a fresh start, but Miranda guessed that, in spite of this baring of her soul, she would go home and continue as before.

'You only live once, remember,' she said. 'You mustn't waste it.'

That had been Alice's motto and was probably George's, if he ever stopped to think up a motto. In passing it on to Philippa, Miranda felt a hollow sense of irony. Coming from her, it had little substance. She gave Philippa a last hug and stood back.

'Come on. Whatever you decide, you've always got me on your side. You've got a bolt hole here whenever you want it. It's up to you. Shall we have tea before we go? I made a cake.'

Strangely enough, after the tears – because of the tears – a rapport was spun and in each other's company they were thoroughly happy. They had tea and left before George came home, driving slowly towards Cambridge across the rolling spring landscape. In Philippa's company Miranda felt secure. She was like Meg. She told Philippa her worries about Sally.

'Henry Beenbeg? Is he the eldest?'

'That's right. Not that he behaves with any responsibility at all. I'm rather afraid Sally is bedazzled by him and he has no moral scruples at all. Nor has she, I'm afraid, but she's so young!'

'She's seventeen now.'

'Yes. A month ago! And your father just laughs. "What do you expect? A pretty girl like Sally," he says proudly. She hates her schoolwork and I'm sure she'll fail her exams. Then what?'

'She'd get a job easily – she's got so much drive and charm when she turns it on. Why worry? Sally can look after herself – she's the sort.'

'Yes, that's true. She's really brainy though, if she would work. She ought to go to university.'

'Why?'

Miranda couldn't think of an answer.

'If she went, she'd carry on the same – tons of boys at university. If she doesn't work now, she won't work if she goes.'

It seemed a perfectly sane presentation of the facts.

'All the same,' Miranda said, 'education is a good thing. Look at me. I don't know a thing.'

'And look how well you've done.'

'How well? Good heavens, you're joking!'

'Oh, Mum, you hold the whole family together. Dad and the boys, and old Alice, what would they have done without you? And for me, knowing you're there – I can't tell you . . . Why do you think it's so negligible, to mean so much to so many people?'

'It doesn't seem much to me. I'm sure they could all get on without me very well.' But Philippa's words were comforting, even if she didn't agree with them. 'It's nice to be wanted, I suppose. That's pretty basic. Even if only for making dinners and doing the washing.'

Five miles farther on she said, 'There must be more to it than that.'

Listening to Paul playing the piano, she let her mind wander on the subject, aware that Paul, who made her daughter so unhappy, undoubtably had the skill to impart great pleasure to other people through his playing. Paul could argue that his life was very worthwhile. Yet he seemed himself an unhappy, overwrought man. The music he imparted, through his skill, was written by a man whose life must have given more pleasure than almost anybody ever born, if her own experience in this crowded hall was anything to go by.

'Was Chopin a happy man?' she asked Philippa in the interval.

'I suppose he had his moments, but at the end, coming to Scotland, alone, in the winter, to play concerts to make money to pay his doctor's bills, dying – God, I always think of that.'

'What did he die of?'

'TB of course. They said of him that he was dying all his life, although I suppose that was cattiness. But it was true.'

'It doesn't sound like the music of a sick man.'

'No, it doesn't. Nor of a weak man either, yet he used to play all those pieces himself.'

'How old was he when he died?'

'Forty.'

Miranda was deeply impressed, and aware that all this was what was missing in her life. 'All this' was actually something difficult to define. When she looked around, the hall was filled with what she thought of as 'very nice people', well-dressed, well-spoken: they all looked on top of whatever it was they did in their lives, in command, relaxed, knowledgable about what killed Chopin and what his music was all about. Her son-in-law Paul had the capacity to impress these impressive people; on all sides she could hear only appreciation of his talent. She remembered meeting a woman at Meg's once, who had come to buy free-range eggs, and they had talked about parties, and the woman, not knowing Miranda's background, had said, 'Over Christmas we were invited up to Leicestershire to stay with some old friends, and one evening we went to a party. It was a beautiful place but, as soon as I went into the room I had a sense of not wanting to speak to any of the people. There was something quite alien about them all, although they were perfectly friendly and amusing. Quite soon I realised they were all *hunting people*! Wasn't it extraordinary, that I felt this antipathy before I knew the reason why?' Clever Meg had adroitly changed the subject, and Miranda had been left thinking, yes, I had the same feeling once going to a strange party, a sense of stultifying boredom the moment I entered the room, and she had discovered she was amongst lawyers, solicitors and doctors. Now it seemed to her that there was something quite natural about the woman at Meg's being repelled by a roomful of hunting people, whereas because she was bored by roomful of extremely clever people, there was something wrong not with them but with her.

These very disturbing and rather inconsequential thoughts occurred to her during the first étude of Paul's second half, the opus twenty-five. Miranda, knowing nothing about music at all, was set adrift by Paul's playing and went into a fantasy about living graciously and having parties where her son-in-law came to play, all sweetness and light, and their stock was raised in the neighbourhood – 'those *clever* Fairweathers!' – and George grew benign and intelligent and wore a suit and a tie like Jasper. When she came down from this cloud, she found herself thinking that it wasn't surprising that Paul didn't like them or find their company even bearable, but it was rather a dreadful indictment coming from someone so patently clever whose company was so much desired by all these well-educated people. No doubt he smelled the uncongenial atmosphere as soon as he came in at the door, like the lady she met at Meg's.

By the end of the recital she felt slightly drunk, her brain so far out of its normal rut that it could hardly find its way back. A storm of applause picked up the whirlwind sound of the last piece and everyone was cheering and shouting 'Bravo!' Dazed, Miranda turned to Philippa and found her smiling.

'Oh, he's wonderful!' Philippa said. She started to clap enthusiatically. 'You must admit, Mum—'

'Yes.' Miranda clapped too.

Paul bowed, standing by the keyboard looking very romantic, slightly dishevelled, pale and sweaty.

'We'll go round behind and see him – then we'll go on home. He'll be ages – they talk after these things and someone'll probably ask him back – sometimes he's not home for hours.'

Philippa was now animated and happy, quite obviously pleased for Paul's success. They fought their way through the scrum of people into the small room behind the stage (Miranda's natural instincts thought of it as the collecting-ring but Philippa called it a green room; it served the same purpose) and found Paul surrounded by a group of decidedly up-market admirers. Philippa went up to him and put a hand on his arm and said something quietly. She was still shining and proud, but he scarcely glanced at her, engaged by an extremely smart, persuasive woman who was praising his technical skills in very obscure language. Miranda saw exactly Philippa's problem, looking like a nice lady at the Women's Institute when Paul's hangers-on were so dashing and dynamic. In horse terms they were all in the first three and Philippa was quite patently an also-ran. And Paul who depended on her like a dog its keeper did not even introduce her, hardly acknowledged her. Miranda's throat rose up in a hard lump to see dear Philippa at such a disadvantage. In his moment of glory surely he could include her, put an arm round her, acknowledge a partnership? But Philippa came out, back to Miranda, and they went outside to find the car. She had not even expected it.

When Miranda made a tentative criticism of Paul's reaction Philippa said, 'But that's what I mean – you saw it exactly – I can't compete with those people! Some of those women are vultures. They have such style, they are clever and witty. And the others, the music buffs, they are very sweet but so earnest music buffs, they are very sweet but so earnest and I can't make conversation with them; they find out immediately that I can't make their sort of conversation. So I've opted out. Perhaps it's a mistake, not to compete. If Paul had given me the slightest encouragement I would have tried, but he never did.'

They drove home, Miranda thinking: us two doormats, what a pair! The moon was shining between serene clouds, a fine spring night, full of promise.

As they came home up the drive Miranda said vehemently, 'You mustn't go on like this, Philippa! Promise me!'

Philippa did not reply, gazing bleakly across the moon-white fields.

CHAPTER NINE

DURING HIS WEEKEND stay Paul managed to see remarkably little of his family by marriage. He came home in the small hours of Sunday morning, long after everyone but Philippa was in bed, and when he got up he had to go back to Cambridge for a coffee morning to meet the music society. Miranda scheduled her Sunday dinner for two o'clock to accommodate him, and Meg and Martin arrived a few minutes before he returned. George was into the drink early, to see him through this family duty, and pressed sherry on Meg and Martin. Miranda shooed them all out of the kitchen – why did all entertaining at Violets, and Lilyshine before that, take place in the kitchen, for God's sake? Proper people entertained in the sitting room.

When Paul came in, Miranda hissed at Philippa, 'Take him in to the others. Sally will help me dish up.'

'Where is Sally?'

'Drinking sherry of course.'

Philippa always helped as a matter of course. As a

matter of course Sally didn't. Miranda flung a tight smile at Paul through a cloud of steam and Philippa led him away. A sulky Sally presently came back.

'What do you want?'

'Put the wine glasses out and see that they're clean. And some paper napkins – find some that aren't all creased. I think there's a packet in the lefthand drawer.'

'Paul's awfully dishy,' Sally said. 'I never really noticed before.'

'Not your type, I'd say.'

'What is my type?'

'Well, I'm hoping it's not Henry.'

'You've got a down on Henry. He's really sweet. He's terribly kind to me. Much kinder than Dad is to you.'

Miranda didn't feel the moment was opportune to philosophise over Sally's taste in men. As she drained the sprouts she knew that Sally could scarcely be criticised for appreciating kindness as a virtue. Kindness! Kindness was exactly what both she and Philippa were starved of. Lucky Sally for finding kindness! She thought of the competitions in women's magazines where one put various qualities in order, to make the perfect husband. A sense of humour always seemed to be paramount but Miranda thought she could do without that if she had kindness. Not to mention honesty. Honesty was so essential that she took that for granted, and what was the good of Henry being kind when it was always with someone else's money? She decided to change the subject.

'Shall we have the blue plates, or the ordinary ones? What colour napkins have you found?'

'A sort of dirty purple. And there's some with Father Christmas on.'

'Oh dear. White plates then.'

This was something else she had never got together: enough matching tableware, and gracious touches – the centrepiece of little flowers, candles and the right-coloured napkins. She never seemed to get farther than the actual dinner dished up with minimal cutlery and ancillaries. Not like Ianthe. Even the white plates didn't go round seven and she had to give herself a blue one, hidden at the bottom of the pile.

'Go and tell Dad to come and start carving, will you?' (She had decided Paul could make do with vegetables and gravy.)

George was a terrible carver and needed plenty of time. Sally went out and came back with Martin.

'George wasn't keen so I'm offering.'

'Oh, great! George only ever makes quite a big joint go round about four, I don't know why.'

'His generous nature.'

If anyone was kind, it was Martin. It struck Miranda

forcibly, seeing his genuinely affectionate smile, the total willingness to help, not martyred like George or grumpy like Sally. He was sweet, yet not effeminate; although slender and not over tall, he gave the assurance of an oak. He was quiet by nature, but always shrewd; an easy smile came often but not at anyone else's expense; like his mother he was without malice. He was, Miranda decided, quite the nicest person around.

He was also an excellent carver.

Sally went to fetch the others and Miranda dished up. If it hadn't been for Paul she would have loved this family occasion, with everyone present save Jack, but if it hadn't been for Paul it wouldn't have taken place. And Martin, sitting next to Paul, fended him admirably, keeping the family from savaging him with their ignorance, giving him support. Philippa, sitting opposite, palpably relaxed. Miranda knew then that she would say no more about leaving Paul.

Meg sat next to Miranda, taking it all in. Miranda could see her shrewd eyes (Martin's eyes, amber-green, very attractive) considering Paul, then Sally who, in spite of being dressed to the nines ready to go out with Henry after lunch, looked about fourteen. Her long slender neck, head bent over the roast beef, looked to Miranda as vulnerable as Anne Boleyn's. Henry knew exactly what he was doing. He wasn't bowled over by his new young love, but exploiting her willing, innocent devotion. He had told Sally that he had 'interests' – a few acres of land, a share in a marina – in the South of France, that he might go out there in the summer. There was no way that Sally's interest in a university education was going to compete with dabbling in business (inevitably shady, if Henry was involved) in the South of France.

After lunch the children cleared the table and washed up.

'You'd never know your two girls were sisters,' Meg remarked. 'Are you sure the milkman took no part?'

'I've always thought the same about you. Martin, I mean, being so lovely, considering the captain.'

'Amazing, isn't it? He's just as selfish, mind you. Only thinks of one thing, his work. The captain all over again.'

She sighed deeply.

'We've really nothing to say to each other, Martin and I. Funny, isn't it? At least when the captain was around we talked, we had fun.'

Miranda remembered very well how the captain had talked. The captain and George had got on famously during the increasingly short periods when the captain was home from sea but Miranda had found his company overpowering and had been glad to see them depart for the pub. Marriage and the Merchant Navy did not mix, and Meg had tried going to sea and hated it. She was the archetypal earth lady and could not change her nature.

'Funny we still call them children, why do we?' Miranda asked, sitting by the fire with Meg.

'There's no word for it, is there? One's grown-up children. When they're sixty and we're eighty-something I suppose they'll still be the children. Do you think other languages have a word for it?'

'Probably. There's words for most things, after all.'

Meg stared into the fire, smoking her cigarette. She wondered if Miranda knew Felix was having an affair with Ianthe and George with Sandy Fielding-Jones. Miranda often did not talk about what she did not want to know about. She had the gift of burying unpalatable home-truths, rather than spilling them out to implore reassurance. It was very noble, but probably not good for one. It caused cancer, she had read somewhere.

'How's Jack getting on with the woolshop?' Jack was the only one of Miranda's four children not presently enmeshed in sexual crisis so the only one fit to raise conversation about.

'You've been listening to George. Jack doesn't actually sell the wool. George is so terribly sniffy about it, but I'm sure it's going to be a great success. It's open and doing very well, they tell me. Jack's now fitting out the flat above it. Carol's all right, you know. Such a relief after all these descriptions of a hard little blonde. She is a hard little blonde but she's all right. Even George has to admit it. After he's got over how hard-done-by he is by Jack leaving he'll get on with her very well.'

'He must miss Jack.'

'Yes. But most farms this size are run by one man these days. What can he expect if he doesn't pay decent wages to his own sons?'

'And buys expensive horses? How is The Druid?'

And Miranda's face lit up at the one subject on which there were no reservations.

'He's what the Irish call a real Christian. Which is more than you can say for any of the human beings I know.'

Except Martin, Miranda thought as she spoke the words. But did not say, for Meg would not agree.

'I love you when you ride that horse! A real hero! I shout myself stupid.'

Felix was amused.

'Jasper thinks it's because I've put my money on.'

'He doesn't guess?'

'Heaven knows. He's never said anything. How could he find out?'

'My mother knows. I think Meg knows. She's seen

our cars. She's not stupid. Several people must've seen our cars.'

'Does it matter?'

'Not for me. But it's dangerous for you, I would have thought. All this—'

Felix gestured to their luxurious surroundings: the best spare bedroom at Lilyshine, once old Alice's room. Gone was the fusty furniture, the smell of dust and old leather, stale air and stale bodies. All was now pink and white like sugared almonds, smelling of rose petals and Ianthe's scent, the bed a celebration of crisp new linen, flower-scattered duvet and deep eider-feather pillows. It was out of a film, Felix thought, or an advertisement: it only needed a cameraman. Ianthe propped herself on one elbow and stared at his naked body with her amazing violet eyes.

'You are so beautiful,' she said.

Felix felt himself blushing.

'I'm supposed to say that. Men aren't beautiful.'

'Of course they are! You are thick, Felix. Why do you think I love you? For your mind?'

'Well—'

'For your body, I'm sorry.'

Felix supposed there were worse things. Not for his money or his possessions, nor anything else he didn't have, like a brain.

'What did you love Jasper for?'

'His money. And he's quite sweet really.'

'Does he know you do this?'

'I don't know. How do I know he doesn't?'

'What, in the morgue?'

They giggled and played about some more. Then, because Felix had had a late night with Jack and Carol the night before and Ianthe was getting careless, they both fell asleep.

They were awoken by the sound of the front door slamming, and Jasper's voice.

'Ianthe?'

Ianthe was out of bed and into her jeans and sweater before Felix had quite taken in what was happening. She ran a comb through her dishevelled hair.

'Don't move. Don't do anything,' she said and went out.

Felix heard her running down the stairs.

He lay, only half-awake, blinking, slowly becoming aware of his ridiculous situation. It was the stuff of pub jokes, not funny at all, hearing Jasper's voice quite plainly in the hall directly below. Felix knew the floorboards creaked, and decided it was safer to stay in bed for the moment. As least he was in the spare bedroom and not Jasper's own. It was unlikely Jasper would look in, unless something in Ianthe's demeanour alerted him. Yet for all this cool reasoning, Felix felt the sweat rising. How the hell did he get out without going down the stairs? He knew only too well that there was no easy way out of the bedroom windows, not even a garage roof to get down by, only the scullery roof beneath the bathroom window and that was close to where Jasper would be eating his dinner. Miranda had kept a coiled rope in their bedroom in case the house ever set on fire, but Felix doubted whether the houseproud Ianthe still had this desirable piece of equipment. The prospect of staying the night seemed imminent.

Jasper came upstairs. He went into the bathroom. Felix heard him pee and pull the chain, then he ran the taps into the basin to have a wash. He had left the door open, and Ianthe had left the guest room door ajar in her haste so that Felix could hear his every move. He pulled the duvet up over his face and felt slightly better.

Jasper went into his own bedroom next door, and Felix heard some drawers being opened and closed and some rustling. Then a long silence. What was he doing? Felix felt himself relaxing slightly, picturing Jasper innocently cutting his toenails or even staring out of the window at his improved garden. A wardrobe door clicked and Jasper went out. He went to the head of the stairs, and there stopped. Complete silence.

Felix felt the damp sweat of fear clamming his stiff body. The whole thing was ridiculous, yet he was as frightened as if his life were in danger. He had never had occasion to feel like this before; it was repellent.

The door of his room creaked very slightly.

Felix held his breath.

'Felix?'

Jasper's voice was soft, enquiring.

Felix lay like a stone. His mind was panicking. What was he supposed to do, sit up and smile? He was sweating, rigid with humiliation. He did not move.

There was another long, quivering silence. Then Felix heard the door shut. He heard Jasper going down the stairs.

He threw the duvet aside and sat up. His clothes were all over the floor. Jasper must have seen them. He must have recognised the rumpled state of the guest bed: one pillow was on the floor and Ianthe's shoes were lying kicked off, one on its side and one under the dressing-table, abandoned and guilty.

'Bloody hell!' There was no point prevaricating. He got out of bed and creaked across the old floor to retrieve his clothes. What sort of a husband was Jasper, that he hadn't thrown back the duvet and slammed him one? He had been expecting it. But perhaps undertakers behaved differently from Young

Farmers: a lifetime of placating had dictated conciliatory habits.

He dressed angrily and went to the door. All was quiet. There was nothing for it but to go downstairs and out by the front door. The kitchen door was mercifully closed and he could hear voices, but not well enough to distinguish the mood, save that it was quiet. Were Jasper and Ianthe so extraordinarily civilised that such a situation could be discussed without rage and hysteria? Felix found his mind boggling. He walked across the hall and unbolted the front door. The bolts slid silently. He went out and closed it softly behind him.

It was a cold evening and raining. He walked back to Violets, sick with anger at his humiliation. It was all his own fault, having become so careless, and bewitched by the wonderful sex provided by Ianthe. The pure pleasure of it in what he now saw was a pretty boring life had become a drug and the prospect of giving it up made him feel quite desperate. If this was love he could see why it spurred great deeds, feuds, literature, art, crime and general mayhem: it had never hit him before, not until the imminent demise of his amazing affair stared him in the face. He had been living in a dreamworld, lulled by Ianthe's assurance that there was nothing amiss in their behaviour.

When he got up to the house he remembered

his van was down in the stableyard by Lilyshine.

His mother thought he had flu coming on and advised him to go to bed early with a hot drink and a couple of aspirins.

Two days later George came back from market and said, 'What the hell is Jasper up to down the drive? There's a load of fencing material been delivered from Thomson's – all good stuff. But I can't see what on earth he's going to fence.'

The next day the fencing contractors arrived to start work, and built a three-railed wooden fence across the Violets driveway, blocking the Violets access on to the road. George drove out after lunch and came back, apoplectic with rage.

It took some time for Miranda to understand what had happened. When she did, she found it extremely funny. Her amusement made George madder than ever.

'He can't do this! I'll take the bucket down on the tractor and smash the fence down. Go through his bloody front door as well while I'm about it!'

'Wait a bit. Ring up the solicitor first – the one who did the house conveyance – Peter whatsit – Holmes, was it? You've got to find out if he's got a right first.'

'Right! What bloody right? To seal us in? He's gone raving mad—'

'You sold the place to him – you must have decided the boundaries.'

'The house and bloody garden – that's all!'

'But the garden goes across the drive to the stream – it used to, at any rate. There used to be a shrubbery on the other side of the drive, when I was little. Didn't you tell the solicitor we needed access?'

'I can't remember. I just said the house and the garden, sell the house and the garden.'

'That's what's happened then. If you didn't explain the layout, that we needed access, then Jasper owns the bottom of the drive. It's part of the garden.'

'So why's he fenced it off all of a sudden?'

'You must have offended him.'

'Me? It haven't set eyes on the bloody man for weeks.'

'Ring him up and ask him. When he comes home from work.'

'I want to go out now, not at seven o'clock tonight!'

'Ring Ianthe, she'll know.'

Even as she gave this advice, it dawned on Miranda what the reason might be.

'Ask Felix. He might know something about it.'

'*Felix?*'

'For heaven's sake, Felix has been screwing Ianthe for weeks! Jasper's probably found out.' Miranda flared up, thinking of George and Sandy, and George's decades of infidelity. 'You should understand!'

George was pole-axed. His mouth dropped open, and the apoplectic rage drained away. His high purple colour faded perceptibly.

'You may not be the only one,' Miranda said bitterly. 'But you could say you've set an example.'

'Jesus Christ!'

George sat down. Miranda saw his amazement changing to the sullenness of jealousy; he seemed to shrink, and looked for a few moments drained and old – Miranda was almost alarmed. She had never foreseen George old.

He drove across the fields and out through the tractor gate and went to see the solicitor. The solicitor confirmed that George had sold Jasper the land that gave Violets access to the road.

Three days later Lilyshine was put up for sale. George instructed the solicitor to buy his drive back, but Jasper, via his solicitors, informed him that the price was twenty thousand pounds.

'That's a thousand pounds a bloody yard!'

George set Felix to collecting hardcore to make a new track out of Violets. He railed at Felix. 'All your bloody fault! Screwing in your own backyard – anyone'd have more sense!'

'What if it was you she'd made a set at, Dad? Would you have turned her down? You're a bloody hypocrite!'

Felix was suffering withdrawal symptoms and was in a blacker mood than George. Both Ianthe and Jasper had departed to London and Lilyshine was empty. Felix heard not a word from Ianthe, nor expected to. He knew he didn't mean a thing to her beyond a bit of fun.

Miranda thought the Pertwee reaction, selling up and departing, was surprisingly overexcited, considering the prevalence of Ianthe's sin in the surrounding countryside, but as the price put on Lilyshine was four times what George had asked, and interested parties seemed to be in and out all day, she supposed a business element came into it. Certainly making a home out of tatters seemed to be Ianthe's speciality: another ruin to go at and she wouldn't have time to spare for extra-marital sex. Perhaps it was a pattern with them. From something Meg said, which she'd heard from someone who knew the Pertwees in London, they never stayed anywhere long. The only stable thing in their lives was death.

Miranda, surprised by the turn of events, wondered if the exciting life she thought she was missing was any improvement on her own predictable round. Ianthe had been bored rigid once the house was finished. She didn't even garden. She didn't do anything at all, as far as Miranda could remember. At least, if not excited, Miranda was never bored.

'I think you're pushing Felix too hard,' she warned George. 'He'll go if you're not careful, like Jack. Then where will you be?'

'Go where? Where else would he get free board and lodging, come and go as he pleases? You tell me!'

'Oh, come on! It didn't keep Jack!'

'That girl – she was the trouble with Jack. He had somewhere to go to.'

George's logic exasperated Miranda. She would not be drawn into an argument, for George only shouted if the argument went against him. She tried to remember all the nice things about him, but these days it was difficult.

Felix could not get Ianthe out of his thoughts. He thought his life was in ruins, without prospects, without sex. He kept seeing Ianthe's jokey face in all the strange places they had made love: the haybarn, the garden shed at Lilyshine, the pathway into the cow pasture, behind the cricket pavilion. While the affair was going on he had quite happily known it was only temporary: he would have been frightened to death if Ianthe had wanted to leave Jasper and live with him. He knew this now, yet perversely it made no difference to his yearning for her. He went over to see Jack and Carol and was even more depressed by their obvious satisfaction with life. Jack's work was going well, the woolshop thrived and the flat over the shop was extremely comfortable. They were thinking of getting married.

'You should clear out like me,' Jack said. 'Dad's impossible.'

Felix called in for a lunchtime drink with Jack when he went to buy a new tractor part. On the way home, deeply depressed, he crossed the canal and saw a boat just entering the lock below. It wasn't the usual narrowboat, crewed by holidaymakers, but a small yacht with its mast laid on deck, very shapely, old-fashioned, with a laid wooden deck and a bowsprit sticking out in front. It appeared to have only one member of crew, a youth about twenty who, seeing Felix, shouted up, 'You wouldn't give me a hand, mate, just for a minute?'

Felix went down on to the tow-path and caught the warp thrown up, just in time to take a turn round the bollard and prevent the little yacht's bowsprit smashing into the lock gate ahead.

'Thanks, mate, great! That was a bit of luck, catching you! I can't get the engine in reverse, didn't find out until too late – thought the bowsprit was a gonner.'

'What's wrong with it?'

'The prop's slipping. Don't know why. I'm not much

good with engines. I use the sails most of the time.'

Anxiety did not lie heavily. He gave an engaging grin and climbed up to close the lock gates. Felix closed the one on his side and had a good look at the boat while the boy went off to open the paddles on the far gates. It was about eight metres long, the hull painted black, the varnish-work around the cockpit and cabin-top peeling sadly. The boom and gaff lashed to the deck were wooden, not alloy, and red sails were stowed neatly to the boom. A glimpse through the open hatchway showed a kettle swinging in gimbals, a few tumbled cushions, a book on a bunk.

The boy came back as the water started gushing into the lock and shortened up one of the warps, then stood by Felix, looking down.

Felix said, 'Where're you going?'

'Out to the coast. There's a boatyard owned by a friend of mine – says I can leave her there till I get a buyer.'

'Do you live on her?'

'Yeah, most of the time. But I've got a girlfriend now—'

For a moment, Felix had a vision of making love to Ianthe inside this little boat. It was just her style.

'Do you mind if I look below?'

'Help yourself, mate. She's not very tidy mind.'

Felix sat down on the lockside and slipped down into the cockpit. He stepped through the hatch and down the companionway and found himself in a small saloon with bunks on either side. A bookshelf full of colourful reading nestled over one of the bunks; a few clothes were strewn about and, forward between the two bunks, a small bogey-stove glowed cosily, giving a thoroughly domestic air. A tattered red Persian mat lay over the cabin-sole.

Aft, on either side of the companionway steps, a small galley crouched on one side, a chart table on the other, presently covered with a motoring map. Behind the steps lay the recalcitrant engine, now ticking over in neutral.

Felix sat on a bunk for a minute, taking in the atmosphere which was so different from anything he had met before: a tiny shell of domesticity, designed to go out into the ocean. It was difficult to adjust to.

'Have you been far in her?' he asked when he emerged.

'Been round Brittany, the Channel Islands. To Holland once. Yeah, she's been around.'

Felix was impressed. To spin out the interest, as the lock gates were ready to be opened and the little ship to depart, he said, 'I might be able to fix the engine, if you like.'

The boy's face lit up.

'That would be great, if you could! With no reverse, it means I'll have to go so slow into the locks – it'll put hours on.'

The boy, who said his name was Ginger although his hair was a mousey brown, went below and motored the yacht out of the lock while Felix kept hold of the stern warp and followed her out. They moored her up to the wall outside the lock and Felix fetched his toolbox from the van and went below. He noticed the yacht's name, *Clover*, incised and picked out in gilt, across the stern.

'Cup of tea?' Ginger put the kettle on top of the bogey-stove as Felix got down on his hands and knees in the stern to discover the mysteries of the ancient engine.

'Yes, fine.'

'It's pretty useless, that engine. You'll see.'

But Felix rose to mechanical challenge. It was said in the neighbourhood that there was no engine the Lilyshine boys couldn't get going between them, and although Ginger's engine was definitely vintage and suffering from neglect, he had little trouble fixing the defect. For good measure he cleaned it up, spinning out the time.

'Why are you going to sell her?'

'Girlfriend.' Ginger shrugged. 'They don't mix with

living on boats, not boats as small as this at any rate.'

'What sort of price will she fetch?'

'Well, she's sound and seaworthy, but old wooden yachts don't fetch much these days.'

Felix wiped a rag around the plugs.

'Can I come down to the next lock with you? A test run – we'll try the reverse again.'

'Great. Yes.'

Ginger was obviously not a loner by nature. Felix knew perfectly well that the reverse would now work, but was curiously loath to leave this funny little cockleshell of a yacht, travelling all found through the heart of the country to the sea where she belonged. She seemed incredibly romantic. He had never given a thought to the narrowboats, ponderously at home between lock and lock, but this little craft was something different altogether, at home on foreign shores, signalling adventure. He took the helm and piloted her along the canal, watching the familiar shores from this unfamiliar angle, stirred by equally unfamiliar thoughts. Ginger's complete independence fascinated him.

Six locks later he was still on board, listening to Ginger's life-story. Three locks farther on they moored up by a pub and went inside. It was dark and Felix's dinner was dished up at home and waiting to be reheated in the microwave.

'It's not like Felix,' Miranda said at nine o'clock. 'Did he go and see Jack at lunchtime?'

'Probably. He went to Agrispares, I know that.'

'I'll ring Jack.'

Jack said Felix had left for home at two. He said Felix was very depressed.

At ten o'clock George drove out and found Felix's van, empty and unlocked, by the bridge over the canal. Nobody had heard anything from Felix since he had left Jack's.

By midnight, even George was restless.

Miranda was thinking Felix might have drowned himself in the lock, but knew the thought was only a mother's hysterical imagining. Felix was not the sort to commit suicide, especially with so little reason. He had often stayed away, but not in this unexpected way, leaving his car on the roadside. She knew the police would laugh to scorn a call concerned about a young man of twenty-six who hadn't come home for his supper. So she went to bed, and George followed her up, and tossed and turned beside her.

'You don't think——?' he said.

'No, I don't.'

'He's buggered off like Jack?'

'I think that, yes.'

'Jesus Christ.'

Miranda, with great restraint, said nothing.

'What'll I do, Miranda? I'm not that bad, am I?'

'As you ask, yes.'

'I suppose I'm lucky you haven't left me by now.'

'Debatable.'

'What does that mean?'

'Work it out for yourself.'

'I'm not clever enough to follow the workings of a woman's mind.'

'Exactly.'

George turned over and put an arm round her. Miranda, habitually angry with him, now was sorry for him, the story of her life. She tried to remember why she liked him, and couldn't, but they had shared over thirty years and four children and the ties were strong. She knew, ultimately, that he was completely reliable and strong, and if his overactive sexual juices kept leading him astray there was never any real commitment to anyone else. And nobody had loved like the pair of them had loved in the beginning: nobody had shared a passion like that with him save her – to the best of her knowledge. There were strong historical reasons for loving him, although many practical against.

'If Felix has buggered off . . . bloody hell . . .'

'You'll have to work for a change, George.'

There was a long silence.

'Lots of farms our size are worked by only one man.'

'Bloody hard work,' George said gloomily.

Miranda laughed.

'You're a heartless beast, Miranda.'

'If you were to work hard, I might too.'

'Do the horses?'

'Possibly.'

'Who'll race The Druid? It won't be the same if it's not family.'

'I won't do that.'

'I suppose I could . . .' A long silence. 'I would like that, you know. If I could get my weight down.'

'You're too old.'

'No. It's fitness that matters. Harder when you're older, true, but men older than me ride races.'

'We don't know Felix has left us yet.'

Miranda was uneasy at the thought of George riding The Druid. She thought it would be a good thing if Felix, like Jack, decided to make his own way, and was quite prepared to help George go it alone on the farm, but the thought of his riding depressed her.

'It'll be pretty hard, getting down to twelve stone whatever. You'll never do it.'

'Want to bet?'

He laughed.

Miranda lay staring into the darkness. Good luck,

Felix, she was thinking, it's the only way to treat George, with the same lack of consideration he used on other people. Bugger off.

That only left Sally.

Miranda lay and thought of being alone, and thought how simple it would be, how peaceful. George was soon asleep, but she lay staring into the darkness, considering her various scenarios.

She knew Felix wouldn't come back.

CHAPTER TEN

FELIX SAT IN the small cockpit, watching the sun go down. The sky, for a few moments, was magical, the underside of the drifting cloud glowing rose-pink, as quickly passing, the thumbnail of a crimson sun perceptibly sank below the horizon of flat marsh inland, leaving the reeds silhouetted, the distant grazing a brown-purple gloom. Wading birds cried eerily along the shoreline, louder in the evening than he had heard all day. Aware all his life of the outdoors sometimes looking rather beautiful, this was the first time Felix had ever consciously sat and looked at it and thought so. He also thought his situation was rather beautiful, and wanted to savour it.

Clover lay in a snug cleft in the salting that lined a Suffolk creek, upstream a few hundred yards from the boatyard owned by young Ginger's mate. The voyage was completed. The last leg had been by sea, the mast reinstalled and the faded tan sails stretched to the fresh breeze blowing across the Wash. Ginger took *Clover's* performance for granted but Felix had been enchanted by the feel and the smell and the exhilaration, the land virtually out of sight and the spray flying, rainbowed by sunlight, the long bowsprit curtseying up and down over the waves. The eager tug of the tiller against his hand was like the pull of a fresh horse, and he instinctively knew how to humour it, to get the best out of the spirited little yacht.

'You must've sailed a boat before,' Ginger decided.

'No. Never. I'm a dull farmer.'

A couple of cows stood on the seawall in the setting sun, having pulled themselves up from the ditch-seamed pasture beyond the saltings as if to take in the view. High-tech farming had stopped short of this forgotten stretch of coast, or else modern indignation was protecting it, for the scene was straight out of an ancient oil-painting: it needed only the gilt frame. Felix let his gaze savour it. So peaceful the scene, yet its implications and his new experience made Felix feel heady with excitement. A whole new way of life had been presented to him. He sat feeling slightly drunk, although he had nothing stronger than a mug of tea in his hand.

The tide was retreating, leaving banks of silvery, darkening mud on either side of the channel. *Clover* touched bottom and settled, and Felix could hear the water burbling away from under her rounded bilges and feel the boat canting very slightly to the unevenness of her berth. The leathery silver leaves of the sea-lavender brushed her coamings and the sun disappeared and the sky turned dark blue, patterned with bright stars. Felix thought they looked quite different out here, away from tractor lights. They were for seafarers and navigators, stars for courses, not just for prettiness. Felix had been intoxicated by his voyage.

'He says it's okay. You can stay.'

Ginger's feet squelched over the mat of sea-lavender.

'He doesn't mind the odd guy living on board, if you keep an eye open for scroungers. You know, the kind of guys that'll lift some of the electronic gear, the odd outboard and suchlike.'

'Fine.'

'He's going to give me a lift up to the station in half-an-hour.'

He kicked his boots off and came back on board to collect his tattered hold-all.

'I don't suppose I shall sail her again.'

He sat in the cockpit with a look on his face that Felix equated with the decision to put down an old horse.

'You'll sail another,' he said, to comfort.

'They have a character, the old ones – you get fond of 'em. I've had some great times in *Clover*.'

He was barely twenty by the look of him, and yet had done more than Felix thought he would do in twice twenty years.

'You can stay aboard until I get a buyer – do her good to be kept aired.'

Felix did not answer. Ginger assumed he was homeless: had he given that impression? Was it, in fact, true? Felix knew that his mind had taken off and was telling him to stay with it, cut loose, become a boat-bum himself.

When Ginger had gone, Felix went on sitting there in the dark, thinking about it. There was no hurry to decide. He could make his mind up when he was ready. The evening breeze came coldly now over the mudbanks, but he knew that below there was a little bogey-stove ticking over with a kettle on its hob, and a cushioned berth with a row of books to hand and a lantern to read by. With Ginger's departure, the sense of being the master of this magic little kernel of adventure and independence came again with such force that he heard himself laughing out loud, and the cows, nervous, lumbered off, and a pair of shelducks launched themselves towards the rising moon and flew away.

Miranda was more worried about Sally than about

Felix, who rang up after a week's absence and said he was taking a holiday.

'I haven't had one for years.'

This was true.

'Where, dear?'

'On the east coast.'

He rang off and Miranda wondered vaguely if Ianthe had joined him, but thought the east coast – Great Yarmouth? Scarborough? Southend? – was an unlikely place to attract Ianthe. She presumed he was 'finding himself', a process that life with George seemed to make necessary sooner or later. Only Sally had not yet taken flight, and Miranda thought that this was coming quite shortly, as soon as exams were over and school finished. She kept hinting that Henry wanted to take her to the South of France.

'He's got a place out there.'

'You're going to live with him?'

'It's a *holiday*! Lots of couples go on holiday together!'

'I know that. A group of youngsters, fine. But a seventeen-year-old girl with a man ten years older? It's an affair, and Henry will drop you as soon as the novelty's worn off. I know I can't stop you, Sally, but I hate it! I don't trust Henry an inch.'

Miranda knew she was doing everything wrong,

condemning, nagging, but indignation overcame sense. Sally had grown up too fast and Henry Beenbeg was a disaster. But there was no way to prevent Sally finding out the hard way and Miranda stoically prepared herself for the worst. At least peace might reign at home when Sally was gone – if George would come to terms with the fact that, as he insisted on being the boss, he now had to farm alone.

'Stop spending your time going off in the Land Rover to jaw to people – you know that's where your working day goes! It was always the boys who stayed at home on the tractor getting the work done – now it'll have to be you!'

Miranda could hear herself becoming a shrew. With Felix gone she had a lot more work herself – the horses first thing in the morning and late at night, and the lambing, which she was good at. But she wasn't prepared to take on the sheep which the boys had always done. George was useless with the incessant troubles sheep were prone to.

'When Felix comes back he—'

'Felix won't come back!'

George couldn't take the fact on board for about three months. He slowly came to realise that Felix's holiday was lasting rather a long time. The horses were all turned out, but it was Miranda who was in charge.

'If he doesn't come back, who's going to ride The Druid?'

'For God's sake, that's the least of our troubles! Who's going to do some work around here? There's only you, George. I'll do the horses but I won't do the sheep. Sell the sheep and hire a man, that would be a good start.'

Or sell the whole bloody farm, she was tempted to add, if you're too bone-idle to work it. Alice had driven him, she remembered, when he was young, using the same invective when he showed signs of slacking as she was now using herself. Alice had worked too, shown him the way, a tough old cookie who could deliver lambs, drive the tractor and do the horses better than any man. Miranda knew she was only a shade of her domineering mother but sometimes she thought her nagging was, with practice, almost up to standard. She refused point-blank to take Felix's place.

'You're good with the sheep, just as good as Felix.'

'I've no intention of taking on a herd of sheep.'

Sally asked if Henry could come to supper.

'Does he want a job?' George asked hopefully.

'No. He doesn't work for other people.'

'He wants something?' Miranda suggested.

'He's going to ask you if I can go to the South of France with him when I break up.'

She smiled sweetly. Miranda felt like hitting her.

Henry had charm, whatever else he lacked, and was going to work it on her, and George would side with Sally. She was going to lose her fight. She decided it wasn't worth the struggle.

'Of course he can come to supper. You can cook it, get some practice in.'

'Why are you so snappish lately?' George asked.

'It's her age,' Sally said.

Henry came, driving his new Mercedes. He brought flowers, and a bottle of very good wine. He smiled; George gave him whisky and lapped up everything he said, laughing and radiating charm like Henry himself.

'What a pair!' Miranda hissed. 'They always say girls fall for someone like their own fathers.'

'Henry isn't like Daddy!'

'He's work-shy like your father. But at least George is honest!'

'You've locked up the silver I hope!' Sally snapped.

Oh, what the hell, Miranda warned herself. Does it matter? She knew she was going to lose. Sally, having no doubt failed all her exams (the results would come when she was in the South of France), would laugh. And was the world really going to end if Henry took his pleasure with her on a romantic Provençal hillside smelling of lavender and shimmering with heat with the sea, blue as butterflies' wings, glittering on the white rocks below? Miranda could think of far worse things if she was honest with herself. Even after he had ditched her, Sally would have memories to cherish that her mother would be hard put to match, never having made love anywhere more romantic than in the back of a Land Rover, or, once, in a punt on the river Cam – and very uncomfortable that had been.

'Go and get your father to pour me a whisky,' she commanded Sally, 'and then I'll dish up.'

It would put her in the right frame of mind. She could see Sally hating her, biting her lip. She was all tarted up for Henry, her youth and beauty shouting in spite of it. Henry, by contrast, was already fading, having drunk and done too much too soon, his undeniably lovely features faintly lined and raddled, the British-blue eyes no longer wide and fearless but tired and frazzled, the whites yellowing like old net curtains. He certainly was very likeable on surface acquaintance, but was known (on reliable authority) for underhand practices, even cheating friends.

Miranda drank too much and felt a lot better about it. She convinced herself that Sally would be a lot better off than poor Philippa, chained to her genius. One could only take one's children so far, then it was out of the nest exactly like a sparrow and bad luck if a cat was waiting. The nest remained, if the human child was lucky, that was the only consolation.

Henry brought the subject up.

'A little boatyard – gem of a setting . . . A friend and I, partnership blah blah blah . . . want a – er – hostess, you know, receptionist should say, just for the summer months, July August, lovely little flat blah blah blah . . .'

Miranda had another glassful.

'Just the chance for Sally – holiday really, meet some nice people blah blah . . .'

'How about putting us in the package, eh, me and Miranda?' George thought this a great joke. 'Old retainers, provision the boats, mend the nets, just our style.'

George had also had too much to drink. Henry looked quite worried until he perceived the feeble joke. Miranda despised them both utterly.

'Take her. She's all yours.'

Henry gaped a bit, and George sent her a shrewd, very sober look, over his port glass.

'Steady on.'

'Not at all. It's what you all want. Take the child to the Mediterranean, ravish her, use her, give her a good time, get her drunk every night, get her a reputation, make her work the odd hours . . . she'll love it, better than books. You'll all be happy. I'm going to bed.'

She got up very unsteadily and left the room. She

climbed the stairs and looked out of her bedroom window on to the moon-drenched, still, perfect summer night and saw nothing beautiful at all. Sally is going to have fun and I am a spoilsport, Mrs Grundy born on Sunday: Sally is going to stand naked in the sun and have lovely boys and wine and swim in the blue sea and laugh all day, and I am a spoilsport, a wet blanket, a past-it old woman who never had fun and good times and admiration and doesn't want Sally to have it either. She rolled into bed.

She woke in the cold dawn with a bad headache and supposed she was in this thing called The Change in which the hormones unbalanced the brain and no husband ever understood. She was ashamed of her behaviour and vowed to apologise to Sally for what she had said and give her her return fare to keep in a sock for when she wanted to come home.

But in the morning she found Sally had already gone. George said he had fallen asleep and they supposed Sally had packed a quick bag and gone in the Mercedes. She left a note saying, 'Thank you for saying I can go, you are darlings. Will write. Sally.'

'Did we say it?' Miranda couldn't remember.

'We must have done.'

It drew them together more than anything else since Felix had departed, and George decided to sell the sheep. He was a lot nicer and started to work quite hard.

In August Miranda, foreseeing that shortly the horses would come in from grass and she would be a lot busier, decided to go and visit Felix on the east coast. He sent scrawled notes at intervals from an address she had great difficulty in tracing – eventually she did so on an Ordnance Survey map she read for free in W H Smith's. Even then it was so remote she bought the map to be on the safe side. She lied to George and told him she was going to see an old school friend for her summer break; she didn't want him deciding to come too. He wasn't at all curious, no doubt thinking he could use a bit of freedom himself.

'All right for some, taking holidays,' was the only moan.

Certainly he was working harder, and had found a few casual lads to boss about during haymaking and harvesting. The thought of hunting The Druid during the coming winter and getting him ready to race in the spring enlivened his horizon, and he had settled down more amiably than Miranda had expected. They also received postcards from Sally at frequent intervals, with 'fab' and 'brill' and 'ace' scored heavily against the views of paradisical beaches, which certainly seemed to make a nonsense of the argument for work and university.

George smiled sentimentally and said, 'You're only young once! Grab an opportunity – that's what it's all about.'

He had grabbed her and the farm that went with her, with the amazing mother-in-law thrown in, but Sally, in Miranda's opinion, had only grabbed a few months in the sun. She could have had that anyway. A girl needed a trade to be independent these days; it was no good relying on a man. Reliability was a dying virtue.

So Miranda thought as she drove through Suffolk towards the coast. None of her children had done anything worthwhile so far and she always felt at a disadvantage at dinner parties when everyone else's young had passed out as lawyers and surgeons and deep-sea divers. Felix had intimated that he had work and lived on a boat, but her imagination had failed to come up with a convincing picture. She wasn't spying on him: she had written to say she would drop in and he hadn't protested.

It was late August and the heat shimmered over the land. The harvest was taken, the fields not yet ploughed, and the bleached stubble trembled towards a lilac smudge that was the sea and the horizon. Marsh meadows lay flat beneath. Heavy alien cattle, bleached like the straw, slumbered near the cool ditches, the only sign of life. Miranda wore a rare dress, with shoulders bare, brown from this hot summer, and she drove barefoot and felt curiously young. She opened all the windows and the wind blew in her frizzled hair. She loved this coast, she decided, unencumbered by promenades and funfairs: kept clear and pure for people of discretion who liked music and real ale. There were no swill houses, no fast-food bars, no sickening smell of hamburgers. Only dust and cows and sometimes children on bikes and an elderly couple with their sandwiches in rucksacks.

Beckoned by tiny white triangles of sail apparently travelling through stubble fields, she found a dusty lane which led to a creek. The tide was high and a group of children were sailing small dinghies. A row of rather motley yachts was secured along a rickety pontoon and others lay haphazard downstream, reached by planks tied hopefully to posts driven into the salting. At the end of the lane were a few old sheds, a tractor, a winch, a few cars, a smell of wood shavings, the whine of an electric drill.

Miranda stopped the car and sat taking it in. A small terrier came out of one of the sheds and barked at her. It looked like Carstairs, but was less aggressive, its bark soon fading and a tentative wag swaying its hindquarters. Another dog, a sort of collie, lay asleep in the cool under the curve of a dinghy's hull. A general air of slightly sleazy amiability lay over the place – no Keep Out notices, no proprietor's board, no barbed wire, only a half-full rubbish skip and two battered cars. This appeared to be Felix's address.

Miranda got out of the car and went to the open doors of the nearest shed. It was a carpenter's shop. One young man in cut-off jeans was planing a piece of wood in a vice and two others were watching him, laughing. One of them was Felix. He wore only shorts and was baked brown; his dark red hair, dulled by sawdust, had grown and curled down the nape of his neck in a most engaging fashion. He did not look up straight away, only when she spoke his name.

'Hey, Ma!' His face lit up with real, unrehearsed delight.

He came across and gave her a big hug.

'This is great – I never dreamed you'd come! How did you find it? I was going to send you a map – hey, it's lovely to see you! This is my mum—'

He introduced her to the other two, grabbed a red shirt and said, 'Come to the pub and we'll have lunch. Let's celebrate!'

'Which is your boat? Where do you live?'

'I'll show you afterwards. Fancy you flushing me out down here—'

'I'm not being nosy! I just had a great urge to see you again – not ask you to come home or anything like that. No strings attached. A day out actually.'

'Dad didn't send you?'

'No. I didn't even tell him.'

'How's he getting on?'

They drove to a sleepy pub and Miranda filled Felix in on all the news over a rustic lunch and the local ale. It was lovely to be with him again after all this time, a Felix so patently happy that Miranda was filled with a wonderful maternal content. It banished her doubts and aches over the girls; the boys were finding their way and so would the girls, in time. Children did not grow up until they were about thirty, it seemed. If ever. Had George? Had she?

'Can I look on board your boat before I go?'

Felix hesitated, then smiled.

'Yes, why not?'

Going back in the car he said, 'I've bought her, you know. With Alice's money. Nice of old Alice.'

'She gave you the chance, didn't she? You and Jack, to go away. I bet you didn't save much from what your father paid you.'

'It might be the making of Dad, having it all his own way.'

'We all want our own way. More as we get older.'

'I can't see that you've ever had yours.'

'More than you think, perhaps. What have I ever wanted after all? Not much that I haven't got. Only George being more considerate, and I chose him, didn't I? I knew what he was. I went into it with my eyes wide open.'

They drove back down the dusty track. Miranda followed Felix along the narrow track on top of the seawall to where *Clover* lay in her mudberth. Skylarks flew up singing over the dry summer grass on the wall. What will it be like in winter, Miranda wondered? The little yacht looked wonderfully romantic, not like the plastic buckets that were moored further down; her red sails were neatly stowed under the boom and her laid wooden decks scrubbed clean. Miranda couldn't see Felix being so domestic . . .

'Mother, this is Pip.'

Miranda, one foot just about to leave the gangplank and make a landing on the narrow side-deck beside the cockpit, nearly missed her landfall altogether. Standing in the hatchway, looking rather surprised, was an extremely beautiful girl. She looked about twenty, and had the long-limbed boyish grace of a model, very brown, with large tawny-green eyes and long sunbleached hair the colour of the rain-starved grass along the seawall. She wore minimal shorts and top; her feet were bare and in her hands she held paintcan and brush.

'Pip, this is my mother Miranda.'

They were both as surprised as each other. Pip put down the paintcan and shook hands and smiled a shy, enchanting smile.

No wonder Felix hadn't come back! Dropping below into the small saloon Miranda saw what a magical niche Felix had carved for himself away from home. The nutshell living quarters were freshly painted, with new covers over the bunks, brasswork gleaming, the old stove black-leaded and a jam-jar full of knapweed and yarrow looking extremely stylish on the saloon table. Miranda was bowled over by the desirability of this sunfilled seaside life smelling of hot stones and salt mud and sawn wood. It seemed to have no connection with real life, with care and strife and routine, with traffic and politics and money and divorce and the starving poor. It was like a childhood memory from *Rupert Bear*, a setting of perfect innocence and rapport with nature in her most perfect guise, blue skies and the lapping tide, birds singing all the way. Miranda sat down on the bunk as these heady thoughts filled her mind and found out that there was minimum head-room and very little knee-room either.

'Coffee?' asked Pip. 'Or do you prefer tea?'

'Oh, coffee please.'

Are you close to Felix? she wanted to ask. And knew that, in this boat, they were very close indeed. The girl was gorgeous, moving like a cat in the small space, neat and contained. Her hair fell over the beautiful shoulders like gold lace. Whatever would George think of her? Miranda couldn't help thinking. He would be stunned. She couldn't find a word to say.

'Pip helps out,' Felix said. 'She's painted Clover inside and out. And repaired all her sails – wonderful. I work for the yard. I make a living, Mum, I hope you're impressed.'

Miranda nodded.

'Roger – that's the guy that runs the place – he wants me to stay on when the season's over. So we hope to get a cottage or a room somewhere when the weather gets cold. Roger knows of a place, he says. So it's not bad, is it? You'll have to tell Dad I'm not coming back. I don't want him to think it's only a summer thing, my tanking off.'

'Oh no.'

When she drove away, Miranda's mind was stamped with the picture of the two of them, hand in hand on the seawall, waving goodbye. The sun made an aura of gold round them, as well it should, so golden, fortunate and beautiful they seemed to Miranda, like a pair out of a fairytale.

When she got home she said to George, 'I called in on Felix, by the way. He's got a job in a boatyard, lives on board with a girl. He's obviously not coming back.'

'Bloody hell,' George said morosely.

There was no way of explaining. George would not understand.

CHAPTER ELEVEN

THEY CAME DOWN to the jump much too fast. It was made of heavy bars thrust across a gap in a thick hawthorn hedge, and there was a ditch on the far side with a steep bank – no place to make a mistake. Jasper was no shirker. Miranda had thought him kind and obedient until she had taken him out hunting, and now she found that her bare eight stone was hard put to control him. 'A man's horse' they all said slightingly, but Miranda knew that few of the men could ride like she could and what they did by brute force she did by expertise. Her skilled hands communicated. Unlike the horse in front of her, Jasper got the message to gather himself together ten metres from the jump; then she drove him strongly, judging his stride like a showjumper. He flew it, landing far out, while the horse in front of her pecked and threw its rider out of the side door. Miranda had prepared for such a contingency and steered clear, but the horse behind her was too close and kicked the fallen rider. Miranda heard the shouts and swearing, but couldn't have stopped now if she had wanted to, Jasper having taken advantage of the momentarily long rein to stride off over the inviting grass. Miranda felt an idiotic smile spreading across her face. It was glorious to have the adrenalin running: she had forgotten how it felt after a lifetime in the kitchen. There was frost in the ground, but it was rideable, and the cold air stung her cheeks and made her eyes water. George was somewhere ahead of her on Maureen, and there were galloping horses dotted all around the landscape, mostly bolting like herself. She stood up in her stirrups and the sheer excitement of it made her laugh out loud.

George who rode like a maniac usually left hunting The Druid to Miranda as, although he wouldn't admit it, he knew the horse would get a better education with her than with him. They all said the horse was too strong for her but she had never failed to ride him successfully and, by not over-taxing him, she had kept him sound and keen right through autumn, Christmas and now into the cold winter. In six weeks the first point-to-point would be held, and The Druid would run.

'Hold hard!'

Hounds had checked ahead, and horses were pulling up hastily, tearing long streamers of turf up with their heels. There were collisions and one horse disappeared through a hedge. Miranda had room to pull her horse out and circle away, getting him back to her.

'You idiot!'

A sudden stab of nostalgia for old Alice hit her as she pulled up, a searing memory of her mother in the saddle, laughing as she had just been laughing. She saw her plainly, the wonderful head of auburn hair bundled up at the back of her head, tipping forward the black bowler, the coal-dark eyes sparking with joie de vivre. Alice had never foregone such pleasure for the rituals of childbearing and homemaking, nor grown old with gracious resignation. But gratefully Miranda acknowledged that Alice had taught her the same skills. And now she was enjoying them with Alice's own ardour and felt, for the first time in her life – and too late for Alice to know – at one with her mother. How perversely life arranged itself! Lush whiffs of horse sweat and stinking leather filled her nostrils as the field jostled for an open gate into the woods; stirrups clinked together. The Druid had perfect manners – she had taught him – and kindly took his place, although she could feel the zest burning in his gorgeous frame. His grey hide glittered with wellbeing.

The fox had gone to ground.

The field gathered in a large glade and the terrier

men were called. The flask-addicted pulled them out and passed round sips of sloe gin or brandy. Miranda refused. She did not need any more stimulant. The picture of shining horses, black and red coats against the bare, frost-touched woodland, entranced her, and the feel of The Druid's quivering flank, aching to go yet obedient, filled her with pride. No one else had a horse to touch hers. She always thought of him as hers, not her husband's.

'I hear a hunting man is interested in Lilyshine?' May Bloom thrust up, shoving her horse through. 'George said he was approached about the stableyard.'

'There's someone, I believe, who says he would like the house if he can have our stableyard as well.'

George had been shooting his mouth off, as usual.

'A Quorn man, I'm told.'

'You must know more about it than I do.'

'Is George going to sell?'

'After Jasper blocked our drive up? You can't expect him to feel like helping Jasper sell his house – you know George well enough.'

'He could ask a big price, if the man's keen! You could always keep your horses in the Violets yard. Save all that walking up and down the drive.'

Exactly what she had told George herself, but George enjoyed frustrating Jasper too much to agree.

'Serve the bugger right if he can't sell it. Hope it's costing him a fortune.'

Certainly Lilyshine had not been snapped up. The market was dull and Jasper's price was high.

'Interesting. I wonder who he is?'

Miranda had no idea. She was hopeful for a good neighbour: it was a bonus in this life, after all.

Hounds were called off and they moved on to draw the far end of the woods. The field moved out into the pasture beyond, and Miranda took The Druid away to stand on his own. George spotted her and came over. Maureen looked as if she had travelled twice the distance The Druid had, sweating and tucked up. George was too heavy for her, a light-framed mare.

'How about a swap?' he said.

'No fear!'

'Who bought the bloody horse then? Thought you disapproved?'

But he smiled, pleased with what he saw.

'I've a real mind to ride him when racing starts. You've taught him the job so well.'

Miranda hated the thought of George riding point-to-point. He was too old and stupid: age had not mellowed his enthusiasm and she knew he would ride as he had twenty years ago, to win at all costs. It would do The Druid no good and likely cause George some damage. At fifty-five he wouldn't bounce back as he had in his youth.

'You can help me get my weight down – salads from now on.'

'What, tonight? After a day's hunting?' She laughed.

'Well, tomorrow. Start tomorrow.'

His face had all the eager anticipation of a boy's. If George had a good project going he was all smiles, but if life stretched ahead full of drudging routine he became morose. He always bucked up towards racing time. Looking at him now, Miranda saw quite plainly the lad she had married, the sky-blue eyes which had entranced her then and which still lit up the leathery brown face, the sensuous mouth so attractive when the good times were upon him, so uncompromising when it set in the stubborn line she had come to know so well. Since they had lived together at Violets without the family they had become closer, more friendly. The Druid had brought them together, just as their children had set them apart.

Miranda knew that she was happier than she had been for a long time.

When the day was over they rode home in the remains of daylight behind the huntsman and his hounds. Fog was closing in and their breath clouded the air when they spoke. The bare hedgerows dripped moisture, soon to freeze. The hounds streamed along at the heels of their master's horse in the great rippling wave that Miranda loved to watch, as if bound by an invisible wire. No longer the individuals casting and scenting through the covert, but a tired obedient pack, their pads made a soft clicking passage over the tarmac surface. They were scratched and bloody and covered with mud. It was a dog's life, but of the best, Miranda thought, used and working, not a bored house dog with only a trip to the supermarket to look forward to. Strange how hunting people were thought of as cruel, when their lives were bound up with animals working as nature intended, strongly and with great joy in their natural environment.

They said goodnight at the kennels and rode the last few miles alone, coming home over their own land. Dark and shrouded, the wet plough stank of honest earth. The elemental day had been good and the night and the fog and the weariness were bound into a rare sense of wellbeing. Miranda felt optimistic about the future for the first time in years.

In the evening, when they were both slumped in front of the television by the fire, the phone rang. Miranda answered it.

'Philippa, how nice!'

Yet her heart sank. Philippa generally rang when she felt low.

'I'd love to see you, Mum.'

'Can't you come down? I'd love to see you too.'

'I suppose – it's difficult. You know. You couldn't come up, could you? Meet me for lunch somewhere?'

Miranda hesitated. 'Well, why not? There's no reason why I can't.' She warmed to the idea. 'Of course I will. When would suit you?'

'Thursday?'

'Fine.'

Philippa stipulated a restaurant in Covent Garden at twelve-thirty.

'There's nothing wrong, is there?'

A long pause. 'I'll tell you. How I've been thinking. Just the same thing . . . you know. I'd just like to talk to you, it would help.'

'Yes, fine, darling. I'll do anything I can.'

George looked up when she returned, raising his eyebrows.

'Philippa.'

'Moaning about her lot?'

Miranda did not answer, feeling her maternal hackles rising. Sympathy for his young (save Sally) was not one of his virtues. She explained.

He yawned.

'She should leave that bloody wimp – should've left him years ago. Play the field like Sally.' He got up. 'Noddy time for me.'

Female troubles did not interest George. There were chasms between them still, in spite of jolly times out hunting. He went to bed, and left Miranda worrying, staring into the dying fire.

Philippa was her own worst enemy. Over lunch, Miranda felt that George perhaps was right to take her 'moaning' in his stride.

'You can't go on like this,' Miranda said. 'It's crazy. So unhappy, and doing nothing to make it any better.'

Philippa had lost weight which actually improved her looks quite a lot, although the haggard expression and shadowed eyes were light years from her sister's bright image. She crumbled her bread roll nervously.

'I suppose that's why I asked you here . . . really . . . to make me make my mind up. I thought . . .'

The look of stark misery on her face overcame Miranda's brisk approach. She melted hopelessly, remembering her little laughing Pony Club girl of twenty years earlier. Only a brute could have changed her to this damp rag of a woman.

'Well, of course you must make a clean break! It's ridiculous. I will certainly encourage you.'

'I'd like to get a place of my own, just a room

somewhere. And then a job. But I've no money to tide me over.'

'What about Alice's money?'

'It went into the flat. I've got no actual cash of my own I can lay my hands on, that's what's so difficult.'

'Philippa!'

Her idiocy, her enslavement, knew no bounds. But this wasn't the moment to discuss it.

'So, if I lend you some—?'

'I would go.'

'No bluffing? You promise?'

'Yes.'

'Very well. I will. How much would you want?'

They worked it out. Miranda had no idea where she would get it from, her financial situation being much the same as Philippa's, but she gave Philippa the confidence she needed.

'We can pawn Alice's jewellery! That should fetch enough. Pawn shops are back in fashion I've noticed.'

'Oh, Mum, I promise I'll pay it back! If I had it, I could go next week, when he's in Paris. I've already sounded out a place to go where he won't come looking – a girl I met, with a flat in Richmond – she said I could have a room for a few weeks, until I get myself together . . .'

Philippa started to get quite animated. Miranda

encouraged her, knowing how easily she could slip back from her resolution. Getting Alice's ten thousand back could wait till later, when the divorce was worked out. One step at a time.

'Tell your friend you will move in next week. Give me her address. The minute you move, I'll give you the money. I'll come up again and hand it over.'

The conspiracy was having quite an intoxicating effect. They started to giggle together. Miranda ordered two glasses of dessert wine to finish off with, to seal the arrangement, and they parted on a high.

It was only two o'clock and Miranda, excited by the London zizz, decided to have a look round before she caught the train back. She walked towards Oxford Street, enjoying the traffic and the weird people. She had dressed up to visit London but obviously no one else had, and she felt isolated by her setfast country ways. She could remember her mother off to Bond Street in furs, high heels and a hat, but when she got to Bond Street there were no signs of the grandeur she remembered as a little girl. It was busy, workaday, and aloof from her staring, her sense of alienation. She browsed in Fenwicks, coveted shoes in Russell and Bromley's window (not designed for mud and far beyond her means) and homed in by instinct on an art gallery selling pictures of hunting and racing. If she ever had any money to spend, this is what she would spend it on: a canvas by one of the old sporting masters depicting 'The Chase'.

What caught her eye was a vast picture of a Derby finish, dated the early nineteen hundreds. It was not great art, but it was full of felicitous touches and inside knowledge. The room was empty, save for a well-bred lad seated at a desk keeping a bored eye on her. The hum of traffic was sealed away behind the tall windows, and the sympathetic pictures in this oasis of what Miranda thought of as intellect both soothed and stimulated. Miranda felt, suddenly, fantastically happy. She stood in front of the picture actively enjoying the full stretch of the gleaming horses, the expression on the jockeys' faces and the portraits in the crowd.

A voice behind her said quietly, 'I see you're enjoying my favourite picture.'

She hadn't heard anybody come in. She turned round, smiling.

'It's a real treat, isn't it?'

The man was very tall, elderly. He was lean, wiry, his face lined and worn but the eyes demanding: hypnotic, Miranda would have said (held by them), not aggressive and challenging like George's, but kindly and totally engaging. They were grey, deepset under hollowed brows. The man looked ill, she thought, yet gave the impression of great strength. He wore an old but very good suit and old-fashioned, beautifully polished shoes.

'You like racing?' He smiled as he spoke.

'Point-to-point. And hunting. I've never been to the Derby.'

'Who do you hunt with?'

She told him. She told him about The Druid, about teaching him to jump, about hunting him, about Maureen, George, Felix going, needing a jockey . . .

'Oh, gracious, I'm sorry! Rattling on . . .'

'Why be sorry? I enjoy it.'

'I must go, else I'll miss my train.'

'You're not buying the painting?' He smiled again.

'If only I could!'

'They are having great difficulty. It's not expensive, but too big. Buyer collects, I think is the stipulation. It won't go out of the front door.'

'Really? How did they get it in?'

'They had to dismantle the whole doorway. Then it caused a total traffic disruption of central London, manouevring it across the road. The thought of doing it all again distresses them.'

'What fun! Are you considering it?'

'I would love it, if I can find a wall big enough. I'm biding my time.'

'Good luck. It deserves a good home, not a vault.'

She had no excuse for lingering, and he gave a faint bow in farewell. If he had worn a hat he would have raised it. Miranda went out into the street and made for the tube station, bemused by the meeting, surprised by her own sense of having been dazzled, disarmed. How had he managed to extract so much out of her, merely by standing there quietly, smiling, nodding? Did he have such a sympathetic air that all women spilled out their life-stories to him, or was it just something in her own make-up that found him so charismatic? He was too old, after all, gone sixty she guessed, and not vibrant and noticeable in the way George was. Had there been a military background in the aura of quiet authority? How unlike George! Yet she had found him disturbingly attractive. Always afraid of challenge, she had hurried away. Alice wouldn't have hurried away. Miranda caught sight of herself in a shop window, slight and wiry like the man, dressed (like him) in an old but good suit of unexceptional colours, her head bare, the cropped red hair curling close like a boy's. Her face was sharp-featured with its lack of spare flesh, but her expression was dreamy and in no way challenging.

On the way home she spun stories. She had lingered, and he had taken her out to tea, and suggested another meeting. She started an affair. He had a country estate in, say, Norfolk (she thought he had mentioned

Norfolk) and she drove out there to see him, telling George she was going to see Philippa or Felix, or even Jack. Perhaps he had a title; his manners had been so noble. There was really nothing to stop her these days, as long as she arranged with Sam to do the horses. There was no Alice, no Sally. (Sally could teach her a thing or two. Sally, true to form, had not come back, but had thrown over Henry Beenbeg for a nineteen-year-old Greek, according to her spasmodic postcards.)

Over dinner she told George she had met a lovely man.

'Like me?'

'Not a bit. That's why he was so lovely. So kind, so well-mannered, such a gentleman.'

'Must've been pretty boring.'

'I fell for him.'

'You fell for me once, remember? Those were the days, eh, Miranda? No, only one potato. I'm slimming, don't you remember?'

'What if I went off and had an affair?'

'What if?' He looked at her rather keenly. 'Well, I couldn't really say anything, could I?'

'No.'

'I bloody well would, though. I'd beat the bloody daylights out of him.'

Miranda noted he said him and not her. She laughed.

He might be bigger than you.'

'In that case I'd shoot him.'

'A crime of passion. Do you care that much then?'

'I like having you around.'

'To look after you. Cook your dinners, do your washing?'

'That's right. A chap needs someone.'

'God, you are a hypocrite, George.'

He did not reply.

Philippa left Paul three days before the first point-to-point. Her timing was very bad.

'I can't come up this weekend, it's impossible!' Miranda exclaimed on the telephone.

'No, well, I understand. I daren't come down – I'd love to – the point-to-point would take my mind off it nicely, but he might come looking.'

'If he does, I'll say I don't know anything. Not even that you've left him.'

'That would be best.'

'You might be flattering yourself. That he'll look for you.'

'I might.'

She sounded quavery. Miranda tried to imagine how she must feel, and failed. She loved him, foolish girl, that was the rub. But one could only take so much. She should know.

For herself, she looked forward to having Philippa as a companion, down for weekends, for meeting in London, without the guilt complexes ruining the day.

She told Meg what had happened. Meg approved.

'Bloody men!'

Miranda didn't agree with blanket disapproval.

'Some women give men a hell of a time. It equals out, on the whole. It's people, after all, not sex or colour or religion or all those things.'

'Tell that to the world!'

'It's always people, treating others with respect. Do as you would be done by. You don't really need any other code but that.'

'Gracious me, Miranda, are you running a women's column?'

'Sorry.' Miranda was embarrassed. 'Sorry.'

'That's why I like living on my own, quite frankly. One can be so happily selfish.'

'I never thought of you as selfish.'

'I'm set in my ways. Martin's threatening to come and live at home while major works are done to his flat – the front wall's falling off or something dire, and he said it might be an opportunity to do some composing

– of what, I'm not sure – his mind or his music – he didn't say.'

'I always think he has a very composed mind. It must be music.'

'That's what I'm afraid of. I can't stand his scraping. I thought he could use the church.'

'It's too cold.'

'Or do they compose in the head? Perhaps he just writes it down, and knows what it sounds like without actually playing it.'

'I've no idea. If you can't bear it, he could come up and use one of the boys' rooms. It wouldn't disturb us.'

'That might be a good idea. You know we don't get on for long, shut up together.' She changed the subject. 'Is George riding on Saturday?'

'I'm afraid so. He's terribly excited.'

'Are you?'

'No. I'm worried.'

'I never dreamed he'd get that weight off.'

'He's still a few pounds over, but he says airily The Druid won't be worried. True enough. It just leaves the rest of us.'

'Are you worried about George or the horse?'

'Both, save that George is supposed to know what he's doing, and The Druid's never raced before. He needs an easy. You tell George that! All that work I've done – George could undo it in ten minutes. You know this, Meg – I don't have to tell you.'

'True. George gets carried away. But age might be telling, Miranda – he might be scared stiff, you never know!'

'Well, that won't be much good either. The horse wants a confidence-giving, enjoyable race. George is not the man.'

'Felix is the man.'

'Not any longer. He's made a new life for himself and I don't blame him.'

'Your children are doing awfully well for themselves all of a sudden, aren't they? Late starters, but now – out from under George – no stopping 'em.'

'They're happy. The boys, at least. Philippa might be now. As for Sally—'

'How can she not be? She's just like old Alice, isn't she? Sexy and independent and go-getting. It's all in the genes, Miranda, you don't stand a chance.'

'She seems to change men a lot. She's just a trollop really. I can't help being old-fashioned about it. AIDS and all that too.'

'They know how to look after themselves these days. Far more than we ever did.'

'It's very peaceful, giving in, letting her go. I do

worry, but only as a sort of habit. If she'd gone to university, I'd be in a frenzy of worry, I should imagine, knowing she wouldn't be working, only out looking for a man.'

'Well then, you're spared that. Worrying . . . it's pointless, gets you nowhere.'

'Wait till Saturday then!'

'I'll come and hold your hand.'

'Oh, yes, I shall need you.'

'Any news of Lilyshine being sold yet?'

'No. It's hanging on. George won't wear the buyer who wants the yard, just to spite Jasper. I think he's stupid not to do a deal, get the drive back and some cash in hand. But – oh, I don't have to tell you! Don't set me off! George!'

'Dear George,' Meg said, smiling. 'Always runs true to form.'

Miranda wished she could feel more nobly towards George and his having taken up race-riding again. Everyone else was full of admiration, tinged with envy, for his courage. Miranda never knew where bravery turned into stupidity: the dividing line was indistinct. George was both brave and stupid.

On the morning of the race she woke up late, having slept badly.

'Oh my God!' She looked at the clock in dismay and

switched back the covers. George was lying awake with his hands behind his head.

'What's the matter?'

'I should've been down there half an hour ago!'

'It won't kill them, half an hour. What about me? It's me you should be cosseting, worrying about. Do you love me, Miranda?'

He reached out and grabbed her as she sat on the side of the bed. She fought him off.

'Don't be daft!'

'What's wrong?'

'Your timing. Your timing's hopeless. We've overslept.'

'Another ten minutes won't make any difference.'

'I can't think about it now. There's too much to do.'

'You always used to say that.'

'In the morning. I like it at night.'

'I'll be too tired tonight.'

'That's your problem. It won't bother me.'

'I should've listened to your mother. She always said you—'

He stopped.

Miranda pulled her jersey over her head and looked at him. Waited.

'What did she say?'

George grinned. 'Nothing. I shouldn't have

mentioned it.'

'Go on, tell me.'

'Come here.'

'No.' But she hesitated.

George lay there grinning, his blonde-grey hair tousled, his blue blue eyes amused and challenging. He was the George she married long ago, still full of spirit, bold and funny and with the power to hurt undimmed.

'My mother was very sexy. You should have married her, not me. Did you ever make love with my mother?'

George opened his eyes very wide.

'What a thing to ask! Your own mother!'

'Deny it then.'

'I wouldn't dream of discussing it. What a question!'

'Tonight. Tell me what she said about me.'

'I shall be drunk tonight – all that champagne. I won't remember.'

'Champagne! You're not out to win, you fool! Just get him back safe and happy. That'll be worth a bottle of champagne.'

'You'll treat me?'

'If you're good.' She grinned. 'As good as Felix. Then you'll tell me about my mother, when you've got drunk.'

He laughed.

She went out, curiously disturbed. She never fancied making love with George any more, cursed by visions of Sandy Fielding-Jones. God knows, she should have got used to George's philandering by now; the scar tissue was so thick she wondered any hurt could still get through, but it did. She had taught herself, by a great effort of will, to eschew jealousy, that totally destructive and evil sin, remembering the pangs she had suffered when the children were small. She would not want to live through those years again. The agony had been appalling. As one grew older, more hardened, one coped much better, but a certain bitterness surfaced at times. Perhaps she was bitter. She had good reason. But lately, in spite of the children's comings and goings, she felt more carefree than she could remember. She was beginning to be her own person after all these years.

'Thanks to you, my darling boy!' she said to Jasper. But he was only part of it, the catalyst.

When she went in to make breakfast, George was no longer in the same mood but, understandably, edgy and short-tempered. There was no way he couldn't be nervous; even Felix, with everything in his favour, had been nervous on the day. And she too . . . she could feel the sweat clamming her body at the thought of the afternoon ahead.

Sam came in to muck out and groom and she went

down to the stables again, anxious to be out of George's path. Sam had forgotten Sally at last and was now blooming: a clumsy gentle giant of a lad, entirely reliable. They had come to depend on him, could set the clock by the spasmodic roaring of his motor bike as it bounced over the badly-made new track out to the road. Even he was nervous.

'I hope he won't take off with 'im, like.'

Miranda rode the horse out round the farm, just walking, to make him think it was just an ordinary day, but he seemed to sense the tension and spooked at broken branches and abandoned fertilizer sacks. It was a good day for racing, cold but not freezing, the going slightly on the soft side, but that suited The Druid. A fair wind bowled grey clouds across the horizon, occasionally opening out a patch of blue, and the blasted crows coasted like black sailing ships across the sky. When she got back she threw a picnic basket together and hunted out the bottle of champagne she had kept from some celebration that hadn't happened. If George and Jasper got back safely – that would be worth celebrating.

She went to the course in the box with George and Sam. She felt sick and wildly excited, but said not a word. George was morose and equally silent. He was still five pounds overweight, but looked better for his dieting, if slightly haggard around the jaw. When they got to the course he abandoned them entirely, to find support and relief with other tensed-up performers in the farmers' tent. Miranda felt better without him.

The Druid was running in the fifth race, the Restricted Open. There was plenty of time, worse than getting ready straight away. Sam reassured Miranda.

'I'll keep an eye on him. Get him out in plenty of time.'

'I think Jack said he'd be here. He'll help saddle up. I'll look for him.'

She needed Meg more than anyone, to temper her twitchiness. She found her by the paddock, ticking the runners for the first race. Meg grinned.

'I've seen George. He looks as if he's regretting it, silly idiot. He'll never learn sense.'

'It was bad enough with Felix. It's ghastly with George. At least Felix knew what he was doing.'

'The horse'll look after him. He's such a Christian. Don't worry.'

But Meg had her maternal face on, knowing exactly that there was little comfort for Miranda in the circumstances. Old Windy Fielding-Jones came up to wish her well with The Druid, and Sandy was demurely at his side, in stunning tweeds.

'Aren't you riding today?' Miranda was surprised.

'No.' She blushed slightly.

'Her riding days are finished for a little while,' Sir Henry bumbled, putting an arm round her shoulders. 'You should congratulate us!'

'Oh, Henry, shut up,' Sandy said.

They sailed away, leaving Meg and Miranda gaping.

'But she's had her two, surely?' Meg said.

'I'd have thought the old boy was past it by now.' Miranda couldn't help freezing over at the thought that came into her head. She looked at Meg for her reaction, but Meg was now in control and studying the horses with sudden interest. She had seen them all before, Miranda knew; they both knew the likely winner, the second and the third. But they discussed chances. Miranda felt her disturbed bloodstream hammering in her temples, staring at the card.

'Hi, Mum. We've come to cheer Dad. Where is he?'

Jack and Carol were suddenly at her side, warm and smiling. They looked such a nice pair, so ordinary and reliable; Miranda felt a surge of love for her eldest boy and his girlfriend.

'Oh, good, I'm so glad you've come! Are you going to help Sam later? We need support! I'm terrified!'

'Oh, come off it, Mum! After all these years—?'

'That's the trouble – all those years – too many years—'

'Life in the old dog – come on, Mum, he'll ride him a treat! Enjoy it!'

They all conspired to soothe her twitches: Napoleon and Eleanor, old May Bloom, hearty but sympathetic. They understood. Racing was all about stirring the adrenalin, after all. Jack came down to the horsebox park and they unloaded The Druid. George was nowhere to be seen.

'I hope he's not drinking.'

'It might help,' Jack grinned.

The Druid stood looking about him, surprised, strong, his long ears flitching to the sounds of excitement from the course. He trembled under his warm rugs.

Horses which had raced came back, heads down, nostrils flaring, grooms despondent, or laughing, shouting to each other. Anxious owners trotted alongside, trailing gear; children capered, dogs barked from parked cars. It was all so utterly familiar and yet, this time, quite different. Miranda shivered.

'Mother, go away. We'll do the work.' Jack was kind, and firm. He was back in his old guise, no longer the woolshop man, but dependable, farming Jack. Miranda loved him. She went away with Meg, and Meg gave her a strong drink from the boot of her car, and then the preamble was over and they were all in the paddock, ready for the race, minds on the job.

There were eight runners. Of the eight, The Druid looked outstanding, so assured with his long stride, his eager interest in all around him. For a beginner, he was well fancied, up in the betting. He walked like a king, towing the sweating Sam with him, yet he seemed in no hurry. He seemed more in charge than any of the rest of them.

George came out to a chorus of whistles, cheers and jeers from his friends. He looked astonishingly slim in his white breeches and colours, Miranda was amazed. His face was pale and he wasn't laughing.

'You've got the best horse, Dad, you can't go wrong.'

'You bloody shopkeeper, what do you know about horses?' But it was a joke, kindly meant. He was pleased to have Jack's support.

Miranda held the horse and the men girthed him up and legged George into the saddle. He gathered up the reins. Miranda looked up at him and saw the old gleam in his eye, the smile breaking. Once you were under way, everything was all right – it was always the way. His red silk cap sparked against the gathering grey clouds of the late afternoon.

'What a handsome couple you make,' she said, and laughed.

'Got that champagne ready?' he said.

The huntsman was waiting to see them down to the start, horn to his lips. Everyone cheered George as he went, and the young jockeys called out as to who should give 'old grandpa' a lead. The Druid pranced, pulling hard. Jack put his arm round Miranda's shoulders and gave a squeeze.

'You have to take your hat off to the old devil, eh?'

I shall have to live with him if he gets it wrong, Miranda thought. She was shivering. But laughing.

She had watched enough races, God only knew, and none dispassionately, but this was something else. George would never settle for mild accomplishment: it had to be the whole works, heart and soul, neck or nothing. Even for the start: no holding back and lobbing along comfortably in train, but The Druid had to be nudged up, held hard, dancing and prancing as the flag was raised, barging across the others. There was shouting and swearing and someone turned round; George swore; the starter bellowed and the flag went down with a cutting swipe. The Druid sprang off with an almighty bound at the boot from his rider and swung immediately into the lead with his great raking stride, coming to the first some six or seven lengths ahead of all the others. Miranda heard herself screaming, but wasn't the only one. The grey horse flew it, leaving George in mid-air for an uncomfortably long time, and tore away with his head down between his knees in the general direction of the next jump. He was completely out of control, but heading in the right direction.

'He'll fall if he doesn't get a hold of him!'

It was all exactly as Miranda had feared.

'He's a clever horse,' Meg said comfortably, 'George'll manage.'

'If he stays on!'

Going with that much abandon, at least the horse would ease up well before home. He would exhaust himself. George would then blame 'the old devil', no doubt – it all came back to Miranda as she watched, the memory of George's bad tempered post-mortems, blaming everyone except himself – the bloody horse, the blind starter, the upstart young jockeys . . . Racing with Felix riding had been a rest cure by comparison.

At least The Druid had a clear view of the fences and jumping was his game. Up the long hill round the top of the course he started to settle, George having gathered himself together, and at every jump he put himself another length ahead, such was his fluency and precision. It was a beautiful performance, but George was misjudging the pace and Miranda knew that The Druid would start tiring where it mattered, in the last half-mile. After one circuit the others were starting to come up. This was where The Druid needed a fit young rider to hold him together, but Miranda could see only too clearly that George was fast becoming exhausted. The pace had told on him too.

'He should pull up,' Jack said doubtfully.

'They've done well – yes, he should be satisfied – the horse has jumped superbly.'

'He won't, though,' Meg said, and laughed.

At the top of the hill on the last circuit two horses were challenging The Druid. They jumped abreast, but as they came down the hill to the penultimate jump one dropped back and one went ahead. The Druid, rapidly tiring, badly needed help to get right for the tricky, downhill jump. He was asprawl with fatigue. But George could only think of the horse in front of him, which needed to be passed: he could not think any other way. Races were for winning. Instead of taking a hold and trying to gather the big grey horse together, to make him see the jump, shorten his stride and get it right, he gave him a wallop with his stick and booted him on faster.

The Druid came to the jump all wrong. He tried to take off boldly but was too close. He caught his knees in the thick brush and turned a somersault. Such was his downhill impetus he rolled over twice on landing and came to a halt in the natural hedgerow behind which a large crowd was standing.

Miranda saw the crowd bow out, shouting with alarm; then there was a long, agonizing delay before The Druid's grey head bobbed up above the hedge. He was on his feet and away at once, pounding on up the hill.

'He's all right!'

Miranda started to run, almost cheering with the flooding sense of relief at seeing The Druid regain his feet. No doubt George was still swearing in the ditch. He had only himself to blame, throwing the race away by his idiotic tactics. The horse had run really well, no disgrace and with luck the fall would be quickly forgotten. He wasn't a nervous horse by nature.

Someone had caught him and a little crowd had collected round him. The winner and second were being cheered in and everyone was moving off away from the rails. Miranda had to shove her way through.

'I'll take him – thanks!'

Sam was there before her.

'He's cut himself, like. We want the vet, that'd be best.'

Blood was running copiously down the hind leg from above the hock, welling out in surges from a deep cut. Miranda felt for it and held the edges together momentarily.

'It needs stitches! Let's get back to the box.'

'We'll put a call out for the vet,' someone said.

'Tell him the dark blue Bedford.'

The wound looked dramatic, but was not on the joint and unlikely to prove disabling for long. One of the stewards produced a bandage and Miranda did some swift first aid. Sam loosened the girths and held the horse and when Miranda was ready they started off back for the horse-park.

'I suppose I ought to see if George is okay, but the vet might be waiting. George'll come on down. He always bounces.'

'A shame, that,' Sam said.

'Yes, George was daft, the way he rode! But they did well, I suppose, up till then. He jumped a treat, didn't he? He's got a future, I'd say.'

'Yeah, he was great.'

They were keyed up, spurred by the urgency of the dripping blood, but not dismayed by the way things had turned out. Miranda felt slightly light-headed, deeply thankful that her paranoid worries were now at rest; her body felt as if it were singing with joy and relief. The Druid walked out calmly; the cut did not seem to be troubling him, although he left an impressive trail of blood across the grass.

The vet came down in his car and arrived a few moments after they did. He was an old friend. Sam held the horse and Miranda stripped off his saddle and put his rugs on. It was cold now. The horses had gone out for the last race, and the place seemed suddenly quiet and subdued. Beneath the grey cloud the last of the sun was flaring over the wooded horizon. Miranda straightened up. She felt suddenly as if a goose had walked over her grave.

Meg was coming down the field, alone. She looked very strange, hunched up.

'What's the matter?' Miranda said.

She knew it was bad.

She shut her eyes and took a deep, quivering breath.

'What is it? What's he done?'

Back . . . spinal cord, wheelchairs. Brain . . . a vegetable . . . She had been through it all, with Felix, that moment when they fell and lay still. But this time, with George, she had never given it a thought. Only the horse, the horse was all right.

'Collarbone?' She smiled.

'Oh, Miranda.' Meg's mouth went slack and out of shape. 'My dear.'

She stood there, staring at her, her face working against tears.

'It's finished.'

'Finished?'

Meg couldn't say it. She shook her head. She came up and put her arms round Miranda and squeezed her with a fierce, angry embrace. It was Meg who was sobbing, asking Miranda's comfort.

'He's dead?'

'Yes. The horse rolled – right over him.'

Miranda put her arms round Meg, far more gently than Meg's arms were round her. She had no feelings at all at that moment, save of astonishment. A limbo.

The Druid swung against them, warm and very much alive, knocking them apart. The vet was stooping over his hock.

'Can you hold his foreleg up, make him stand?'

Miranda reached down and caught up the leg. It was something to do, after all. Head down, like the vet, hold on. The leg was strong. Hold on, she thought.

'Miranda!' Meg wept.

'Is something wrong?' The vet, looking up, noticed.

'It's all right, I've got him,' Miranda said.

'I'll give him a sedative if he won't stand. Should be okay though.'

The runners for the last race were coming back, cool and untried. Their grooms were silent, heads down. No one looked at Miranda and The Druid. In the dusk their faces were unreadable. The race had been cancelled.

'Is Jack there?' Miranda asked.

'He went in the ambulance. I don't know why. He said George wanted someone, he mustn't go alone.'

'Quite right.'

'Napoleon'll be here in a minute and — and the others.'

She kept holding on to The Druid's leg. It was her lifeline, taking all her strength as he pulled about. Head down. Deep breaths. Hold on. The horse was all right. George wasn't coming home.

'I'll take you home,' Meg said.

'I'll have to drive the horsebox.'

'No. One of the men'll do that.'

'Okay,' the vet said.

Miranda straightened. She felt slightly light-headed, all that bending. Someone put a strong arm round her and she was propelled away.

'We'll see to the horse.'

'Get you home.'

'Get you a drink.'

'Are you warm enough?'

'Carol's coming. Jack'll come back.'

She did not know how to respond. She wanted to stay with the horse but they wouldn't let her. They took her away across the darkening, emptying fields and drove her home. She said nothing. She felt winded, wiped clear, nothing. All the time she thought it wasn't true; it couldn't be happening. She could look at herself from way apart, playing this role, not real. Napoleon's car was like a palace, all soft purring and warm like the womb, Eleanor's hand warm on hers, firm and reliable.

'If you'd prefer to come home with us?'

'Oh no. No, I want to go home.'

She wanted to go home with George, tell him what a fool he was for getting killed. Don't think that. Blankness. It was better, the brain blank. Peaceful at home, no more arguing, everything her own way . . . always . . . do exactly what she pleased. For ever.

If she'd known she was having all these visitors she would have left the kitchen more tidy. There were still old coffee mugs on the table and the papers scattered around. The dogs put up a terrible racket; she had to shut them in the old scullery. But the people got the fire going, the house warm, The Druid home and unloaded and made comfortable, the other horses fed and mucked out; all she had to do was sit there and watch it all revolving round her. Then Jack and Carol came back, and Meg had made some scrambled eggs and everyone else departed. The four of them sat round the kitchen table. Miranda poured the tea, watching Jack, who kept crying. Jack! . . . He had never cried, not since he was nine or ten.

Carol said, 'Shall I ring up Felix? And Philippa? And what about Sally?'

'Yes, we must tell them.'

'Do you want me to do it? Or would it be better—?' Carol looked uncertainly at Meg, sensitive as to her status, not strictly family. She had seen little of the others.

'Perhaps I should do it.' Meg had seen them all born, after all. Auntie Meg, one of the pillars.

'Poor things,' Miranda said. 'Poor Philippa. There's no hurry. Eat your eggs first.'

To her surprise, she found she was hungry and wanted the food. It was something to do, so awkward to make conversation about what had happened. So empty, the George department, after over thirty years – a big black hole just where you were going to step. Not to look in.

Meg did the telephoning. To Miranda's surprise, Felix and Philippa came. Two hours after the phone call they were both in the house. Martin brought Philippa in his car. Meg made more scrambled eggs, and Jack opened some bottles of wine. After the tears, they started talking about what George would have been like if he had grown to be old and incapable, what he had done in the past that had made them laugh. Miranda laughed as loudly as any of them, and while she was laughing her brain was registering amazement, half appalled, half impressed. It was a party – George would have loved it. George would have approved. George was there, it seemed to Miranda, egging them on.

Long past midnight she flaked out in her own bed. Jack checked the horses; Felix would do them in the morning. Philippa was staying. Meg would come back when the children departed. Miranda's head whirled. She remembered how it had been when Alice had died, all the things there were to do . . . No time, really, to dwell on what had actually happened.

Chapter Twelve

SHE LAY THERE remembering that George had been going to tell her what her mother had said. Or would he have told her? Even after the bottles of champagne that hadn't been needed, she thought the reticence of thirty-two years would have been respected. The two of them could lie easy with their suspect past. No one would ever know.

She turned over and put out her arms to the empty space where George should have been. Everything was different now, in the light of day: George was dead and not coming back. The bed seemed very large and unfriendly.

The others were doing the chores. She could hear the chinking of cutlery and plates, and Felix's car coming back from the stables. She supposed it was commonplace to be surprised that life went on just the same beyond one's own personal tragedy, yet she was surprised. The sun came up, the winter rays shimmered tentatively across her pillow and the same blackbird that sang in the pear tree was singing now, just as he had sung the day before. Nothing was different for anybody else, only for her. For her, the sun should stay below the horizon, the birds should stop singing.

When things had been all right for her, and she had sometimes felt exceptionally happy, she remembered she had stopped in her self-congratulation to remember that while she felt that way, all over the place other people were bereft, in agony, starving, animals were dying of neglect and people of worse. Yet even while she had been remembering that, her own happiness had been bursting inside her like water from a spring. It was not particularly helpful to remember this generous and useless delicacy of awareness towards the suffering multitude, but it seemed fair to remember that, all in all, she had been very fortunate up till now. She wasn't familiar with suffering. She didn't know how to do it, thought she ought to be crying, but somehow felt merely numb. Pole-axed. A bit sick. She had been far more emotional over her mother, which seemed a bit unfair to George.

She suddenly remembered that her father had been killed in much the same way. As she had been so young at the time, it was not a memory that had ever surfaced a great deal. 'Bloody fine way to go,' Miranda could recall Alice saying, and could scarcely argue, recalling the expression of manic excitement on George's face as he belted The Druid into the jump. A bloody fine way to go but a bit too soon, in George's case.

Breakfast continued below. Jack and Carol and Felix and Philippa had put her to bed and gone on talking, as she remembered it. It was a long time since they had all been together, and no doubt they had been arranging her future. She hoped the boys did not feel they had to come back to the farm. She didn't think they would: they had grown away, grown up in the last year, their conversation was altogether larger and more intelligent, lifted above the price of potatoes and how many tonnes to an acre.

'It's my farm,' she thought.

The land was hers.

She wanted it. She did not want to go away, whatever the children were planning.

She felt sad, and very peaceful. She felt like a rag of seaweed come to rest above the highwater mark after weeks of rough seas. Too tired to lift her head. The bed she lay in had been Alice's guest room bed. It had heavy mahogany ends and was unfashionably, beautifully soft and saggy; it was a bed of her childhood, as was the other heavy and unsuitable (for a cottage) furniture of dark oak and mahogany, familiar and old-fashioned, and she loved it. Meg had thought she would throw it all out when Alice died, replace it with trendy, cottagey pine. George had liked it, especially the bed. The hollow his body had made was still there beside her, cold and empty. Very strange. Miranda felt suspended from grief; there would be a time for it, but for the moment she was in a state of limbo, still – metaphorically speaking – holding on to the horse's leg. Holding on. It took all her strength.

Philippa came up with a cup of tea, silently round the door.

'Oh, good, you're awake.'

'Habit,' Miranda said.

'Nothing's habit any more. Paul – and Dad.' She looked dreadful, bereaved twice over. It was only three days since she had left Paul.

'You needn't feel you have to stay with me,' Miranda said. 'I'll be all right.'

'There'll be a lot to do, until the funeral. I could help you with that. I think it would suit me.'

Paul wasn't having a funeral, of course. Perhaps it was worse for Philippa, leaving Paul of her own free will, than it was for herself having George snatched away by fate. You couldn't argue with fate.

'It'll get better, Philippa,' Miranda said gently. 'I would love you to stay, if you'd like to. It would help a lot.'

Philippa looked slightly more cheerful.

'I'll tell the boys. They're being rather bossy down there.'

'It's too early to make plans. But tell them I don't want them back here, in case they're worried. I think I'll stay in bed for a bit. They can check The Druid's leg, can't they? Sam's not all that experienced. It'll need cleaning.'

'Felix has already done it. He says it's okay. You won't shoot him or anything like that, will you? It wasn't his fault.'

'Of course I won't! Good God, imagine what George would say to that!'

'No, I didn't think so. But people are funny.'

She hadn't stayed in bed for years.

It was raining. She pulled the mothy old eiderdown up round her ears and lay thinking about George. Poor old bugger! It was going to take a lot of getting used to. And money . . . The farm ticked over, but George had been cagey about the money. Whether he had paid off all the overdraft with the Lilyshine money was doubtful, knowing how careless he was, and how he despised bank matters. His fine disdain! How he had enjoyed life! He hadn't done much, all in all, but his gusto had made it all seem very important. He would have made a dreadful old man. Hold on to that comfort, because there wasn't much else.

* ★ ★

Martin came to the funeral and told Philippa gently that Paul had moved in with a brilliant young German violinist and engaged a housekeeper-cum-secretary to do all the work. It had been exactly a week since Philippa had left him. Miranda was too worried about Philippa to think of her own troubles. She looked like a ghost. She lost half a stone in seven days. She looked beautiful. People who hadn't seen her for years said what a beautiful girl the elder one was. Funny, they had never noticed.

'It's all my fault,' Miranda said. 'You followed me in the doormat stakes, because that's how you were brought up to see a marriage.'

'I loved him. I wanted to help him and look after him.'

'He kicked you in the teeth for it. You must go back and claim your flat. Change the locks. Throw all his stuff out.'

'I want to stay here.'

'No. You mustn't. The flat's important. Come on, Philippa, neither of us can sit on our backsides! We can't just mope!'

She hadn't even cried yet. She was still in her state of suspension. The funeral had to be huge, like Alice's, because so many people would come, and the work and the worry occupied her completely. Jack and Carol rose to the occasion, and Miranda acknowledged that Carol was now one of the family; her sharp, tartish appearance was matched by a quick competence that had caterers, florists, even Tom the vicar, out and on their toes for a first-class performance. She took Miranda in hand for a black suit and hat, eschewing the stuff she had worn for Alice's big day – 'Rubbish! You could look stunning in the right gear!' She was quite right. Miranda was stunned herself by the ethereal figure that stared back from the mirror. She never wore black ordinarily. They fished out the unpawned remnants of Alice's jewels and Miranda chose, hesitantly, the diamond ear-rings and discreet necklace.

'George would be proud of you!'

Carol hired the church hall for the reception, Violets being too small, and with Meg did the flowers and the arrangements.

Everyone came.

It was a bitter day, with snow threatening. The rooks squawked about the churchyard at the disturbance, the cars discharging all over the village green and every available verge, the villagers all out to crowd the back of the church. It was standing room only and the flowers heaped in piles along the drive.

'Was he so popular?' Miranda whispered to Jack as she came, amazed, to the gateway.

'He was a character, Ma. A bit larger than life.'

Felix said, 'You got most of the stick. And us. Other people only saw the jolly side.'

Jack and Felix were on either side of her. She was the frail little thing in the middle. She felt it. Everyone stared, and she did not know it was because she was almost unrecognisably striking in her black, with her white face, violet-shadowed eyes, and close-cropped red hair. Large blonde Jack and tall foxy Felix, her outriders, set off her fragility. Behind came the equally ethereal Philippa and the shining, shattered Sally with her young Greek by her side. They had flown in the same morning. Miranda had not had time to speak to the boyfriend, only gape in passing. As a family, they were at their most handsome best, and the congregation was impressed and full of admiration. They liked style and this was style. Trust old George, they were all thinking. George knew how to go. Knew how to do things with a flourish. They were all warm with affection and a feeling of fraternity, eternity and a confounded reverence.

Miranda was afraid she would break down now, with the organ playing and the coffin heaped with flowers, containing George, right beside her. She knew it would be bad form in front of these people, in public. She tried to think of how badly he had treated her, how grumpy he was, how stupid, how bossy, how mean. She bit her lips tightly together. She thought of The Druid's leg and what the vet had said, of Sally's amazing Mediterranean escort, of Martin (why Martin?), Sally's green finger-nails (why green?) and where and when the next meet was. She would have to go, and The Druid would have to run again next Saturday. It was the done thing, after tragedy, to carry on. The Druid would need a jockey. She shut her eyes tightly against the feeling in them. Tom's cousin Alexander played the organ exquisitely and it would do for her if she didn't think of something quickly. Sandy Fielding-Jones! Sandy's big stomach. Sandy's baby. The bloody philandering hypocrite! She made a gargling noise that could have become a howl.

Felix bent down to her quickly and said in her ear, 'There was a young lady from Hickstead . . .'

This was a family joke from their childhood.

'Who said, "Steady on with your dick, Ted."'

'Through pastures green he leadeth me, the quiet waters by.' The congregation was in great voice, drowning Miranda's gulps. The bad moment was over. Felix put his arm round her shoulders and gave her a hug. She suddenly thought, without George, they might be closer as a family.

Afterwards, of course, it was quite jolly, although not

as jolly as Alice's because, after all, George had been a young man. Fifty-six is nothing, was the general consensus. Bloody bad luck.

Martin sought out Miranda.

'Are you all right?' He looked anxious.

'Under the circumstances, yes.'

'You look stunning.'

Miranda was taken aback.

'Really?'

'Yes, really. Diamonds become you.' He smiled. 'I want to ask you – Mother said, about my using your place during the next few weeks, can I? She said you wouldn't mind.'

'No, not at all. You can have one of the boys' bedrooms. Or Sally's den over the cowshed, if you want to be really alone.'

'That would be great. I know I drive Mum up the wall.'

'Funny, that.'

'She's always wishing I was something else.'

'Parents are funny that way. Like me and Sally – trying to insist she went to university. I can see now how wrong I was. How could university compare to the likes of him?'

The Greek boy – 'Call me Andreas' – was a vast improvement on Henry Beenbeg. Another charmer, at least he wasn't wrinkled. They weren't planning to stay – 'A few days, that's all. Andreas wants to see London.' 'What does Andreas do?' 'He's a waiter.' 'What do you do?' 'I work in the bar.' 'Where?' 'Antibes.' Oh, well. All that education.

Sally, to be fair, was fairly shattered by her father's death. She cried a lot. The boys felt guilty.

When everyone had gone and life was suddenly back to normal, but without George, they sat round the fire and the boys tried to make Miranda decide what she was going to do.

'It's too soon.'

'You want to sell the farm, Mother.'

'I could work it with contractors. You can't say I don't know how!'

'All that work and worry. If you sold it you'd have enough to live on for ever.'

'Doing what? The Over Fifties Mystery Tours?'

'Leave her alone,' said Philippa. 'Nobody can decide straightaway.'

'I take it neither of you want to come back and be a farmer?'

Jack and Felix looked at each other.

'We talked about it. The answer is "No fear",' Felix said.

Miranda smiled. Poor George.

'Is there still an overdraft?'

'George paid it off with the Lilyshine money. I found out two days ago. He never told me. I must say I was very surprised.'

'If you sold it you could live on the interest. You wouldn't have to work.'

'Can you see me not working? It's the only thing that will keep me sane.'

'You could get used to it.'

'One day perhaps. Not now.'

They departed one by one, guiltily. 'You're sure you'll be all right, Mum?'

Philippa took Sally and Andreas to London with her. She was going to lay claim to the flat, coerced by Miranda. Sally and Andreas would stay there too, and be supportive if Paul turned up. Felix departed for Suffolk and Jack and Carol were left.

'We'll stay the night, happily. If you want us.'

'No. To tell you the truth, I would like to be on my own now.'

'We're only down the road, after all. Just come over, whenever you like.'

'You've been marvellous. Thank you.'

It was true. Her young had risen to the occasion. She had felt much comforted by their loyalty and coherence and kindness. Without George, she could enjoy them more. He had never liked her leaving home.

Miranda waved Jack and Carol down the drive and went back into the kitchen. It felt like the aftermath of Christmas, the remains of the party food to be eaten up, the festive air left behind from evenings round the fire. The big teapot was still warm on the table. Usually, now, George was pulling on his gumboots and his leather waistcoat, as likely as not grumbling, swearing. It was raining: but he had never minded the rain.

His presence was extraordinarily tangible. Miranda almost spoke to him: 'This rain'll make the drive impassable. It needs a drain digging by the big oak tree. That's where it collects.'

But the drive would flood; the calves would bellow; the tractor would fail; George's side of the bed would remain empty.

She sat down at the table and shivered. She pulled the warm teapot towards her for comfort. She still felt desperately tired, although she had done very little; her head was heavy and aching and, in spite of her brave words, being alone, the way it was now, was terrible. She had known it would be. The habits of a lifetime were severed. She had not died with George, but her will to get on with life was at present paralysed. When she had said she wanted to be alone, at last, it was really to get on with facing the awfulness. She knew it was going to be dreadful, in spite of the fact that George had been a tyrant and had lacked any sort of understanding or sensitivity about other people's needs and feelings. She had been dominated by stronger people all her life. Now she was free she wasn't afraid of it, but she was afraid of the long passage of learning to handle life alone. Habit was deeply engrained. Just to know the house was empty, would remain empty day by day . . . no one to pour another cup of tea for, to tell things to, to – ultimately – depend on . . . It was going to take a very constructive line of thinking to overcome. And at the moment she didn't feel strong and constructive. She felt physically ill and mentally weak.

She made herself a strong coffee and sat by the Aga. If she had been a smoker, she would have smoked. One wanted comfort where no comfort was to be had. Jack had fed The Druid early, before leaving, and now he was turned out till Sam came back in the evening. He had fed the calves. No one wanted Miranda or needed her. I am alone, she thought.

Funny, but once it would have been bliss. To stay in bed, knit, not make meals, listen to *Women's Hour*. If she became a farmer she could listen to it while she was ploughing. If she became a farmer . . .

She thought she might go and dig a drain for the bad bit of drive.

Then she realised there was now no impediment to getting their own drive back, if she could do a deal with Jasper about the stableyard, in exchange for the drive back. She would bring the horses up to Violets whether she sold the stableyard or not. She rang the house agent who she knew was handling Lilyshine, and told him to see if he could do a deal. 'Tell Mr Pertwee my husband has died,' she said. 'The situation has changed. I would like the access back, if possible.' Jasper might call with his professional condolences. She doubted it.

Two hours later, having achieved nothing, she put on her anorak, collected a spade and went out to dig drains. It was still raining. Huge puddles needed channels making to lead their contents into the ditch. It was fascinating, making the channels from the ditch towards the puddle, then breaching the last impediment with a fine swipe of the spade and releasing the contents of the puddle in a splendid whoosh down the new waterway. She got very wet and, in the end, rather tired. She straightened up and found herself stiff and sore. 'But I am only young,' she thought. 'I am only fifty-four.' They had all said how young George was to die. 'I am young.' She felt a hundred.

She went home and had a hot bath and listened to the radio. The room was warm and quiet, the fire flickering happily. The grey afternoon light waned unenthusiastically. She had to do the calves as well as the horses, but without a dinner to cook there seemed to be plenty of time. There would always be plenty of time now, considering what a lot George had taken up. She had hived off all her commitments one by one: her mother, Jack, Sally, Felix and now George. It had taken less than two years. On the day of her mother's funeral she had never envisaged being alone, not for another thirty years or so, if ever, considering how rooted the boys had seemed then. How very strange, the way things had turned out: how she had longed then for the hour's peace she was experiencing now; how empty and pointless, in fact, it felt now she had it. How perverse! . . . The times she had wanted to be rid of George, and now the longing for him to walk in at the door . . . The tiny sounds of the running of the house – the clock ticking, the boiler humming, the wisteria branch clicking against the porch tiles in the wind – they were never apparent when George was there with his huffing and puffing, crashing and banging . . . what a *loud* man he had been . . . and how tiny the world had become without him. A miniature life was now hers, orderly, unhurried, unbothered, to be arranged how she pleased. It was hard to take in. After fifty-four years she could do exactly as she pleased. She didn't know how.

You learn these things, she thought. You learn to live alone, not to talk, to please yourself.

But at the moment her brain was numb. She had listened to a whole hour of radio, but could not say what on earth it had been about.

CHAPTER THIRTEEN

A MAN WAS standing there, absolutely still and silent. Outside the kitchen door, in the dusk. The figure was sinister, waiting. Miranda, coming back from her new stables – once the cowsheds – stopped, and felt a cold sweat of fear rising out of her innards.

She hadn't been frightened of being alone, but Meg had been saying why didn't she get a lodger, a companion, a student perhaps, to share the empty house, and give her a bit of security.

'You're terribly vulnerable up there, alone, and so far away from the road.'

Miranda thought Meg was getting a bit funny in her old age. But Meg had put the thought into her head, so that since then the odd 'bumps in the night' had disturbed her. If once the imagination was allowed to roam, it could call up all manner of nastiness. Her nerves were jangled since George's death – part of the inevitable mourning, according to her doctor; she got very tired and sometimes felt she was going to fly apart. So far she hadn't.

'Hullo?' she said tentatively.

The figure did not move.

It was between her and the door, and she thought it was waiting for her. She was, inexplicably, shaking with a quite unaccustomed panic.

'What do you want?' she called out.

Her voice shook, and she felt scared in a way she had never experienced before. Shit-scared. Her whole body trembled with fear.

Then, as suddenly, she recognised the figure as the empty gas-bottle which she had man-handled out of the porch only two days before, waiting to be collected. She had passed it several times in the daylight, and never seen its likeness to a man's figure.

Instead of being amused, she felt her terror dissolve into a furious anger, over which she had no control. She launched herself on the cylinder and knocked it to the ground, screaming oaths like a soldier practising a bayonet charge. She kicked it and thumped it with her fists with such force that she thought she was breaking bones. Then she was crying, raging, hysterical, fighting with the gas cylinder in the dusk outside her own kitchen door.

She went blindly indoors.

The black, empty kitchen was like a tomb. There was no one for miles to hear her scream.

'George! *George!*'

The dogs watched her with their heads on their paws, softly, anxiously, waving their tails.

'I want you! George, I want you back!'

The house was so empty she could hear the spiders breathing, the dust gathering, the walls growing older. She screamed and sobbed to cover up the silence, and her noise came back from the woods beyond the orchard with an echo that hollowly mocked her ridiculous tirade. The woods screamed back, mimicking her pain.

'For God's sake, Miranda!'

A voice in the doorway, soft, startled, familiar. She ran to it and flung herself into the man's arms, sobbing hopelessly. The arms held her with a beautiful comfort, strong and tender at the same time. George had never held her thus, only with passion. She did not know what it was to break down and be comforted, until now. She had never broken down; she had never needed comfort.

The man took her into the house and into the warm back room by the fire and laid her on the sofa. He brought her a glass of brandy from the barely stocked cupboard and sat down beside her and hugged her again. The brandy glass clattered against her lips. She drank it down, and buried her head in the soft jersey front, against the strong, hard bones, and cried.

She wasn't a crying woman. It came flooding, like a dam burst, and the man kissed the top of her head, and pressed his lips along her hairline, her forehead, and on to her wet eyelids. She started to tremble, and felt herself opening up, like a flower to the sunshine. She lifted up her face and looked at him, incredulous, and he kissed her lips, at first softly and then, as she responded, with increasing passion. Miranda thought it was all a miraculous dream: she was adrift, operating on instinct alone, intoxicated with what felt like the love of decades rebuffed and petrified by callous George and now pouring out in a fountain of gratitude to this lovely person who actually wanted to love and comfort her. His hands came down to her poor starved breasts so gently, so magically, and caressed her thin, shivering body with such tenderness as it had never known, so that it responded with a power outside Miranda's control. She felt she was coming apart from her body, watching her passion with the incredulous eyes of her real boring self. And her passion was so great that she was astounded, surfacing afterwards with an awed embarrassment that made her turn away her face. She cried again, with gratitude, with the joy of relief, with incomprehension.

'I've always loved you, Martin, but – I thought I loved you as a son—'

'I could never understand why you had married that swine George.'

'I loved him!'

'Love's very funny. I loved Philippa, you see, and she loved Paul.'

'Philippa's free now.'

'But now I love her mother.'

'Oh, come off it, Martin!'

'I've always loved you.'

'Like a mother. Like I loved you.'

'Yes. But we've just changed it, haven't we? Don't say that wasn't the real thing?'

'Yes, it was. It was the real thing.'

'You can't go back on it, not now. You know I've come to live with you? I've got all my things outside.'

'As my lodger.'

'Yes, your lodger. And your lover.'

'You can't!'

'Why not? We're both free agents. Didn't you like it?'

'Yes I did!'

'Why not then?'

'Your mother – my best friend—'

'Needn't know. Simple.'

'George—'

'Was unfaithful to you, has been for years. Now dead.'

'Only two months.'

'So what?'

True. So what? The habit of years knitted her natural instincts into a tangle of contradiction. There was absolutely nothing to stop her being Martin's lover, yet she could not accept it. Meg would die of shock; her children would fall about – old Mum, with *Martin*! Martin their old playmate. With their mother! How ridiculous could you get?

'You are lovely, Miranda. Lots of people think you are lovely. Why are you so shocked? George crippled your self-respect.'

She could learn to accept it. Take. She had never taken.

'You are beautiful. Now George has gone, you will blossom. You are free. You should be grateful to be free of them both at last, your mother and your husband. They were dreadful. Both of them.'

She couldn't believe him, yet she loved to hear what he said. It was balm, honey, to the sharp-edged bitterness which had been increasingly taunting her. She had thought no one else had noticed what a non-person she had been all her life. It had seemed to her too late now to bloom, this faded flower, thrown on the tip before it was dead, yet still desiring admiration. Instead of growing stronger in her newfound freedom since

George's death, she had found it almost unbearable. She had thought total independence would be highly desirable, but up to now it had been nothing but a burden, taunting her, destroying the routine of her existence. Her life had become increasingly pointless. Screaming out there by the gas-bottle had been her protest.

And like magic had come salvation. Instant salvation.

It wasn't possible.

She smiled.

She had known Martin all his life. Of all the children, he had been the sweetest. He had his father's innate charm, which Meg had always regretted. Meg equated charm with dishonesty – with good reason, after her experience with the captain – and would have preferred the roughness and rudeness of the Lilyshine boys, as encouraged by George. Both Meg and George thought boys should be aggressive and, presumably, overbearing. Miranda's had been a voice in the wilderness. Martin had come to her in those days for comfort, more easily hurt than the others, both physically and mentally. As a sensitive teenage boy he had depended on her to support him against his mother who would rather have had him captain of football than leader of the school orchestra. Miranda remembered his white face after Meg had put him down, calling him a pansy-boy. Miranda had taken his side in the arguments about his going to music college. Gentle and obedient as he was, he had stuck out with great stubbornness and courage against his mother when it came to choice of career. When she refused to top up his grant he worked hard to pay his way, with far more resilience and moral courage than Miranda knew her own boys would ever find in similar circumstances. When Miranda tried to point out his virtues Meg got very grumpy, unable to refute the evidence. Sometimes Miranda thought Meg had even grudged his success. He had never been out of work or noticeably short of money since graduating yet Miranda had never heard Meg boast about him in the manner common to parents nor even offer up a good word. It was always his inadequacy in milking the cow that she came out with, or banging in fencing posts.

'When you came in then, and I was screaming . . .' She hesitated.

'Yes?'

'You were arriving as my lodger?'

'Yes.'

'And what happened was quite unpremeditated?'

'Yes.' He smiled. 'Lovely, wasn't it?'

'You've never thought before, "I love Miranda"? It just happened – then – because I flung myself at you?'

'All my life I've thought, "I love Miranda". Ever since I can remember. Then you threw yourself into my arms, and I took advantage. Is that so bad?'

'The love we've had for each other has never been sexual, surely?'

'Not until now.'

'This changes things terribly.'

'Not terribly. Wonderfully.'

'Can't it be like it was before? Can't we go back to how it was?'

'Why? Do you want to?' He suddenly looked rather cross. 'I don't think we ought to dissect it. It was wonderful. I want it to happen again. Why do we have to debate it?'

'It changes so much.'

'Look, Miranda, that's your trouble. Don't think about it. If you want to, do it. Don't think about whether you should, why you shouldn't, what will happen, who will find out. For once in your life – other people don't matter. You're alone, that's what you were crying about. Love me.'

She was fastened in self-doubt, the legacy of her upbringing. She looked at Martin, straight into his dear, clear green-gold eyes that she remembered from years ago imploring her support, filled with tears, and his words made sense: it was his turn now to smooth the rocky path, keep away the fear and pain. He seemed to be offering her the sort of love she had only dreamed about. She found it hard to believe.

'All right,' she said.

'Free trial for ten days,' he said. 'If not satisfied, your money refunded.'

He carried her up the stairs.

'You are light as a feather, like a little girl.'

'No big bosoms. I'm not very sexy, you know.'

'No?'

'Well—' Confused, she realised she had not demonstrated this trait with any conviction. But she wished she had more to offer Martin. The older woman in such an affair was surely a voluptuous sexpot, who excited a young man with her carnal knowledge? She knew little beyond the basics of sexual intercourse, both George and herself having found satisfaction very easily. She had always supposed it was the farming background. The extremes one read of occasionally were hard to take seriously: hanging from the rafters by a rope round the ankles came to mind, but she was unsure whether she had really read about this, or imagined it. She could not help laughing. Was it true, that she was being laid on the bed by a lover almost half her age?

'What are you laughing at?'

'Not at. For. Happiness. I can't believe it.'

'Do you mind? George's bed and all that?'

'No. It's my bed now. Come in.'

She had not lain in bed with a passionate lover since the early days of her marriage. After the first few years there had been no playing about, no caressing afterwards, no soft, silly talk; only the act, and then instant sleep, with snoring accompaniment. With the small children to care for, she had been no more imaginative. But she was in bed now not for sleep but for love, with the night ahead of her, like an eighteen-year-old girl. Like Sally. The warmth of his body was bliss against her bony pelvis: their two bodies pressed close, tentative, gentle. In the light of the bedside lamp Martin's hair shone gold, his eyes to match, Prince Charming, Miranda thought, to fire her tired spirit. Her own red-gold hair was half grey now, could he not see? And her skin netted with wrinkles.

'You are beautiful, I've always thought so,' he said. 'Did George ever tell you?'

'No. He didn't think so. He thought Alice was beautiful.'

'What, with that great nose and chin? I always thought she looked like the figurehead of an old ship. She terrified me.'

'He should have married Alice, not me. She was

fifty-eight when we were married, and they adored each other.'

'Did they sleep together?'

'I've often wondered. I don't know.'

Martin's hands were soft, violinist's hands. The Lilyshine men all had farmers' hands, like leather, rough and cold on a woman's body. Miranda kissed his fingers, long, beautiful fingers, and his lips and his face and his ears. She could feel him trembling.

'I love you,' he said.

She could not say it back, it was ridiculous. Yet she had known him all his life, from birth. Of course she loved him. But this flowering of sexual love was like a dream. Starved of tenderness and respect, she responded to his sweet love-making with passion; then was ashamed, and wept. And slept. And woke to an ashen spring morning with a sense of relief and bliss which frightened her.

George was scarcely departed two months, and she was away on the wings of an affair with the rapidity of a Sandy Fielding-Jones or Ianthe Pertwee. It was no dream. Martin lay asleep in the bed beside her with the morning sun creeping towards him, touching the disarray of his thick, soft hair and the turn of his cheekbone where the old freckles still faintly spotted the pale skin – as lovely a lover as any young woman could possibly hope for, let alone one old enough to be his mother. And Miranda laughed, sliding out of bed and silently dressing. Lover or not, there were horses to be fed.

CHAPTER FOURTEEN

'WE MUST SAVE it up for night times! People drop in. They walk into the house without knocking. What would −?'

He kissed her. She could not speak, their mouths joining, her protests melting into the fiery desire that flooded her. His hands ran down her warm flesh inside her clothes and he started pressing hard against her and tearing at the zip of her jeans, pushing her backwards. She could protest no more: she wanted him so badly. She heard him gasp as her nails dug into the flesh over his shoulders. He picked her up bodily and carried her up the stairs.

This was the third day since he had moved in.

With maturity she had learned, and her need, reawakened, was now more urgent than a girl's. Martin thought she was amazing and wonderful.

'Oh, how I love you.'

He stroked her in the aftermath of their loving, his long pale fingers exploring her inadequate breasts and the flat stomach swung between the bony knobs of her pelvis: she had no curvaceous delights with which to woo him, only her boyish, active frame – 'Like a golden fish,' he said, 'out of water.'

'All washed up,' she agreed, sighing. 'Where do we go, Martin?'

'Wherever, it doesn't matter. We've all the time in the world.'

'We've all the world. No one to answer to.'

'We're very lucky.'

It seemed a waste of time to go to sleep. It was three o'clock in the afternoon.

'You should be playing your violin. Practising.'

'I still can. I can play it in bed. It's neither here nor there.'

Miranda went and fetched it.

'Go on. Play.'

He rolled over on to his back and reached out for the instrument.

'What would you like? A romance?'

'That would be very suitable.'

She rolled herself up and lay with her head on his stomach. He had golden-red hairs thickening downwards towards that lovely part of him; beyond, his legs were brown and hard. He had a lovely body, slender and hard, and eyes like a cat's, sometimes gold, sometimes green. No wonder she loved him. It was so easy. Her life was transformed. People would notice: she kept laughing and she knew it was in her eyes and the way she moved; she had noticed it herself in young people, a sort of glow. She felt radiant. Knowing how drab she had been the last few weeks, she could not exhibit her new self without some notice being taken.

Martin started to play the violin, lying naked on his back in the rumpled bed. The romance was very sweet. The liquid sound, perfectly inflected – 'scraping'? How could Meg call it 'scraping'? – flowed over Miranda's relaxed body, serenading her senses. She felt her emotions lifting off on to a plane hitherto unexplored, touching hysteria, as if she were in the throes of first love like an adolescent girl. She curled like a shell in the bed and heard the vibrations of the music in the flesh against her cheek.

'Yoo hoo! Anyone at home?'

The voice bawled from the kitchen below, along with a crashing on the back door.

'Christ!' Miranda shot upright. 'I told you!' she hissed.

With great presence of mind Martin went on playing. He was silently laughing.

'I'm practising,' he whispered. 'I'm in the clear. It's you, you hussy—'

'What shall I do?'

'Get dressed. Creep into the loo, pull the chain, then go downstairs and make out you were having a crap. I'll go on playing.'

'It's Jack. Jack and Carol.'

She was dressing already, feverishly. Martin sat up and went on playing. Miranda groped for her shoes, dragged her jersey over her head and rapidly combed her hair. Her face was flushed. She tiptoed out on to the landing and into the lavatory. Martin's romance crescendoed as she pulled the chain. She ran downstairs.

'Jack?'

Jack was sitting at the kitchen table reading her newspaper. Carol was leaning against the Aga.

'Hey, Ma! We were just passing – been to get some timber at Agnew's. Carol's day off so we thought we'd call. How's things?'

'Fine. Nice to see you. Sorry, I was in the loo.'

'So, the lodger's arrived? We saw his car. It's okay, is it? He's a much nicer chap than us lot, better manners you always used to say. She used to hold Martin up to us as an example, Carol – gets up when a lady comes into the room.'

'Did I?' Miranda was amazed. 'Meg did a better job than I did, in that case. Yes, he's very pleasant company.'

As she said this, she felt herself blushing furiously.

Her heart was hammering with nerves. Agitated string-playing floated down the stairs. She turned her back on Jack and Carol, making nervous moves to fill the kettle.

'A cup of tea? There's a cake in the tin. Is everything going well?'

'It's great, Ma. You don't want me back as a farmer, I hope?'

'Oh, no. Gracious me, we could get as much for set-aside as all that labour you used to expend.'

She made a genuine effort to turn her mind to affairs of state: her plans for the future, her financial situation. Jack took quite seriously his role of father figure, wanting her to tidy up the legacy of George's hopeless book-keeping and make decisions.

'You seem much more cheerful,' he said. 'You look better.'

'Well, I'm coming to terms. The worst is over, I think.'

'You look younger. Must be getting rid of Dad.' He laughed. 'It took years off me, leaving home.'

'Oh Jack!'

'He was a tyrant, Ma. When you get used to the idea, I bet you'll be a new woman.'

She was losing no time . . . Miranda had to turn her back again in confusion. She could see Carol's sharp eyes taking in her flushed face. She rattled about in the cupboard for the cake tin.

The violin-playing had turned into virtuoso scales, a practising sort of sound, and had not yet ceased for a moment. Miranda pictured Martin playing, still stark naked, and had to fight down the instinct to giggle.

'How long is Martin here for?'

'As long as it takes the builders to fix his flat. Two or three weeks, I think.' What would she do without him? Two or three weeks was no time at all. Whatever would happen? 'Cake?'

'Thank you.' Carol pulled out a chair and sat down. 'He plays very well. He must be a professional.'

'Oh, yes. He plays in an orchestra. And teaches. I'll call him – he might like a cup of tea.'

She went to the bottom of the stairs and called. 'I've made some tea, Martin! Jack and Carol are here. Are you coming down?'

She dared not look at him when, after a brief interval for getting dressed, he appeared at the kitchen door. She busied herself pouring the tea, eyes down. Her body kept sweeping fire, her face burning. She prayed Carol wouldn't notice.

Martin was totally charming and at ease. Was it a clever pose or was he so practised at deception? Miranda had no idea what sort of a sex life he led, how many girlfriends he had had, or hadn't – she couldn't remember him ever having brought any home. Meg always said he was a conundrum. Miranda had had no cause to concern herself before, but now she realised she really knew nothing about him at all, not the way he lived nor about his work, his London life, his sex-life. She knew about his childhood but not his manhood. Was he a practised seducer of mature women?

She asked him when Jack and Carol had gone.

'One a week.' He laughed. 'Shall we go back to bed?'

'Yes, let's.'

Having an affair without anyone knowing was incredibly difficult. People kept calling. Meg kept bringing eggs, paperbacks, the church magazine.

'Let's go away.'

'Yes, good idea.'

Even going away was terribly difficult, to go at the same time as if it were a coincidence, making up two different stories without getting in a muddle. Miranda was so congenitally honest she found the deception appalling. To Meg, to Sam, to Jack, to Philippa . . . 'Oh, heavens, it drives me mad! They want to know *everything*—'

She put it about that she was going to drive off and find a few nice places to stay and explore and eat and think about things. Martin said he was going back to check up on the builders and would stay with a friend – he had a bit of research to do in the London Library.

'We'll go to Paris.'

Miranda had thought Blakeney or Hunstanton.

'*Paris!*'

Martin didn't think it mattered if everyone knew they were having an affair.

'Martin, they'd think you were off your head! Your mother – I just couldn't face her! Please. I'd die.'

'If it goes on, we can't keep it hidden for ever.'

'What do you mean, goes on?'

'I quite like it. Don't you? Has it got to stop when I go back to London?'

'It's just a flash in the pan, a novelty – surely? For you, at least. You can't be serious, thinking it could last?'

'I could be serious. I think you're being rather rude.'

She saw that he wasn't joking this time.

'Miranda, why don't you give yourself a chance? You don't have to live under a stone all your life. Come out, for God's sake. George has gone now. Have a look round. Why should I do this to you, if I'm not serious? I'm not like that. Give me credit. I'm not playing.'

'I'm fifty-four, Martin! Too old to have children. When you're only fifty I shall be seventy.'

'You won't be seventy for ages! There's all the time in the world! Why can't you take it as it comes? Let love run its course, give it a chance! You get fed up with me . . . I fall for a fat opera singer . . . Give it a whirl until something happens to break it up. And if nothing happens to break it up, why shouldn't you be seventy and me fifty? There's no rules against it.'

'No.' She could not argue. She was a born wet blanket. 'You are quite right.' But it took some getting used to, being a born-again committed lover. She had declined to take it seriously, thinking it was some sort of a whim to comfort her in her bereavement, possibly a bit of an experiment for Martin who might be on the rebound from a jilting or rejection.

'Do you fall in love often?'

He smiled. 'Not these days. Not counting adolescent passions, I've only fancied myself in love once before, and that was with Philippa. Before she met Paul.'

'But Philippa's left Paul. She's free now.'

'Times change, Miranda.'

Miranda's old dream that Philippa should marry Martin surfaced with Martin's admission. Now the scene was set for the dream to come true, it was she who was wrecking it. The thought of Martin making love to Philippa made her feel ill. And the fact that the thought made her feel ill made her feel iller. Perhaps Martin saw this, for he actually shook her, and said, 'Take, Miranda. It's your turn.'

They went to Paris.

Miranda shed twenty years in a week. Her joy in her new experiences was ecstatic, her love for Martin a revelation. Perhaps she had loved George as much in her early days, but she had not had the experience then with which to exploit it and it seemed tame compared with this late flowering of passion. George had never sought out delights especially to please her as Martin did; George would never have seen romance in a view from the bed of the tumbled silver roofs of old Paris and the white flowers of the chestnut trees rubbing the window sill, nor in an evening walk along the bank of the Seine to the floodlit hulk of Notre Dame, with silky talk and laughing and a nightcap of coffee and brandy and the French smell of cigarettes in dark staircases and the flash of lights from the *bâteaux mouches* on the bedroom wall. Martin took her to the cemetery of Père LaChaise to see Chopin's grave and they embraced in a tangled bower somewhere near the Caliph of Baghdad; they went to Balzac's house and had omelettes for lunch in a bar nearby and in the evening to a concert in the crypt of a church on the rue St Germain. She sat in the dark shadows with Martin's arm round her, adrift on the strains of Vivaldi, at one with the ghosts and spirits she felt beyond the curve of the vaulting, beneath the massive stone flags. 'Oh God, I love you, Martin,' she whispered between movements, and he bent and kissed her to the strains of an adagio, as if the music was tempered to her ardour.

George would have laughed.

Miranda remembered days in the rain at point-to-points, days of weeping when he was having an affair, long weeks of helping out when they were short-handed, driving the tractor to get the hay in and the dinner still to be provided, the bad temper, his nights away, his boozing with Martin's father. It had taken fifty years to know happiness, yet she had never considered herself unhappy. Now it seemed she had lived her life in a shroud, bound and fettered. Martin had woken her up. Yet she had been content. This excess of feeling that overflowed in her was something she could not have imagined herself capable of. It transcended reason. It was what she had rebuked Sally for; it was what drove Sandy Fielding-Jones – the coarse drive of physical desire. Lust. I am full of lust, she thought, trembling under the Norman pillars of the ancient church.

'It's great, a bit of lust,' Martin agreed, when they reached their magic bed.

And Miranda lay in the dawn listening to the street cleaners crashing away below and flushing the cleansing streams of water down the gutters – what a din they made! – and wondering whatever was going to become of her, awash on her sea of love, and so happy, happy – they would all see it when she got home. She would have to tell them of her tour round the Norfolk coast and her visits to the treasures of the National Trust . . . It was impossible. She was never going to cover it up. She would have to go away again, or stay away.

'I have to start work on Monday,' Martin said, when the week was nearly over. 'Can you come and live with me in London?'

'How can I?'

Who would feed the dogs, she wondered? She wept.

'I don't know what to do!'

'Stay at home then, and find out how miserable you'll feel! And I'll feel the same in London. You're a glutton for punishment, Miranda.'

'It's only three weeks since you came to Violets! We started the minute you came in the door.'

'We did indeed.'

'Are you sure you didn't come intending to make love to me?'

'No, it never crossed my mind until you flung yourself into my arms. You've only yourself to blame. And then you were so wonderful it dawned on me how much I had always loved you.'

'Like an aunt?'

'Yes. I've always loved you like an aunt. But then it changed into something different.'

'It changed into lust.'

'Yes. Great, wasn't it? I like this way better.'

'What shall we do?'

'We'll just see what happens. You're a great one for wanting plans, aren't you? We'll go home. I'll collect my things from Violets and go back to London. Then we'll both be miserable as sin, and when we can't bear it any longer we'll get back together again.'

It didn't sound too good, but Miranda felt some time apart would bring her to her senses again. She thought she had gone mad. She thought after a few days she would see the past three weeks as a magic interlude with the two of them under some bizarre influence which would quickly disappear with a return to work and to normality. She had been slightly hysterical at the moment of Martin's appearance, and had stayed that way ever since.

'I will get back on an even keel,' she thought. 'This is all quite ridiculous.'

Paris did not help. With a grey Heathrow appearing below, she felt her time in the clouds was up, she was coming down to earth.

'You'll just take me home, collect your things, and go back to London immediately,' she said.

'Yes, Auntie.'

He did exactly that. Just before he got into his car to leave Violets, he took her in his arms and kissed her passionately.

'We could go to bed before I go?'

'No! No!'

She pulled herself free and screamed at him.

'Go away!'

He went.

She went indoors. A week's post was lying on the table where she had taken it out of the letter box. She sifted through it distractedly, throwing out brown envelopes and boring advertisements. There was a letter from Sally with foreign stamps on. She peered at them, absently. They weren't French. They appeared to be Mexican.

She opened it curiously.

After a few ritual sentences of how are you and hope you are feeling better, Sally wrote, 'We have found a little paradise on earth here. We are renting a palm hut on the end of a beach, furnished with hammocks and two candles in baked bean tins. We live on pineapples. I got up early this morning to watch the sun rise and went for a poke around in the woods. I met a buffalo and saw pelicans and humming-birds and strange parrotty things. Also found a tarantula under the mat this morning! It's really great here. See you before too long. Love Sally and Dave.'

Dave? She seemed to remember the Greek was called Andreas. Sally, at seventeen, had reached the point it had taken Miranda fifty years to discover. Good old Sally! She had tried really hard to stop her, she remembered. Sally was a bad girl, full of lust. Philippa was the good one, who should marry Martin. Philippa was having a really bad time.

Miranda was just as hysterical as when Martin had arrived three weeks ago. She wanted to take the dogs for a walk but thought Martin would ring as soon as he got home. She sat drinking whisky and waiting for the phone to ring. The house felt like a morgue.

The phone rang. She leapt to it, trembling.

'Hullo!'

'Mum, is that you?' It was Philippa.

'Yes. Philippa.'

'You sound funny. Are you all right?'

'Yes, of course! Sorry! Philippa, how lovely! How are you?'

'I'm fine. I was just ringing to see if I could come down next weekend? I haven't seen you since I started my new job. Is Martin still with you? I'd love to see him again too. Did you have a good holiday?'

Miranda's mind was a complete blank as to what she

had told Philippa about the holiday. She only just stopped herself from saying, 'Where did I say I was going?' Philippa coming next weekend was a disaster. Martin had only been gone an hour and she was frantic to see him again. But if she said she was coming up to London Philippa would expect to see her just the same.

'Lovely, darling, do come,' she heard herself saying. It was like putting an electronic beam on the gates of paradise and watching them shut in her face.

'Oh good. I can't wait to hear all about it. It must be the first holiday you've had since we went to Westgate when I was ten.'

'Yes, I've got some catching up to do, haven't I?' Fifty years of it, and she was on her way. 'I could get addicted.'

'Where did you go?'

'Oh, all over the place. I'll tell you when you come.'

'Blakeney's gorgeous, isn't it? Walking for miles across the sand with the sea making channels all over the place. I went there once with Paul. Did you go to Norwich? Isn't it the loveliest city — and those wonderful Cotmans in the Castle! You saw those? It's amazing how you've never been anywhere, Mum. I hope you've got the taste for it?'

'Yes, I have. It was wonderful.'

'Did you take any photos?'

'Er — no — my camera's packed up.'

'Oh well. Anyway, next weekend. You're sure it's okay? Will Martin still be with you?'

'No. He's back in London. Unless he comes down.'

'I could ask him. Would that be a good idea?'

Miranda dithered, panicking.

'No! Yes. Why not?'

Why not, indeed? It was the only way she was going to see him, unless she pursued him during the week. But no, the idea was to stand off and see how she felt. Her idea. She knew how she felt already and he hadn't been gone two hours.

'Yes, ask him.'

'We could come down together. I'll let you know. I shall really look forward to it, Ma.'

'Lovely, darling.'

'Goodbye.'

Perhaps Philippa now had designs on Martin?

Martin did not ring. Miranda thought he was punishing her, or that he had had an accident. No, Meg would have told her if he had had an accident. He was punishing her for not saying yes yes yes all the time. What had she got to lose? There was no one to talk it over with, only the dogs. Sam had always said he would have the dogs any time she wanted to go away. The horses were out now and needed no attention. Meg would keep an eye on them. All her thoughts were turned to working out how she could leave home to be with Martin. He had been gone four hours.

Two days later Philippa rang to say yes, Martin would like to come down and they would drive together. He sent his kindest regards.

The thought of being in the house for the whole weekend with Martin, deceiving Philippa, was too much for Miranda, so she invited Jack and Carol, Felix and Pip and Meg to the various meals, and to stay the night. This gave her plenty to think about and lots of shopping and arranging to do, which she assumed was good for her lovelorn condition. Meg came round and asked her how her holiday had gone.

'I don't know why you went alone. It can't have been easy. Did you enjoy it?'

'Yes, very much. It was very relaxing.'

'Where did you go?'

Miranda had worked out her route on a motorway map and been into the public library to look up all the places she might have stayed at. She had done it very thoroughly, right down to the National Trust handbook and which houses were open in April and what were the specialities. She read all the county books and studied photos of the landscapes, and felt herself well prepared. It was the only way she felt able to face the weekend. She practised on Meg, who wasn't much better-travelled than herself and Meg lapped it all up amiably.

'Sounds good. Pity I couldn't have come with you. It's the cow that's the stopper. No one can milk these days. They'll feed the hens and the goats and what have you but they won't milk Elspeth. I might get rid of her, I suppose, give myself a rest. I must say, Miranda, you look tons better for your holiday. Quite a different woman. It must be dawning on you that it wasn't all roses with George. I've seen quite a few women blossom after their husbands have departed, you know – start to live their own lives. I always went my own way, made no difference to me, but you always danced to George's tune, didn't you?'

'It made for a peaceful life, yes.'

'He could be a charming man, but he was a real bastard, wasn't he?'

'Shall we have brandy in our coffee?'

'Why not? Good idea.'

'Yes, he could be. I've made a lemon cake. D'you want a piece?'

'Yes, I like your lemon cake.'

This is the life Miranda had dreamed of, no hurry, no waiting on hungry men, no clock-watching – but all the time to chat and have coffee with Meg. It now seemed incredibly boring. She kept looking at Meg's face for signs of Martin: the eyes were alike. Meg's were that funny colour that looked different all the time, roughly brown, but sometimes green and sometimes amberish. She kept thinking of saying, over the lemon cake, 'I am having a passionate affair with your son.' But then perhaps she wasn't, for he had not rung and nor had she. She felt how she knew Sally had felt when she first met Henry. She was ashamed when she remembered how unsympathetically she had treated Sally. Sally had gone off Henry quite quickly. How long would it take her to go off Martin?

'I have to tell you, Miranda, as you will hear the news pretty quickly anyway, that Sandy Fielding-Jones has given birth to a son. Thirteen daughters old Windy has begotten, and the fourteenth is a son. He is over the moon. The baby looks – I have to add – exactly like George.'

She looked anxiously at Miranda to see how the news would be received. Miranda, to her surprise, didn't see that it mattered at all. She felt, in fact, a rather proprietory warmth towards the infant, for being George's. She would take a keen interest in its future. Perhaps she could be a godmother?

'How sweet! Will he be called George, do you think?'

'Highly unlikely, I would say. I am afraid the family name is Ambrose. This cake is very good.'

'Was the captain Martin's father?'

'Oh, yes.'

'I can't see very much of either of you in Martin. He's a puzzle.'

'That's what I've always been telling you, and you always stick up for him so. He's so unphysical, and both of us are on the go all the time.'

Miranda dared not answer this remark, Martin's physical prowess being exactly what was possessing her. She should have left his name out of the conversation, for Meg then pressed her, 'You got on well with him while he was your lodger? He didn't drive you mad?'

'No. Not at all. He was very kind.'

'Yes, he's kind. But such a layabout. All that reading and listening to music.'

'Well, it's work to him.'

'I always think for work you need a spade. I suppose I'm very primitive.'

She took another piece of cake.

'Any news about Lilyshine?'

'Well, yes, it seems to be proceeding, slowly. The agent says this buyer still wants the stableyard and doesn't seem to be averse to swapping it for the drive, or part exchanging. They are haggling over it now. I suppose it would be nice to have the drive back. The maintenance on the other one is going to be frightful. It's so long, and very badly drained.'

'You've no one to do these jobs for you any more. Just like me. You'll find out, Miranda, why I envied you your hunky boys.'

Miranda concentrated on making her preparations for the weekend. The shopping and cooking and sorting out the sheets passed her time but only occupied a small part of her brain; the main part of her brain was possessed by seeing Martin again. He was to arrive on Friday evening with Philippa. He made no contact.

By the time the familiar red car bounced up the drive in the spring dusk, Miranda was shivering with an uncontrollable excitement. Setting eyes on Martin again was like coming home to roost after an interminable journey: a quietening of her fears and a great resurgence of the sexual delight that fed on seeing his familiar figure moving towards her and the light in his eyes.

'How are you, Miranda?'

They exchanged an auntly kiss in front of Philippa, lips scarcely brushing. What did he feel, Miranda wondered, seeing his composed smiling face giving nothing away? She turned and embraced Philippa, anguished at the instinct that cursed her daughter for being there, making herself more affectionate because of it.

Philippa looked wonderful, all her brooding fat misery transformed into a positively sparkling gaiety that Miranda hadn't seen in her for years. She wore jeans and a bright pullover, and her once dull hair shone and curled; her skin glowed.

'You look fantastic, Philippa! So well!'

'And you too, Ma – you look years younger than when I last saw you!'

'Getting rid of one's menfolk seems to do wonders for married women,' Martin murmured drily.

'I should have left Paul years ago,' Philippa said. 'How stupid I was!'

She gathered her things out of the boot of Martin's car and went into the house. Miranda suddenly saw her as her sexual rival and the pain of blazing jealousy shook her. The unpleasantness appalled her. She could not believe she was capable of such animal feeling. She made a great effort to be motherly, fighting down her beastly instincts.

'You must be hungry – the dinner is almost ready to dish up. Go in by the fire. I'll put another log on – they burn up so quickly! You've got Jack's old room, Philippa, and Martin the one at the end. Felix and Pip will be staying tomorrow night so they can have the big room.'

'I'm dying to meet this Pip,' Philippa said.

'She's really lovely to look at, and seems very sweet.'

Miranda saw them all suddenly in her mind's eye. Felix and Pip, Jack and Carol, Martin and Philippa – tomorrow night they would sit up late and talk and drink and play music, and she would lie in bed listening, stranded by the generation gap. Sometimes her children seemed very close to her, but when they got together and talked she felt an age away, amazed by their opinions, their confidence, their brashness. If she sought to join this generation in marriage, or in a serious relationship, how could she come to terms with being friends with her children in this context? It was impossible, a gross intrusion.

She felt, during the first evening, that Philippa saw her way clear to a relationship with Martin. Not once did Martin betray by a private look or word to Miranda their past weeks of loving; not once were they left together without Philippa. He was charming with Philippa, not less to herself. He gave nothing away. He was both intimate and relaxed, the epitome of an old family friend. Miranda knew she was besotted by him; his restrained manner towards her inflamed her hopelessly.

By the end of the evening she knew it was her place to go to bed and leave them together. She did so. She undressed and lay in bed, shivering with self-disgust at the feelings that rampaged through her body. This was exactly what she had always wanted, what she had dreamed of, that Martin and Philippa would fall in love and marry, cementing her own long friendship with Martin's mother – even the old comradeship between their two erring fathers. She particularly wanted happiness for poor Philippa, and without her own interference she thought it might now all happen. What it might cost her she was barely beginning to appreciate. She could not take seriously that Martin could prefer herself to Philippa.

Everything she foresaw the first evening happened. Jack and Felix arrived the next day with their counterparts and after dinner they all sat round drinking and talking and laughing. She sat with Meg, half listening, enjoying in a totally maternal way the satisfaction of one's children having come to terms with life: with partners, with work, with a way of living, demonstrating compassion, intelligence, humour and kindness – she was proud of the products of her life with George. They were not politicians, judges, film stars or high-flying scientists, but in their modest callings they were happy; they were nice. What more could one ask? And Sally in her paradise, taking enjoyment while she could – Miranda no longer disapproved, but envied and admired.

Jack and Felix had taken admirable girls, full of sharp

fun and a great will to make something of their partnerships, working alongside, equal, yet losing nothing in femininity and charm. Even the astringent Carol, relaxing, had charm of a sort; her initial abruptness and bossiness seemed to have been tempered by good-natured Jack. Philippa, not having been allowed to enjoy her family for years, made up for it now, exhilarated by her freedom from fear. She laughed and joked and once or twice touched Martin's hand with what Miranda's sharp eyes saw as a proprietory air.

As the evening drew on, Miranda found she could not take this new angle on Martin, in his element with the witty, abrasive talk and the in-joking. She and Meg were bystanders. She felt completely outside. This was the real Martin, this young man talking about films she had never seen, music she had never heard of, friends she could only know as somebody's mother. She went out to the kitchen on the pretence of looking for something to eat. The dogs lying in front of the Aga lifted their heads and waved their tails in their eternally comforting offer of friendship, and she sat at the table and put her head in her arms and wept. It was all hopeless, her idyll with Martin.

Presently Meg came out, and assumed she was crying for George. Miranda looked up and saw through her tears the lined, sympathetic face, the unkempt grey hair, the wrinkled hands reaching out for hers, and thought: this is my contemporary, Meg is the same age as me, how can Martin be serious in professing his love? This is how I look, give or take a few wrinkles. And how on earth could she ever break the news to Meg that she was having an affair with Martin? It was beyond the bounds of friendship, suggesting that her withering body and mossy brain were attractive to the virile and gorgeous young man that Meg, in spite of her grumbling, thought the apple of her eye.

'Come on, Miranda, you've got so much! Yet I know only too well how lonely it can be. It takes time.'

Time the great healer, the biggest cliché of all, and the most true – but did she need it for overcoming her loss of George or for recovering from her affair with Martin, which she now concluded was ended? When she went to bed she lay alone, as lonely as she had ever felt in spite of the house being full of people.

On Sunday they all went for a walk with the dogs, except Philippa who stayed behind to help Miranda prepare the roast lunch. The boys still had farmers' appetites and wanted all the trimmings, as in the old days. Miranda had almost forgotten how to cook after her weeks alone. She bothered very little for herself, existing on cheese on toast and baked beans, and her present condition did not lend itself to an interest in food. If it hadn't been for Martin, Miranda would have been overjoyed to spend a domestic morning with dear Philippa in her new happiness, in a companionship they had not enjoyed for nearly ten years.

'My time with Paul seems just like a bad dream now,' Philippa confided. 'I just can't believe how quickly I've got over it. It's absolute magic. I can even meet him again and be quite friendly – he's still friendly with Martin, you see, and it's as if nothing ever happened between us. All that time I wasted – what a fool I was!'

'It was good at the beginning – at least you loved him initially.'

'Do you ever think you should have left Dad?'

'I couldn't, with four children. No mother to run to, as she was living in the same house. Not having children was your great good luck, the way it turned out.'

'I did – do – want children. It's just a toss-up, if you meet the right person, isn't it?'

Miranda couldn't help herself: 'Are you going out with Martin?'

'Oh, Mum, he's lovely, isn't he? We went out last week, and met Paul, as they are going to do a recital together. They talked, and afterwards we went for a drink, just the two of us, and walked by the river. It was one of those really beautiful spring nights – you know, how we've had recently, all smelling marvellous and the stars coming and going – it was so lovely. I felt as if I have a future all over again.'

Miranda kept her eyes resolutely on the Yorkshire pudding mixture, which was whirring round with her electric beater. The jealousy was terrible, evil, bringing tears to her eyes. The smell of Paris, and the Seine, and the feel of his arm round her shoulder, flooded back into her senses. It was all she could do to keep herself from breaking down.

'Have you heard Martin play? He always does himself down, but he's very good.' Philippa prattled on. 'Of course – you must have, because he stayed here, didn't he, while his flat was being refurbished? Did you enjoy it – his company I mean?'

'Yes. We got on very well.' The understatement of all time.

'He has this chamber quartet, and that's what the chat with Paul was about – they want Paul to play the piano bit in the Trout quintet at the end of the month. They're playing at the South Bank – the Queen Elizabeth Hall. Do you want to come, Ma – it would be lovely if you could? You would enjoy it. And you could stay the night afterwards – we could all go out for a meal. Will you?'

'Yes, I'd like that.' It would crucify her.

'Are you all right, Mum? You look queer.'

'Yes, of course!' She laughed brightly.

'That pork smells fantastic! It's lovely to be back again – what a pity Dad's not here just when I've been liberated – it's so strange without him. I never got to know him properly, did I? We didn't get on, but we might have now, if we had the chance. I'm not so stupid any more. I feel I'm just starting to grow up.'

'Your father never did.'

'I suppose that was the trouble.'

'We had our good times.' A hundred years ago, she felt, when she was young.

The lunch and the afternoon went past her in a blur. She felt she was staring at Martin all the time, aware of every nuance in his movement, his conversation, his attention to Philippa. She pretended she had drunk too much, as they all remarked on her strange mood. She had hardly touched a drop, but she could not help herself. Felix and Pip departed, then Jack and Carol, and she went out to the car in the evening with Martin and Philippa. They threw their bags in the boot.

'Oh, I've left my boots in my room,' Philippa exclaimed and ran back indoors.

'Martin!'

He stood like a statue.

'What do you want?'

'I can't bear it!'

'Say the word, Miranda, and it's tickets for two to paradise, just like Sally.'

'You're crazy!'

'I'm not crazy, Miranda. I could tell you who is.'

'You don't mean it?'

'If you say so.' He shrugged. She could not divine his expression in the dusk, but his voice was cool, slightly scornful.

After they had gone, she kept trying to recall his words, exactly, but could not get the meaning right. He had sounded perfectly sincere, she remembered, but had made no move towards her. Because she had revealed her feelings to him in her uncontrolled and childish way, he had been compelled to say the obvious thing to her, knowing that she was too dull and set in her ways to accept.

And besides, Philippa wanted him.

CHAPTER FIFTEEN

SHE THOUGHT IT was her age, the rebound from George's sudden departure, her hormones awry. She set out to fill her days with physical exercise, taking on the job of breaking in a difficult filly for – of all people – Sandy Fielding-Jones, wholly occupied with her new baby. Ambrose was indeed the picture of George. 'You little bugger!' Miranda thought, entranced, but only smiled indulgently. Sandy, in showing her, was plainly embarrassed. Miranda's kind reaction provoked a grateful rush of conversation, mainly about not being able to get the horses schooled, which resulted in Miranda getting herself the job.

The sale of Lilyshine went through to 'the old codger', as yet to be seen. Miranda learned that he was a widower, and hunted. Everyone said, 'Great, Miranda, just the thing for you!' 'I can't wait!' she laughed, as required. Some workmen came and rearranged the fencing, opening up the old drive to Miranda's decrepit car, and arranging a path from the house into the stableyard, through the hole in the hedge made by the adventurous Ianthe. The boys had always driven to the yard from Lilyshine in their cars by the driveway, a distance of all of seventy metres. What a long time ago that seemed! Both Jack and Felix had decided to set the seal on their partnerships by getting married, but seemed in no hurry to set a date. 'At the end of the summer, perhaps,' they said, and then, 'All together – how about that? Two for the price of one.' Miranda was happy to let them get on with it. 'Why not three?' Jack said once. 'Philippa seems to be setting the pace with Martin.' Miranda drove home and instead of weeping went outside and did a vigorous work-out on the aptly named Indian Summer. 'It's all in the mind,' she convinced herself, as once she had told Sally. She had never believed that it was inevitable to fall in love with an unsuitable person. One saw it coming and nipped it in the bud. So she had believed. Sally was in New York with Hank.

It was a bad time.

Martin came home for the weekend and stayed with Meg. Meg told Miranda, thrilled, that he seemed to be seeing a lot of Philippa. Miranda wondered if he kissed her and went to bed with her. It was George all over again, loving mother and daughter in a joint package. Philippa remained buoyantly happy, and reminded

Miranda that she had tickets for the Queen Elizabeth Hall at the end of the week.

'You will come up? You'll enjoy it, Mum.'

'Yes, of course.'

She arranged to go up in the afternoon, stay the night with Philippa and go home the following morning. She knew it would be better not to go, for she would merely reaffirm her manic passion for Martin. She could not wait to set eyes on him again; she was aflame like the filly Indian Summer at the smell of Napoleon's young colts. It was biology run amok. Like a teenager she spent hours deciding what to wear, and going shopping to find something new to flatter her. She experimented with make-up and her hair, and bought a hair-colourer to get rid of her grey, then was too nervous to use it, in case they laughed.

She arranged to meet Philippa in the foyer of the Royal Festival Hall before the concert. It was warm and sunny, and she was able to wear the new dress she had bought, a slender, simple jade-green silk slip which combined perfectly with Alice's jade ear-rings. Even without the colour rinse her hair was still a good deal redder than grey, and green was a good colour for her: she had rarely bothered in the past with her dress, George never having given her enough money to splash about. With the light behind her she could pass, at a glance, for forty. The ladies' cloakroom in the Festival Hall was kindly and its mirrors encouraged her. For a moment she even saw in herself a likeness to Sally, the vibrancy of the love condition, a set of the lips – dear Sally! Miranda's heart leapt with sympathy at the thought of all her children presently in love, doing the right thing.

'Philippa!'

She embraced her daughter as she came across the foyer. Philippa too looked radiant, as Miranda felt.

'Mum, you look marvellous!'

'And you too!'

'You've been shopping – about time! That dress is gorgeous – wonderful colour!' She glanced at her watch. 'They're all going to eat after the concert and we're invited – some cellar place, you know the sort, noisy and smoky. Are you game? If not we could have a good meal here, beforehand. But if we go with them we'll just have a snack now. What do you say?'

'You'd rather eat with them, wouldn't you?' Miranda cleverly put the onus on Philippa. 'Yes, of course. Coffee will do for now, and a sandwich perhaps.'

'Yes, good. It'll be fun afterwards.'

They went to the coffee bar and sat talking for an hour. Philippa talked about her job – 'Nice people, that's what really matters, and lots of coming and going. Not a bit boring.'

Miranda told her about Indian Summer and, hesitantly, about Ambrose Fielding-Jones.

'Don't tell the boys. I thought I would mind but, funnily enough, I'm rather touched. Now George isn't here any more, it's rather sweet to have a baby George around, to take an interest in. Of course nobody says it isn't Windy's, but if you saw him – well!' She laughed. 'Not the only one, I daresay, did I but know.'

Philippa was shocked.

'He was a shit, wasn't he?'

'Over-sexed.' She must have caught it.

They went across the concourse to the Queen Elizabeth Hall and took their seats.

'Paul will only come on for the Schubert. It's mostly just the Quartet. Martin's the leader. They've been doing rather well lately – some good reviews.'

She was very knowledgeable, earnest, touching. Miranda was adrift, knowing so little. She felt like a parrot in her green dress. The hall was fairly full, and the murmur dropped suddenly and applause broke out. From the side of the stage the four musicians appeared, led by Martin. He was in evening dress, black and white and shining gold as far as Miranda was concerned, leading his group to the platform and making a modest bow. The others looked quite ordinary, youngish, settling on their chairs with their instruments, turning up the leaves of their music, shuffling themselves into a state of readiness. Miranda had only seen Martin playing his violin in his old jersey, or naked; she wasn't prepared for this showpiece musician with the light shining on him. Into the reverent silence Martin introduced the first poignant strokes of his bow. The melting sound transfixed her. She listened in a trance, hearing only Martin, eschewing viola, cello and double bass.

The concert passed over her rather than entered her appreciative conscience. During the interval she refused Philippa's suggestion that they should visit backstage.

'You go! I'll wait till afterwards.' She was now dreading that she was going to make a fool of herself, her feelings so hard to keep hidden. Philippa departed and Miranda sat commanding herself into a state of dullness and decorum. When Philippa came back she said Martin had asked if she had come and said he was looking forward to seeing her. Polite conversation, Miranda registered. The rest of the music passed in a dream, its romantic nature inflaming still more Miranda's lust – she could not think of it as anything otherwise, disgraceful in a mature woman.

The concert was very well received, with loud applause, stamping of feet and several 'bravos', which elicited an encore or two. These seemed to Miranda to go on for ever. Then at last they were in the crush of departure, and fighting their way down the stairs to the side of the stage. Action helped. Miranda was grateful to see that she was not going to stand out in the crush: the backstage room was crowded and the conversation was loud. Philippa made for her ex-husband's entourage. Miranda went towards Martin like a star bound on its course and found herself face to face with him scarcely knowing her feet had moved. She stood there looking at him and smiling. It was all she wanted, to look at him. He was talking to someone but turned as if he sensed she was there.

'Miranda! Philippa said you had come. Listen, I want to say something to you, in private. It's important.' He turned to the man he had been speaking to. 'If you'll just excuse me a moment. I'll be right back.'

He grasped Miranda's wrist and almost dragged her out of the room and down an empty corridor. He opened another door and pulled her in. He spun her round to face him as if she were a naughty child.

'I have tried not to think about you. I haven't rung you or written to you because I wanted to see if the whole thing was a passing infatuation. I have been going out with Philippa to try and cure myself. But it makes no difference at all. I adore you, Miranda, and I don't want anybody else. Do you still feel the same way?'

'Yes!'

'Then you must come to me and stop being frightened of what people will think. Including my mother. She loves you, for God's sake – she'll take it, after the first shock. Come and live with me, come away with me. I can get those tickets to that place where Sally was, paradise she called it, the Pacific coast – I can get them tomorrow! I keep thinking about it! I keep thinking about you the whole time.'

'Yes, and me about you.'

He put his arms round her and they kissed passionately. Someone knocked on the door. Martin lifted his head. 'Coming!' he called.

'Will you?'

'I don't know!'

'You've got to decide. We can't go on like this. If you want to go on shovelling manure all your life, do so, I can't make you come. You can still live at Violets if you want, but it's got to be with me, Miranda. You've got to come out of the closet – let them all laugh and gossip! Why not? This secret way is useless. Say you will!'

Someone opened the door. Martin walked out and back down the corridor to the crowd in the room by the stage, hurrying. Miranda stumbled after him.

'Oh, there you are!' The man he had been talking to

initially turned and saw him and Martin said, 'So sorry. What we were discussing, I think it would be best if . . .' He did not look at Miranda again. She stood in a daze, feeling the roughness of his kissing on her burning face, and found that Philippa was introducing her to the other members of the quartet, and the taut-faced Paul was actually cracking his face into a smile to greet his erstwhile mother-in-law. She tried to come to, make the right signs, but nothing signified, save what Martin had said. Martin kissing her. Martin.

They went to a restaurant. She did not know where. It was, as Philippa had prophesied, hot, crowded, noisy and smoky. They were very happy. They laughed a lot, shouted even, and drank, and the food was very good.

'We must go, Ma, or we'll miss the last tube,' Philippa said eventually.

Martin fetched their coats. As he held out hers for Miranda to slip her arms into he said, 'You'll let me know tomorrow? I'll need to know by late afternoon.'

It was as if it were about cabbages, or ordering a taxi. He did not lower his voice. What if the others knew it was about flying to paradise with their arms wrapped round each other? This can't be happening to me, Miranda thought helplessly. She rode on the underground to Richmond with Philippa and Philippa talked brightly about the other members of the quartet and their plans and how Paul was getting on. She was full of a bright happiness that Miranda had never seen in her before: mature, optimistic. Even when she married Paul she had not been so happy, sure of herself. It was growing up, coping. Miranda was grown up and she couldn't cope.

They left the station and walked towards the bridge which they had to cross to reach Philippa's flat. It was a warm starry night and the river ran sweetly beneath the old stone arches on its way to the Festival Hall and the Thames barrier and the sea beyond. They stopped halfway across to lean over the parapet. There was no wind and a smell came up to them of wet countryside and weeds and mud and earth and all the things Miranda was at home with. She sniffed it in, thinking about her place in the pattern of things – suddenly, strangely, terribly homesick for George. It was almost as if he stood beside her, so close, so real. Laughing. After so many years with George it was ludicrous that she could be acting in the way she was, like a neurotic girl; it was a reaction to losing George, being temporarily in a state of shock. It was a comfort to see it this way, it helped. It steadied her. It was a great compliment to her that she had bowled Martin over, but it had no relevance to her real life. She felt very calm, and loving towards Philippa.

'Is there anything between you and Martin?' she asked. 'He is a lovely person.' She was able to say this without embarrassment.

Philippa smiled.

'Yes, isn't he? I've always loved him, you know – he's very special. I think it might come right now. It would be so wonderful.'

'You're serious?'

'Yes, but it's too soon . . . I need to be on my own a bit. And he's not pushed anything, it's just friends. I appreciate that. I hate this idea that you have to leap into bed instantly.'

In the darkness Miranda felt herself burning with shame. It had taken her a mere hour. Her own daughter was talking her into sanity, as she had tried in vain to talk to Sally. She looked down into the dark water and saw life as it really was, not on this hysterical high that had possessed her, but running smoothly along its prescribed course. Philippa and Martin were made for each other, and events were proving in their favour. Once Martin knew that she had come to her senses, that there was no future between them, he would settle down and put their wild affair down to experience, a course of rehabilitation for her in her loneliness after George's death. She felt calm at last, and very loving towards Philippa. It was wonderful to have her companionship back, her favourite child. And things would go right for her now.

They walked on and Miranda felt very intelligent and calm, glad that she had decided on her answer to Martin without going crazy. She would start getting her life in order and decide what to do with the farm. And prepare to greet her new neighbour who was supposed to be moving in shortly. He was bound to be more congenial than the Pertwees, especially if he was a hunting man.

Miranda slept well and in the morning awoke with a great sense of relief that she had made her difficult decision. As if she could have faced Meg, for heaven's sake! It had never been on the cards. She and Philippa parted affectionately and Miranda caught the train for home. It was as if a weight had been lifted from her back, a black cloud from over her head. She felt free and back to her senses, as if from a long illness.

It was another warm summer day, and she drove home from the station taking in the unfailing beauty of her familiar surroundings, the progress of the crops and the readiness of the hay for cutting. She came down the lane towards Lilyshine, and saw the bulk of a very large removals van just turning into the drive. She slowed down, and saw Meg coming out of her cottage. She tooted and pulled up.

'Look, my neighbour's arriving!'

'I hope he fits in better than the last one,' Meg said. 'He could be just the boyo for you.'

'My luck – eighteen stone and seventy if he's a day. I had a lovely evening listening to your lad.' Poor Martin, she thought as she spoke, with a pang for his ardour, how sweet he was! She was lucky beyond belief.

'Oh, the scraping!' Meg said, and laughed. 'I just can't take anything without an actual tune. I've tried, I really have. I just can't imagine people paying to listen to that stuff. I mean, "You Are My Heart's Delight" – you know where you are. You can sing along. Philippa okay?'

'Blooming. A new woman.'

'Good for her.'

Miranda drove on. She thought she could squeeze round the huge lorry now parked in the driveway but it meant going up in the freshly dug flower bed. She pulled up and got out. The back of the lorry was down and it appeared to be carrying not furniture but what looked like an enormous picture. The corner of a heavy gilt frame was revealed where the dustsheets that shrouded it had come loose. She got out curiously. The driver was lighting a fag, standing in the drive.

'I'll pull up a bit, sorry,' he said.

'Whatever have you brought? You're never going to unload that on your own?'

'No, there's a gang coming over in a car. I'm a bit early.'

'Can I have a look?'

'Help yourself.'

Miranda, with a very strange feeling of déjà vu, walked up the ramp and lifted up the bottom of the sheet. She held it away from the picture, peering underneath, and saw the painting of the Derby finish that she had so admired in Bond Street.

The driver said, 'He wanted this moved in and hung first. The furniture and the rest of the stuff is coming tomorrow. I'll move up and let you through.'

'Thanks.'

Miranda got back into her car. She felt mesmerised. She could not believe the coincidence. Life wasn't like that. She drove up the hill and saw her horses grazing in the orchard and the woods beyond green and budding in the sun, and heard the thrushes singing, as if her own home were on its best behaviour to delight her and prove to her that her place was there, where she had always belonged. The dogs, let out and fed by Sam, came racing to meet her. What a fool she had been.

She went in and made a sketchy lunch and changed out of her lovely green dress. As she hung it on the hanger she felt it was a symbol of her madness, and would remain so, to remind her like an old theatre programme or racecard of a memorable period of her life. She pulled on jeans and a T-shirt and went out into the garden and lay in a deckchair looking at the sky, reflecting on the extraordinary events of the last few months. A fresh start was exactly what she had needed, and it was as if her mother's death had set her own life in train, at last, after all those years of servitude. It was so warm and peaceful that she fell asleep. She wasn't used to late nights.

She came to to hear the phone ringing.

Startled, she got up and went into the kitchen.

'Hullo?'

'Miranda? Have you decided?'

'Oh, Martin.' She heard her own voice full of regret.

'You will come? I'm waiting for you.'

She looked out of the window and saw a pair of house-martins flitting up to their nest in the eaves. She did not answer. She was calm, she remembered, and sensible, and everything had slotted into place for her. Her bad times were over.

'Miranda, are you there?'

'Yes.'

The house-martins hovered, swooped, several pairs all engaged in home building. They were a sign of good luck.

'For God's sake, Miranda — yes or no? We can fly tonight if you say yes. There's time.'

She saw the green dress, shimmering on its hanger. Made for hot places, and Martin with the gold light shining on him, Philippa on the bridge looking into the river.

She knew then that she could only be true to her own nature, to the people who had made her and to the people who depended on her. She had far too much to throw away.

'No, Martin.'

For once she would be utterly selfish. She would not think of anyone else's feeling, only her own. She was more important just now than anyone else in the world.

'No, I'm not coming. I've got too much to do here.' To please myself. To live my life. She rang off quickly before he could say anything else and went back into the garden and sat down in the deckchair. She was trembling slightly.

She lay back and looked up at the sky. Paradise was where you made it. The sky was as blue over Lilyshine as it was over the Pacific and it was going to stay that way if she had anything to do with it. She cried for a while, but that was only natural, and then she felt marvellous and started to weed the rosebed.